Touching her, even through her clothes, made him tremble.

"I am going to do all kinds of things to you," he said. "Like make you scream for me until you come, again and again."

"Niles." Her throat sounded dry.

Beneath his hands, the soft skirt of her dress slipped up easily until he felt lace at the top of her stocking, and satin where garter met lace. Leigh pushed her fingers into his hair and held him to her tightly. He felt the rapid beat of her heart.

He hiked the skirt above the edges of her white lace panties. She made a little sound when he started to unfasten her garters and he paused, looked up at her face. She bit her bottom lip.

"Are you ready for me—for us? Once we really get going on the journey I have in mind, there won't be any turning back."

"Welcome to a thrilling new world where suspense runs *wild* (literally)! I devoured this book, I drooled over the hero, and now I'm panting for the next one in the series. Sexy, spooky, and suspenseful! Read this inside with the doors locked!"

—Kerrelyn Sparks, *New York Times* bestselling author

DARKNESS BOUND

A Chimney Rock Novel

STELLA CAMERON

FOREVER

NEW YORK   BOSTON

Copyright © 2012 by Stella Cameron
Excerpt from *Darkness Bred* copyright © 2012 by Stella Cameron
All rights reserved. In accordance with the U.S. Copyright Act of 1976, the scanning, uploading, and electronic sharing of any part of this book without the permission of the publisher is unlawful piracy and theft of the author's intellectual property. If you would like to use material from the book (other than for review purposes), prior written permission must be obtained by contacting the publisher at permissions@hbgusa.com. Thank you for your support of the author's rights.

Forever
Hachette Book Group
237 Park Avenue
New York, NY 10017

www.HachetteBookGroup.com

Printed in the United States of America

First Edition: March 2012
10 9 8 7 6 5 4 3 2 1

Forever is an imprint of Grand Central Publishing.

The Forever name and logo are trademarks of Hachette Book Group, Inc.

The publisher is not responsible for websites (or their content) that are not owned by the publisher.

For Mango and Grendel
Somewhere over the rainbow—fly free.

DARKNESS
BOUND

chapter ONE

W E'RE GOING TO *highjack this woman, body and soul,"* Niles Latimer said. *"I feel like crap about it but we don't have a choice—unless we give up and wait to die, one by one."*

Standing in the bed of his truck beside a small stone cottage, he spoke telepathically to his second in command, Sean Black, who was several miles away, leaping through great, dark trees on agile feet. Sean was in his werehound form and at the speed he moved would arrive momentarily.

Niles paused, flexed his shoulders. From behind him he heard the familiar sounds of the powerful animal grazing past branches, using the dense forest as cover to allow him to move freely, hidden from any inconvenient and curious eyes. Even in his human form, Niles wasn't tempted to turn around when Sean arrived—werehounds recognized each other instinctively.

"We appear to have no choice about the decision we've

made," Sean mind-tracked. *"Unless, as you say, we scrap this plan completely and accept the inevitable. There's still time for you to leave before she gets here. She doesn't know you, doesn't expect you to be here, so if you pass her on the way out you can say you took a wrong turn."*

Niles understood reverse psychology when he heard it. *"Accept that our numbers will continue to shrink while we cling to the fringes of human society, never allowed to live among them openly, you mean? I'm not ready to do that."* Okay, so he had cold feet about the woman, but they wouldn't get the better of him.

"We're living among them now," Sean said.

"Carefully," Niles said. He looked over the waters of Saratoga Passage sweeping in beneath the bluff where the cottage stood. Wind spun dead leaves and grit into the cold air. He sighed, loving this place, hating that he and his kind could not find peace there. *"We consider every move we make. If they knew what we are we would be forced to leave."*

"Or stand and fight."

Niles swallowed a curse. *"Fight the human world we want to be part of? Back to reality, Sean. We are sworn never to harm a human unless they threaten us. Without them we have no hope of getting back our own humanity. We are not like the werewolves—they are animals and they like it that way. We're not the men we were meant to be either, dammit, but we're not giving up, not now. Not ever."*

"They are too quiet," Sean said. *"The wolves. I keep expecting them to interfere with our plans somehow."* On these occasions he wished hounds could hear wolves' thoughts, but they couldn't, just as the wolves couldn't hear them.

"If they knew our plans, Brande and his pack would have every reason to stop us. We know too much about them. He knows we could make their lives hell."

"It's getting late," Sean said. "Are you sure Gabriel gave you the right day for her arrival at Two Chimneys?" Two Chimneys was the name of the cottage the woman had inherited from her dead husband. She was about to come back for the first time since that death.

Niles rarely noticed fading light. He preferred the darkness and had perfect dark-sight, but he glanced around and wondered if Sean might have a point. "Gabriel ought to know. He's going to be her new boss. She's supposed to start in his office in the next couple of days and she'll need to settle in here first. Gabriel said she'd come today."

"This thing you're doing could blow everything apart," Sean said. "It could totally backfire. What if she goes running for the nearest cop the minute she finds out what you are?"

"I'll feel my way. If she isn't receptive to me, we'll forget it—for now. We'd have to anyway."

"How will you know if she's receptive?" There was laughter in Sean's thoughts. "When she arrives, you say, 'Hi, I'm gonna be your new mate. All the females of my species have died giving birth. I need you—'"

"Knock it off, Sean."

Sean wasn't done yet. "I need you to have my offspring, and find more females to do the same thing with other members of my team. We want to restock our ranks. Oh, and we can't be sure you won't die the same way our own females did."

"Get back to the rest of the team and bring them up to

date," Niles said sharply. *"They've got to be on edge. I'll check in later."*

Niles felt Sean close his mind, and heard him go on his way.

A flash of silver caught Niles's attention. A small car passing the cottage on the far side. Leigh Kelly had arrived. He stood absolutely still, his eyes narrowed.

He had waited a long time for this day, this meeting. If this woman knew his plans she wouldn't even get out of her car.

The thought of what lay ahead scared the hell out of him.

Leigh left the front door of the cottage open to let in fresh air. The little house had been closed up for eighteen months since her husband, Chris, died, and a musty smell inside made her eyes sting.

Or she told herself it was the smell that caused the start of tears.

Can I do this? She had thought she could, thought she was ready.

She glanced at the open steps leading up to the sleeping loft and nearly lost it completely. A recollection shouldn't be so clear you could see it. But she could see Chris climbing down those stairs early in the morning, his dark blond hair mussed, beard shadow clinging to the grooves in his cheeks and the sharp angle of his jaw—and that half-sleepy, half-sexy and all impish smile on his lips.

Leigh shivered and hunched her shoulders. No matter how hard this was at first, she would get past the waves of hurt, even disbelief. She had come too far not to make it all the way back to a full life.

For a few moments she leaned on the doorjamb and made herself take in the main room of the cottage, and the two fireplaces, one on either side. This would be a happy place again. Sure it would take time, but Chris would want her to make it and she would, for both of them.

They had almost two years of wonderful time together before their marriage—only days together after they had married. But she wouldn't wipe out a moment of that time, except for losing him.

Shaking away the memory, Leigh walked inside, dropped her bag, and had started shrugging out of her green down coat when a thud, followed by another, and another, froze her in place. Her dog, Jazzy, still sat on the edge of the cottage porch, unperturbed, even though his head was turned toward the noise. Nothing moved beyond the big front window.

The thudding continued.

Carrying her coat, her heart thundering, Leigh tiptoed into the kitchen to peer through the window over the sink, then the one in the door, covered by a piece of lace curtain held tight at the top and bottom of the glass by lengths of springy wire.

Her stomach made a great revolution. Late afternoon had turned the light muzzy but in front of a wall of firs that was acres deep in places stood a shiny gray truck with a long cab and a businesslike bed piled high with chunks of wood. In that truck bed stood a tall, muscular man in a red plaid shirt who tossed the logs to the ground beside the lean-to woodshed as easily as if they were matchsticks.

Leigh put her coat back on and crossed her arms tightly.

What was he doing here?

The door stuck and it took several wrenches to get it open. The ground was muddy from recent rainfall. Crossing her arms again, she kicked off her shoes and stuffed her feet into a pair of green rubber boots by the wall, where they were always kept—beside a larger pair.

Leigh glanced away from Chris's boots at once.

"Afternoon," the man called.

Leigh shaded her eyes with a cold hand and squinted to see him. He was very powerfully built, with dark wavy hair, long and a bit shaggy. The sleeves of the red wool shirt were rolled up. His Levis clung to strong legs, a dark T-shirt showed at the neck of his shirt. She couldn't make out much more.

"What are you doing here?" she said. And she felt vulnerable since he could probably throw her as easily as one of the chunks of wood.

"Well—"

"Are you planning to squat here?" she asked, keeping her voice steady and sharp. "Because if you are you can forget it. This is my place. Get on your way."

She wished she weren't alone and kept herself ready to rush back the way she had come if he threatened her somehow.

"Hey, sorry. I'm just delivering wood like I told Gabriel Jones I would. I meant to do all this before you got here." He had one of those male voices you don't forget. Low, quiet, and confident. And now that he had stopped moving wood an absolute stillness had come over him, a watchfulness. He was taking her measure. "I must have my days mixed up," he added.

That explained it, right? Gabriel had asked this man

to bring the wood. "I see." She felt like an idiot, but she couldn't be sure he wasn't trouble and likely to turn on her.

"The shed was full when...the last time I was here." The day she and Chris had left, never to come back together.

"Apparently your stash got borrowed," the man said. He flipped up one corner of his mouth. "With the house empty for so long you probably hosted a few beach bonfires. It's starting to get cold. You'll need this yourself now."

She didn't care about how cold it might get. The man sounded reserved but sure of himself and he made her edgy. He was probably right about the beach fires. Kids from the quiet little town of Langley and the outlying areas needed a way to let off steam and there were worse ways than having beach parties around Chimney Rock Cove.

"I've already stacked some of this by the front door," the man said. "Easier to get it to the fireplaces that way."

She had been too busy forcing herself to go into the cottage at all to notice details.

The man didn't seem threatening—not really. Except for that stillness that didn't feel quite natural. "You sound as if you knew I was coming," she said. Of course he did. He had already said as much.

"You know how things are around here," he responded without looking at her. "Everyone knows everyone else's business, but your new boss, Gabriel, he said you took some sort of office job at the bar. He mentioned it to me when he got me to clean your gutters."

The blood that rushed to her face throbbed. It would look awful, splotchy and bright red around the freckled bits where her skin stayed pale. "Clean the gutters?" she said, and swallowed. "Gabriel thinks of everything."

"I was glad to do it. Niles Latimer—" he hopped down from the back of the truck and wiped his right hand on his jeans, and wiped and wiped, then hesitated and put the hand in his pocket. "I'm in the cabin by the beach." He hooked a thumb over his shoulder. "That way."

Leigh felt his stillness even more strongly. Something restrained by his own will. If he didn't want to hold it back, what then?

A rapid but stealthy current of energy invaded her, touched her in places and ways beyond understanding. She was responding to him. The most subtle yet definite change in light, an intensity, sharpened the lines and shadows of his features.

These things didn't really happen. Fancy had taken over because she was tired and anxious. Strange and fascinating men didn't set out to charm a woman they had only just met—or to possess her. *The presence of danger.* Leigh gave an involuntary shiver.

Shape up!

She advanced on him with wobbly determination, only she'd make certain he never knew she was not sure of herself. "I know the place," she told him, shooting out her own hand. "I'm Leigh Kelly." She used to be so confident, at least on the outside. To a fault, some said. The same people might have called her a "smart mouth" and she knew some had.

He glanced at her face with bright blue eyes, lowered that gaze quickly and yanked his hand out again. He wrapped very long, workman's fingers around hers and she winced when her bones ground together. Niles Latimer pulled back as if she had shocked him.

"Nice to meet you." There was no particular accent that she recognized. He cleared his throat. "I'm sorry you lost your husband."

"Are you?" She closed her eyes for an instant. "Forgive me—my social skills are a bit rusty sometimes. Thank you, but Chris has been gone quite a while now and I'm back in the swing of things." She surprised herself by adding, "Wonderful memories can't be so bad."

She followed his gaze to her left hand where her wedding ring still looked new and three embedded diamonds glinted.

Leigh had never considered taking the ring off.

Once more she felt his unwavering attention on her. That was it—he watched her as if she was the only other person in the world and he had to commit her to memory.

And that, she thought, was a ridiculous conclusion on her part. He paid attention when he talked to someone was all. That was polite and probably too rare.

Niles pushed his sleeves higher on the heavily muscled, weather-darkened forearms of a physical man. "Is it all right if I carry on unloading now?"

"Of course," Leigh said. "Thank you. But tell me how much I owe you for the gutters and the firewood." Whether she'd asked for them or not, both things were needed.

"Nothing," he said airily, sweeping wide an arm. "Housewarming present. Rewarming. This tree had to come down and I've already got enough wood for half a dozen winters. Anyway, neighbors look out for neighbors."

Refusing the kindness would sound churlish but it made her feel very uncomfortable to accept. "Um," was all she could think of to say. Leigh felt iron determination under Niles's calm manner, determination and control drawn as tight as a loaded crossbow. It didn't make her comfortable.

He laughed and it suited him—and made her smile. "I reckon I scared you. That was dumb. I should have thought of that possibility and come to the door to introduce myself," he said. "Sorry about that. But let me get back to unloading. Then I'll stack it."

"Oh, no." She shook her head. "No such thing. Leave it on the ground and I'll do it. I'm tougher than I look and I need the exercise."

"Stacking wood is a man's job," he said, showing no sign of realizing his own reminder that she was alone now. "You'll have plenty to do giving the house a good clean."

She dithered but said, "Well, thank you, then." At another time she would have told him a woman could stack wood perfectly well. Today she didn't mind having a man do something for her.

She only glanced over her shoulder once on her way back and he was already making the first layer of wood in the lean-to. Gabriel would never send anyone untrustworthy, and Leigh decided she liked having Niles there, doing ordinary things and making the place feel less empty.

chapter **TWO**

BLUE STRIPED MUGS and matching plates lined shelves built into a kitchen alcove no more than two feet wide. A heap of clean silverplate flatware worn dull by use remained atop the small chest fitted below the shelves. And white pottery canisters, complete with yellow duck knobs, stood in a cluster on a scrubbed wood counter beside the speckled green enamel sink. One side of the sink was chipped all the way down to dark metal. Everything was exactly the way it had been when Leigh had last left the kitchen—with Chris at her side.

More than eighteen months ago.

Everything was the same? No, everything had changed. Leigh was alone now, had been for what felt an eternity. She and Chris would never again run into this house, breathless after chasing each other around outside, and race for the kitchen to make hot chocolate or pour a glass of cold wine.

But she would start over. She would learn to remember Chris without wanting to cry.

She took the carnival glass vase from the center of the round table and filled its pencil-width well with water. With the New Year firmly settled in, the deep cold of winter turned the ground to stone. The only thing in bloom outside was a hardy fuchsia bush, but she had picked a short branch with a few vivid red flowers that would do just fine. Whenever she and Chris came here, the first thing she had done was to put a flower in the vase, sometimes a purple cosmos, or a snapdragon in summer, a couple of leggy impatiens in fall.

Chris's chair was left pushed out from the table and he had forgotten to take his scarred leather bomber jacket from the back. He had only used the coat up here and kept it on a hook in the broom closet.

Leigh's eyes stung again and she blinked. The brown leather felt so soft beneath her fingers. The inside of the collar was darker where it had rested against his neck over a number of years. She touched the collar, picked up a sleeve, and squeezed the knitted band at the wrist in one fist.

The jacket was cold but she could see Chris wearing it and striding along the beach below the bluff, laughing up at her.

Blinking didn't hold back tears this time.

This was breaking the promise she had made herself. It was okay to feel nostalgic and even a bit choked up, but there could be no falling apart or letting the terrible hurt take over once more.

She fumbled in her pockets until she found tissues and pressed them to her eyes just as they completely misted over. The pain in her throat was as much from fighting for control as struggling not to put on the coat and go curl up with the tears until she fell asleep.

No. This was her new beginning. Choosing to return to the area known as Chimney Rock Cove and the house called Two Chimneys (because of the two fireplaces, one on either side of the same room) might take more guts than to go to a fresh, strange place, but in time she would be glad of the familiarity.

And she had not really had any choice but to return to see how she did here. The power of remembered happiness would eventually pull her back anyway.

The baggage she had brought in, one suitcase, still stood just inside the front door that opened into a well-worn and cozy living room where she and Chris had spent hour after hour. She had left the case there when she heard Niles but if she decided not to stay she wouldn't have far to carry the bag back to her car.

The only sound was the distant pounding of the waters in Saratoga Passage onto the driftwood-strewn beach beneath the bluff in front of the house—and the thump of Niles Latimer's logs. These and some loud sniffing from Jazzy, her Sheltie-Yorkie mix. Jazzy didn't settle until he had explored every corner and cranny of new digs.

Jazzy was seeing the house on Washington's Whidbey Island for the first time.

Chris had never met the dog.

Leigh tapped a foot, summoning up the energy she was famous for. It had been on the rocky beach below the cottage that she met Chris for the first time. She had come by chance, looking for a retreat. A pin in a map was her guide to Chimney Rock Cove, even if she had rejected the first two places her pin landed, and from the moment she saw the place it seemed familiar and she wanted to be there. Chris was the clincher.

Sometimes she had been convinced it wasn't the pin that brought her to Whidbey Island, but fate—not that she believed in fate. Or did she? Even the air in the place felt different and colors took on their own fresh brilliance.

Now there was a job waiting for Leigh at Gabriel's Place, a bar and grill in a forested setting a few miles south of Langley. She had found the help-wanted ad in a discarded newspaper at a Seattle coffee shop and called on impulse before she could change her mind.

Gabriel Jones had interviewed her on the phone and told her she was hired. Just like that. Of course she knew him from the times she and Chris had eaten at the restaurant north of the little stone house Chris's grandfather had built almost entirely with his own hands.

As soon as she had hung up the phone from speaking with Gabriel about the job, and to make sure she didn't find an excuse to back out, Leigh gave notice at Microsoft and took her software engineering skills north to the island she had tried to stay away from in case she couldn't deal with the memories. But after all, thanks to Chris, she owned the house and land at Chimney Rock, and knew the area intimately. And she didn't care if designing a web page for a local bar and eatery, getting the accounts computerized, and generally trying to drag the place out of the red was a huge step down from what she was trained to do.

The measly pay would cover expenses, not that she cared about that either, and she wouldn't be the first woman to be way overqualified for a position.

This was where she had been happier than at any other time in her life and sadness had become so old. She was ready to laugh again, maybe make a friend or two.

She was talking herself into this. Perhaps she was succeeding.

The least she could do was see how she did spending a night alone in the house. She filled her lungs with crystal air and shivered at the tingle that whipped over her skin.

Time to pick up and make a life again, that's what she had told herself, many times, until she finally got the message and knew she was right.

The phone rang, and rang, and rang. She picked it up on the fifth ring, figuring someone didn't intend to leave her alone until she answered—not that anyone was supposed to know she was here.

"Hello." The wintry evening snapped cold outside but she could see a steel blue moon rising beyond the windows, even with all the lamps switched on.

"You okay?"

Leigh didn't recognize the voice. "Who is this?"

"Gabriel Jones . . . at Gabriel's Place. I'll be there in an hour or so. I picked up a few groceries for you. Enough to get you started. Sorry to be so late coming."

Of course it was Gabriel. Who else would it be? Puffing air into her cheeks and holding it, Leigh tried to think coherently but failed. She wanted to tell him not to come, didn't she? Yes, definitely.

"I've got a couple of phone numbers for your neighbors just in case you need to call someone," he said. "You can always reach me if you've got a problem."

She and Chris had only come up on weekends and she didn't recall ever talking to a neighbor. The nearest house, which must belong to Niles Latimer, was built farther south on a piece of land that jutted out to the water's edge beneath the bluff. Chris said he didn't think he would like it there when the tide was in and water lapped around concrete bulkheads built to protect the foundation of the big cabin.

"You still there?" Gabriel said. He had one of those deep, vibrating voices that sounded as if he would sing baritone—and as if he smoked. Leigh didn't know about either. She did know he was an ex-football player who was imposingly huge.

"You don't have to do all this," she said. But she couldn't be rude. "I'd be very grateful for the groceries but you don't need to bother with anything else. It's all fine here."

"I'm not checking the electricity," Gabriel said. "Niles will do that. He knows all that stuff."

"We already met. The power seems fine. Thank you, both of you, for getting the gutters clean and the wood in."

Leigh tried to ignore Jazzy, who was scratching the front door. The dog should not need to go out again.

Gabriel cleared his throat. "Good. Wanted to make sure I told you how glad I am you're here. I couldn't believe my luck when you took the job. It's real different from what you're used to. Could be a breath of fresh air for you. Different air anyway. The pay's not much but by the time you've started bringing in more customers— and I know you will—I'll be able to afford more. You do know all your meals are found. That'll help."

She didn't know how to answer.

"Anyway, Leigh, give yourself a few days to settle in. Start here when you're ready. I'll be over with the groceries."

Leigh opened her mouth to say she intended to begin work tomorrow but Gabriel said, "Bye," and hung up the phone.

The scratching continued, and an uncharacteristic whining. Leigh made her way back from the kitchen and through the living room with its assortment of slightly sagging armchairs covered with a fabric resembling tartan carpet in shades of rust and green.

She let Jazzy run outside, where he only went as far as the edge of the weathered gray porch and sat with his head raised, sniffing. The fringes of blond fur on his ears and above his eyes stood straight up in the breeze.

The open door let in a whiff of air off the water. Very little about the house had been changed since Chris's grandparents' time. He had liked it that way and Leigh still did.

She wasn't ready to climb the stairs to the loft yet. That's where they had slept and felt so cocooned and isolated in their own world—safe in each other's arms and in their love.

Leigh did look up at the patchwork quilt draped over the loft railings. Even that was grungy-looking. Many months of neglect had coated the whole place with dirt, but cleaning would help her adjust and keep her mind busy at the same time.

A while later the downstairs had begun to feel the way Leigh liked it. She had tied her hair back with a scarf and rolled up her sleeves and the legs of her jeans. Sweating from physical labor helped ease the tension.

Illuminated by the yellowish porch light, buckets of dirty, sudsy water made a river through mud near the porch. Leigh wiped her face on a sleeve. The house smelled clean. Within days it would be its old shiny self.

She heard the powerful engine of Niles Latimer's

truck start. By the time she got to the kitchen door his taillights were disappearing through the canyon of firs as he drove up the track leading to the road. Leaving him alone like that for hours without as much as the offer of some coffee stank. She had been so preoccupied she got used to the sounds of him working and now she was sorry he had left. He had been there a long time.

She grabbed a flashlight and stepped outside the door. The woodshed was full and extra logs stood in piles covered with tarpaulins. The whole area was raked free of debris and he had pulled out the jungle of weeds from behind the shed. No wonder he had spent a lot of time there. She would take him some cookies or a pie, or both, and write a thank-you note.

"Neighbors look out for neighbors." His voice came to her clearly, and the vision of a vibrant man with steady, amazingly blue eyes.

Loneliness could become a dangerous companion.

Losing herself in work again was the best way to shut out unwanted thoughts.

Darkness became complete and milky mist rose off the water to curl up over the bank. Seat cushions from the chairs had been vacuumed and stood propped on the porch to air out. If she didn't bring them in they would get damp.

Followed back and forth by Jazzy, she hauled in the cushions and replaced them. The bookshelves were dusted, including the books, and the crystal birds Chris had inherited and liked had all been washed in ammonia until they sparkled. Every table had been polished, the big Oriental rug vacuumed and the wooden floors washed. Leigh had done the dark boards on her hands and knees.

Dragging stiffness dug between her shoulders. She looked up at the unlit loft. If she was to have a place to sleep, there was no putting it off any longer. Clean sheets and the swipe of a duster over the obvious surfaces would have to do for now. She had already freshened up the one bathroom in the place, a shower combination that was downstairs.

Moving rapidly, she climbed the stairs and coughed when she pulled the hanging quilt from the railings. It must go to the cleaners. She would have to do something about getting a washer and dryer here—if she stayed. Not that she knew where they could be hooked up other than outside.

Using a set of sheets she had brought from the condo in Seattle, she changed the bed in record time and gathered everything for the laundry into a pile in one corner.

Gabriel hadn't come with the groceries. Smiling to herself, Leigh went wearily downstairs again. The main reason Gabriel needed help was that he was disorganized and disinclined to attend to detail—like milk and bread for Leigh. She got her keys and bag, hoping there would be somewhere open in Langley. If all else failed, the gas station carried a few things.

"C'mon, Jazzy," she said. "We're going for a ride."

Jazzy rolled his eyes. Leigh couldn't tell anyone her dog did that, but he did—sort of—if there was something he didn't want to do. Jazzy didn't much like riding in the car, particularly not when he was already curled up and comfy on one of Leigh's freshly cleaned chair seats.

She opened the front door and barely stopped herself from falling over a box and a small ice chest. Gabriel must have sensed on the phone that she wasn't ready for visitors. "You're a good man, Mr. Jones," she said aloud, hauling the box, then the ice chest to the kitchen. A potted poinsettia with leaves in two shades of deep pink nestled between coffee, bread, and several boxes of cookies.

Leigh sighed. This was all part of tackling a normal life again, and she had better get used to it. Gabriel was being thoughtful and kind and the plant was beautiful, obviously one of the many that had not been sold over Christmas.

"Doggy treat," Leigh called out, producing a surprising box of rawhide chews.

Instantly, Jazzy raced into the kitchen, his black currant eyes shining behind the wispy fringe of beige hair. He stood on his hind legs and danced, until he could grab the chew and take off.

Leigh put the poinsettia on the draining board and gave it some water. When she turned around, Jazzy was back—without the chew—and standing on his hind legs again, pawing the air like a miniature wild horse.

"Pig," Leigh said, knowing her shaggy friend's penchant for hoarding. "Okay, but don't come back again." She gave him another, bigger chew and scratched his head.

Half an hour later, the groceries put away and a cup of tea in hand, Leigh headed into the living room, sat down, and stretched out her legs. If she wasn't careful she'd fall asleep in the chair, and appealing as that might be, it wouldn't feel so good in the morning.

The front door was still open—just a few inches—and a cold draft slid through.

Leigh got up and trudged across the floor. She could hear Jazzy gnawing on his chew. Arching her back, she listened again and held her breath. The sound of teeth scraping across something hard got louder—too loud to be made by her little dog.

She looked outside and it took all the restraint she had not to scream.

Side by side on the porch lay Jazzy and a new companion. Jazzy chewed the little piece of rawhide. His friend gnawed the other one.

"Jazzy, come here," Leigh croaked.

Her contrary buddy stared at her, then licked the face of the other animal...wolf, giant mutant dog, something escaped from a zoo somewhere, or whatever it was. Leigh wanted to slam her door on the blue-black creature with massive shoulders, hard muscle that undulated with even the slightest move, and lion-sized feet.

It stared at her with soft golden eyes while she shivered and poised herself to grab her silly, trusting little dog and pull him to safety.

The giant rose slowly, backed away a step or two. He was a magnificent dog, she decided, and very scary. With one paw he batted Jazzy on the butt, sending him toward Leigh a whole lot faster than he ever moved by choice.

Back rippling beneath the wiry fur along its spine, what was left of the chew delicately balanced between his teeth, their bizarre visitor lumbered from the porch and was instantly absorbed into shadows.

She thought she heard soft, measured footfalls that entered the forest and kept on loping. Only, of course, she couldn't hear an animal walking on spongy ground from this distance. Or see a faint, gauzy trail of silver slipping from the bluff to follow in the dog's wake...

chapter **THREE**

LEIGH WROTE *ROADSIDE SIGNAGE* on a list she had started in a new, college-ruled notebook.

She found the notebook waiting for her on top of a teetering, foot-high pile of bills in the office at Gabriel's Place. Or she assumed it was for her. The computer didn't appear usable but she would manage for today and bring in her own laptop tomorrow.

Her eyes felt heavy. After confronting the monster-sized dog, followed by a night when she dealt with memories of other times in that bed, with Chris, sleep had not come easily.

The dog would be a puzzle until she could prove to herself that she hadn't been hallucinating.

Thoughts of Chris had been inevitable, but more sweet than bitter. She couldn't hope to move on unless she learned to remember the best of what they'd had without letting grief take away the smiles.

It was a great goal but she didn't kid herself she would always succeed.

Gabriel put his head around the door of what he had called *his* office when she arrived. In the next breath he had told her he was giving the chaotic little room to her—he didn't need that much space for the paperwork he had to do.

There wasn't actually any free space in the disaster area.

"Hey, how are you doing?" he said, just a bit too cheerfully.

"Good, I think." She figured Gabriel didn't plan on doing any paperwork from here on out—evidently he hadn't done much in the past. The office was around ten by ten and littered with stacks of files, opened and unopened envelopes, overflowing wastebaskets, a shredder that couldn't be used because it was jammed and spilling ripped paper, and pill bottles, mostly vitamins and aspirin. "I may need to get a few supplies if that's okay with you." The pen in her hand was one of many she had tried before finding one that worked.

He grinned and she saw him relax his big muscles. "Anything you want. Just take money from the till."

Any gentle lectures about not telling people to *take money from the till* for miscellaneous items could wait—a little while. Money was obviously the commodity that needed most attention around here.

Leigh looked around. When she felt the time was right she would beg to take down the major league football posters that covered every wall—and the ceiling. The one on the door had a hole punched through for the handle.

Gabriel followed her glance over the room. "You're all settled in," he said, inching all the way into the room. "You look as if you've been here forever."

Leigh didn't say that it was everything other than her that looked as if it had been there forever—including the computer with its chunky, bullet-shaped monitor and, she figured, a ten-inch screen. Decorated with many faded stickers—all football related—the monitor sat on top of the box with a keyboard stored behind it. She already knew the entire unit was unplugged. The total absence of response when she tried plugging it in told the whole story.

"I'm enjoying the smell of raw logs," she said. No point getting started here with nothing but a litany of complaints. "Is the whole building made of cedar?"

"Sure is." Gabriel looked pleased. "I wanted a real log place all my life and finally got one. I reckon a man couldn't want anything more."

If he didn't do something about the organizational mess she could already see he was in, he wouldn't have his pretty sprawling building as long as he wanted to.

"You making lists?" Gabriel said, obviously trying hard for a good beginning to their professional relationship. "I like lists. Always put a bunch of things on there I've already done so I can cross 'em off quick."

"I bet that really gets you revved up and going on the rest of your list," she said. "I'm just jotting things as they come to mind. I figure I'll do that each day and discuss them with you before I go home."

The big, craggy-faced man immediately looked uncertain but he smiled and she noticed again that he had a smile that would melt marble, and he was nice-looking in a rough-hewn way. He had muscles on muscles and he was fit. Gray tipped the ends all over his tightly curled black hair, and his dark skin shone.

"I want you to feel free to put your own mark in here," he said. "What you don't want, chuck it out. And let me know what you want to make it feel more like home."

"Thanks." As if she knew where to start.

"It was Sally who talked me into putting that ad in *The Stranger*. She's Cliff's—he's our cook—she's his assistant. I didn't want to do it but I'm sure glad I did. I couldn't believe it when it was you who called. The last time I saw you and Chris..."

"That was a long time ago," she said quickly. Gabriel's Place had been their favorite place to grab a meal.

Gabriel glanced away from her and the smile disappeared.

"Anyway," Leigh said tentatively, "will that suit you? To go over things at the end of the day and—"

"Sure will," he said in a rush. He turned his head sideways to see what she had written so far. "Roadside signage?" He crumpled up his face.

"So people will see we're here and drive in. It's nice to be a ways off the main road but it's too bad if you aren't noticed. You could be losing a lot of custom that way."

His puzzlement deepened. "I've got a sign."

"Yup," Leigh said. "Two by two. Bet that's a nice cedar board you've got down there by the ground where a driver couldn't see it if he wanted to. And I like the tasteful green fir trees and tiny "Gabriel's Place" in black. Black on brown, Gabriel? Think about it. It's just a thought, but could we be going overboard with *tasteful*?"

"What do you want then, neon?"

Offense overtook the puzzled expression. Men had a way of misunderstanding the obvious sometimes.

"There's neon and there's *neon*. Don't worry, 'You

Want It, We Got It!' wasn't what I had in mind. Not even, 'Drop In For A Good Time.' "

Gabriel narrowed his eyes and gave her one of those looks that suggests a meeting with an alien life form.

He would have to be dragged up to date. "Or we could start with a simple, 'Open,' if you want to stick with the elegant approach." She smiled up at him to soften her teasing.

"Yeah," he said, but he cracked a little smile. "I get it. You'll be having your dinner here, too, so you can tell me more about it all then."

"I'll go home and cook for myself," she said gently to take away any sting.

"Some days you will," Gabriel said, unperturbed. "Some days you won't. It's my job to make sure you stay fed and from the look of you it's time someone did."

She didn't reply but nodded. Eating wasn't something she always remembered anymore but that was one more thing she intended to change.

"I'm responsible for you, see," he said, not looking right at Leigh again. He kind of lowered his eyelids and let his gaze slide away. "You're taking a big step to start over and all. It can't be easy to come back here. Your Chris was a helluva man."

Leigh couldn't help blinking. "Thanks. He was a helluva man." She smiled a little. At least there weren't too many people up here who knew anything about her life. Even Gabriel knew very little other than the obvious. "Coming back here could be just what I need. It's not good to keep living in the past. You aren't responsible for me, though. I've been looking after myself . . . most of my life." Out of habit she had almost said: all of her life.

"You think Jazzy likes her new bed," Gabriel said, not changing the subject too smoothly.

Bringing her dog to work with her had been about the only condition she had put on taking the job.

"Jazzy's a boy," Leigh said. "He looks as if he's wearing eyeliner but I think it suits him. And the blond bangs. I think they're cute. It was sweet of you to think of him with the bed—and the treats yesterday. Totally unexpected and Jazzy appreciates it. So do I." She was glad Gabriel was too busy waving off her thanks to notice the scruffy little dog roll his eyes.

"You got here before seven this morning," Gabriel said. "No need to show up until nine or so."

"I'm an early bird." And she hadn't felt like hanging around the house any longer. "I get a lot done before sunup." That was true. The dark Welsh pony masquerading as a dog could not be forgotten easily, but she wasn't ready to risk sounding paranoid by outing her visitor to Gabriel.

She could see him deciding what to say next.

"Leigh," he said at last. "This is no big deal but I'd rather you weren't out in the dark on your own. There's always someone coming past your place who'd be glad to give you a ride in the morning. I can take you home."

Her twin sister, Jan, had been the closest Leigh had to a mother. They had looked after each other, and she didn't need a new surrogate now. "Thanks, but I like driving my own car."

"That's not the point." He closed his mouth in a hard line.

Gabriel was saying a whole lot less than he was thinking and Leigh wondered how reassuring the rest of his thoughts might be.

"What is the point?" she asked, looking quickly behind her and immediately feeling ridiculous.

He shrugged. "Nothing. I'm just fussing. C'mon, it's time you had breakfast."

Leigh didn't like lying so she said, "I'm ready for coffee," rather than pretending she had already eaten breakfast. "I'll get it and bring it back here."

There was something about the way Gabriel talked about not being out in the dark alone that made her uneasy. Darn it, she had never been afraid of the dark and she wanted to feel safe and at home here. She *needed* to feel at home. She told Jazzy to stay and followed her boss into the bar. A big room, it did smell strongly of cedar, with beer mixed in. Tables dotted the room around a tiny dance floor in the center. The fire, only just lit when she had arrived and it was still dark outside, curled its way fiercely inside a huge, brick-faced fireplace. A single downward step led to the area reserved for restaurant customers.

Gabriel pulled out a chair at one of the oak tables and made her sit. The heat felt good. "You relax a bit," he said. "No reason to take a break in the office when you can be out here. Besides, you gussy the place up." He smiled.

Chris had liked to sit by the fire in this room. She stared into the flames.

"Coffee, ma'am?" Cliff Ames had come from the kitchen himself to take care of her. Leigh already knew he was a great cook. Short and all muscle, with a close gray crewcut, he had placed a mug on the table and stood with the coffee pot poised to pour.

"Yes, please," she told him. "Can I call you Cliff if you call me Leigh?"

Cliff turned the color of poppies in full bloom and his brown eyes crinkled up. "That'd be good," he said.

She wondered if all the men around here blushed and immediately doubted if Niles Latimer did.

A woman appeared from the direction of the kitchens and rocked her way rapidly across the room as if her feet hurt and her hips were fused. A tan hopsack apron covered a fair amount of the floral dress and shapeless cardigan she wore.

"This is Sally," Cliff said. "She helps me in the kitchen. Couldn't do any of it without her. She don't say a whole lot when she's busy but she likes seeing people happy with their food."

With one hand Sally slid down a plate of scrambled eggs, hash browns, bacon, sausage, biscuits, and gravy. With the other hand she plopped already buttered toast and two muffins beside the bigger plate. Deftly, she swooped honey, jam, and marmalade from a serving trolley.

"Thank you," Leigh said. "It all looks wonderful."

Sally wiped her hands on the apron and nodded. "Got 'em ready to go right after Gabriel went to get you from the office," she said. "It's a good thing you came back to Chimney Rock."

"A good thing?" The comment confused Leigh.

"It's always best being where you belong."

No less confused, Leigh studied her food. One of the first things that came to her mind when she woke up that morning was that she felt right—comfortable, despite some misgivings about the big dog's visit and the difficult memories of Chris. The sensation, when she isolated it, had felt very strange. Sally's remarks sounded as if the woman had some way of knowing what Leigh felt.

She drank more coffee. Jazzy would make short work of the sausages but Leigh would have difficulty not leaving most of the rest of the food on the plates.

"Cliff here decides what we're doing for each meal," Sally said in a hoarse voice. Except for the roots, her curly hair was white blond and she applied makeup with a lavish hand. "Can't have a big variety. There's not room out there. Cliff's clever at making a few choices sound like a lot. But if there's something special you fancy, just give me the word." She nodded and returned the way she had come, disappearing behind the log wall loaded with shelves of spirits that backed the bar.

"Well, I'll be," Cliff said quietly. "She's taken a shine to you. Sally never says that much to anyone she doesn't know." He followed Sally, muttering to himself.

The logs were stripped raw on the inside as well as the outside of the building's walls. Leigh liked the way it looked, and the snug atmosphere in the place. Last night might not have been easy, but with each passing hour she felt hope grow.

What Sally had said was a coincidence.

The front door of the bar opened and two men walked in. Niles and another man, who was just as tall but leaner. The second man also had a visibly powerful physique beneath the wool jacket he wore open over a T-shirt. But Niles's musculature seemed more massive, more powerful, as if he was no stranger to physical work. The second man wore thick, dark blond hair pulled straight back in a band.

Niles saw her and nodded. She waved and he hesitated before heading for her table. He said something to the other man, who followed but looked reluctant about it.

"You're an early bird," Niles said. "Got your breakfast already, huh?"

"Mine and six other people's," Leigh said. She had hoped to see him today and ask him about a possible stray dog. The stranger with Niles made her less comfortable about asking questions.

Two unsmilingly watchful, very noticeable men, standing close beside her, didn't make for a relaxed feeling, yet when she looked directly at their faces, they weren't actually watching her at all.

Leigh cleared her throat and said, "Would you like to join me? It's nice by the fire." Despite his seriousness, seeing Niles again pleased her. He felt familiar.

Niles sat down at once, tipped his chair onto its back legs, and gave her a slight smile.

He did have the bluest eyes, and one of those rare male mouths you couldn't look away from. Niles had a habit of keeping the edges of his top teeth pressed into his bottom lip. Leigh raised her eyebrows. She was surprising herself. It had been a very long time since she responded to a man but she was very aware of Niles.

His companion shifted from foot to foot a couple of times and remained standing.

"This is Sean Black," Niles said. "He's our next closest neighbor. His place is in the forest—literally. If you didn't know where to look you'd never find it."

Sean's quiet, unreadable expression didn't suggest he cared if no one ever found his house, but it was the way his light brown eyes passed over her, never making total contact, that made the biggest impression on Leigh. She couldn't seem to stop herself from studying him— repeatedly. His beard shadow, brows, and thick lashes were much darker than his hair.

Coffee arrived for the men, delivered by Gabriel

himself. "I need a word with both of you later," he told the men. "I'll give you a call."

From the artificially neutral tone of his voice and the intense look he gave Niles and Sean, Leigh figured he had something important and private to discuss. She also sensed that Gabriel was tense.

"Later," Niles said, breaking his gaze with Gabriel and turning his attention to Leigh again.

She looked at her plate and gamely ate several mouthfuls of eggs, then drank some coffee.

Gabriel walked away.

"I burned the first of that wood last night," Leigh said. Trying to read these people was senseless and not her affair. "Why don't you let me pay for it? I thought I'd bake you something but that doesn't seem enough."

"I'd rather you didn't do anything," Niles said, letting the front legs of his chair smack down on the floor. "It was Sean here who told me that tree needed to come down—and about your woodshed being empty. Gabriel thought you'd be glad to have the logs."

Sean kept his face half turned away and his weight on one leg. "Worked out well all the way around," he said.

"Well, thank you both, then." Leigh wished he would look at her but she could feel how eager he was to get away.

Sean gave her a sudden, piercing stare, excused himself, and went outside.

"He's always quiet," Niles said. He frowned a little. "Interesting guy, huh?"

"I don't know enough about him to have an opinion."

"I think most women would like to know Sean. I have it on good authority that he's a *hunk*. Or so Gabriel's girlfriend, Molly, tells me."

Leigh raised her eyebrows. She wasn't sure why she said, "I don't tend to be impressed by the silent type."

"Really?" His frown disappeared.

"I don't suppose I could get you to eat some of this food?" Leigh said. Talking about her taste in men suddenly felt uncomfortable and she was eager to change the subject. "I don't want to upset Cliff and Sally."

"You aren't hungry?"

She grimaced. "Not hungry enough to eat all this."

Niles actually grinned, and Leigh thought he ought to try it a lot more often. He demolished the bacon. Leigh rolled one of the sausages in a paper napkin. "For my dog," she explained and inched the plate closer to Niles.

He watched her with a little too much concentration for Leigh's comfort.

She couldn't ask him about anything. He was a stranger.

"What?" he said, his blue eyes never leaving her face. "Tell me."

Leigh sat straighter. Goosebumps shot out on her arms. "How do you know I wanted to say something?"

He shrugged. "Just a hunch."

A hunch that made him seem as if he had read her mind.

"Are there a lot of stray animals around here? A really big..." She hesitated. In a low voice she went on, "dog, a really big dog came to my door last night. He was big enough to be scary."

Niles looked at her and said, "Almost black. Shaggy guy with big feet?"

"Huge. Bigfoot with a dye job."

"Blue," Niles said, finishing the last sausage. "That's

the name on his collar. He's mostly Irish wolfhound, I think."

"The rest must be horse," she said. "He really freaked me out."

Niles wiped his hands on a napkin. "Don't be scared of him." He put a hand over hers on the table but quickly took it away again. "He's a pussycat. Hangs around with me when I'm working. If you're worried about anything at all, just give me a shout on the phone."

The door opened again and three men came in, heading for a table in one corner but talking loudly enough about their plans for the day to be heard all over the room. "Amateur hunters," Niles said as if that explained everything. "Looks like they starched their duds. Any wildlife should have a good laugh at that bunch."

Leigh nodded and sipped her coffee, but she was too distracted by thoughts of Blue to concentrate on what Niles was saying. "That dog was massive—biggest dog I've ever seen. But he was gentle enough. I hope he's got someone taking care of him."

"Sure he does. He wouldn't keep all that muscle and meat on him if he wasn't being fed."

Niles's tone was light, but when Leigh looked at him she saw his gaze was locked on the hunters, his eyes slightly narrowed. Leigh decided he looked Slavic, all angles and upward-slashing brows. Handsome—whatever that meant—and she had long ago decided that a positive reaction to male looks was more about the vibes you got from them than anything else.

Gabriel stood behind the bar while Cliff went to take the hunters' orders. Obviously the staff was lean and everyone doubled up.

Niles touched her hand. "Hey, don't talk about Blue to anyone else, okay? I'm always afraid some yahoo will get pie-eyed and pick him off when it's getting dark one evening. They'd probably say they thought he was a bear or something. I keep an eye out for him."

"Pick him off?" Leigh's tummy made a sickening roll. "Shoot him, you mean?"

"Keep your voice down," Niles said. "It's not a big deal. I just wouldn't want to see something happen to him is all."

"Um," Leigh looked for the right words. "He is safe to have around, isn't he? He wouldn't do something . . . to my dog or anything?"

Niles laughed and tipped his head back. "No! Geez, no. If I thought otherwise I'd tell you right off, but, no. So forget that. If anything, Blue would look after your guy." Taking a drink of his coffee, Niles stared at Leigh, all humor in his expression gone. "What time did you get in this morning?" he asked.

"Around seven or so." She hadn't forgotten Gabriel's anxiousness about her driving around alone when things were really quiet.

"Dark then," Niles commented.

"My car does have headlights," she said with a smile. But his frown was back and she had the feeling he was stopping himself from saying more.

"It's a good idea to lock your doors as soon as you're in the car," Niles finally said. "And make sure they're locked when it's parked."

"Right." There was no mistaking the menace in all these warnings, or her own queasy reaction.

They fell silent. Leigh looked at Gabriel and saw how closely he watched the three men at their corner table.

"Gabriel told us you worked for Microsoft," Niles said, his voice returning to a lighter note. "What did you do?"

"Games," Leigh told him, her attention still on Gabriel's watchfulness over some of his customers. "Developer."

"But you just gave it up?"

"I felt like a new challenge." And if she didn't push herself to change, she could spend her forever between an office and an apartment in Seattle where she didn't know or speak to a soul.

"You'll settle here," he commented. "You'll make friends."

Leigh began to wonder if her thoughts were written on her forehead. "I'm sure I will."

"If you organize Gabriel, you'll be doing me a service."

"You?"

"I worry about him. He gives the farm away. Never learned how to haggle over prices with his suppliers so he pays top dollar. And he's got a long list of people who come in here every day to drink his booze and run a tab that rarely gets paid. Change some of that and you'll be making a bunch of us real happy."

Before she could mask her reaction, Leigh realized she'd set her jaw and was giving one of the glares she was told turned people off.

This time Niles's smile was soft. "I take it that look means you aren't pleased?"

"My trouble is I want to cure everything yesterday. I've got to go a bit slowly on this but I'll sort it out. I may look like a wimp but I can be tough."

"I'll remember that," he said, with a mock salute.

"Have you always been a handyman?" she asked, looking straight at him. "If that's what you are."

"Nope. Not always. But I'm Mr. Fixit now. Learned everything I know at my grandpa's knee on the ranch in Wyoming."

"And you just decided to move from Wyoming to Washington State?"

His steady stare let her know she was being too nosy. "It's not my business," she told him, squirming. "Sorry."

"I went a lot of places in between Wyoming and Washington, Leigh. I got back from the Middle East eighteen months ago."

She could imagine him in fatigues, even maybe marching in the sand, or climbing over huge obstacles as if they were nothing; it was the leaping to attention that didn't come easily to mind. "What did you do there?" Maybe he was in one of those groups that built buildings or something.

"I killed people," he said.

chapter FOUR

NILES ALMOST GOT UP and left but he couldn't do that to her. What had got into him to make him go off like that? And why at her of all people? He had thought his control was better now.

It was that last disastrous overseas assignment, he guessed. The guilt he still felt at losing one of their own. The night sweats didn't happen often anymore. But dammit, he had to get past the guilt and past the outbursts.

"I shouldn't have said that," he told her. "I don't know why I did." Impulsively, he caught her hand in his. "Forget it, please."

She coughed. Her brown eyes seemed even bigger and darker in a pretty but thin, freckled face, but her thoughts were sympathetic, not frightened, and her fingers tightened around his for a moment before she let go.

Damn, he should not risk making her afraid of him, not when he hoped to build her trust.

Touching her hand only made him want to touch more

of her, to hold her. How hard would this get if he couldn't keep his mind on the goal, to mate for the good of his kind?

"I expect you were fighting," she said with a faint little smile. "That must have been…hard…" Her voice got weaker and trailed away.

He couldn't believe what had happened. "It's over," he told her.

"War has to be terrifying."

Leaving this dangling wasn't wise. "It's more disappointing than terrifying, although it's that, too."

"What do you mean?"

"People are still killing people because everyone thinks they're right, that they have the only right way." He considered how much more he should say. "When you see humans with all their defenses stripped down to just the will to live, it changes you. I'm not completely over that yet, I guess. I thought I was, but I'm not. Sometimes the anger comes back. It flashes, then it's gone. It doesn't accomplish a thing."

"If it were me," she said, "I don't think I could ever put it behind me."

He had to and mostly he did a good job. "I've come a long way. I'll try not to snap out statements like that again. Sorry."

"You don't have to be." She smiled and he had to stop himself from touching her again. "I'll let you know if you're snapping. Sometimes things just line up wrong and we want to close it all down. It seems kind of like grieving to me."

Niles almost grinned. Though he'd only just found Leigh, something told him she really was the right one for him; that they really could offer each other what they would both need—unconditional understanding. The question was, would he be able to put his duty to the future of the werehounds first if this attraction kept growing? Just looking at her heated him and he was enjoying the burn.

Before Niles could get himself into deeper trouble, one of the men from the corner got up and headed toward Leigh. Pretty slick-looking guy for a woodsy type, Niles thought.

"Hey," the man said. "I just realized who you are. The waiter mentioned your name. You're the Kelly woman from Two Chimneys Cottage, right? Chimney Rock Cove?"

Niles bridled at the pushy tone. "We're having breakfast," he said coolly.

"Just saying hi," the man said without looking at Niles. "I'm John Valley. I've got that information you people wanted."

Leigh looked at him blankly. She pushed her strawberry blond hair behind both ears. Niles liked her straight, shiny hair but he didn't like it that she was considering excusing herself and leaving the table. Her strong thoughts were easy to read. When she became pensive or distant he had to probe harder. He had not listened in much so far and wouldn't in the future, he decided. Some unfair advantages were a bad idea—and dishonest.

He could often hear snippets of human thought, but only those who were sensitives of some kind came through as clearly as Leigh. He figured that could be because they were starting to share a connection that proved they were meant to be mates—or was that only wishful thinking?

"I did a rough assessment on your holdings here on the island," Valley said.

Her mouth moved but she took a while to say, "Who are you?"

"I'm the real estate go-to on this end of the island." The guy's mouth turned down and a nerve twitched in his cheek.

"I don't understand this," Leigh said.

"Hell, maybe I shouldn't have approached you but I wasn't warned to keep quiet. I thought you'd be interested in the valuation. Very nice, too. Who knew the acreage was that big? But I'll talk to your husband."

Leigh had turned white. She put down her coffee mug slowly and with a shaky hand. Finally she said, "My husband?"

"Geez, he's gonna be pissed with me, huh?" the salesman said. But he lowered his eyelids to leer and turned on a smile meant only for Leigh.

"What are you talking about?" She managed to find some steel for her voice and Niles admired her for it.

John Valley bristled. "Mr. Kelly called a few days ago and said you folks are thinking of selling your property."

chapter FIVE

WHAT THE DEVIL WAS the man talking about?

Leigh could hardly breathe. With a sense of unreality, she watched Valley retreat. He pulled a camouflage bucket hat over his pale blond hair and called, "Let's go," to his companions.

For a moment Leigh squeezed her eyes shut. Then something inside her broke free and she exploded after the man, skidding to a halt behind him. "I want your card," she said through her teeth. "The one that says you're the 'go-to' guy for real estate around here."

John Valley spun toward her, his light eyes popping. Color crept up his neck. "Hey, hold your horses, little lady. No need to lose your head just because a man makes a bitty mistake. How was I to know your husband hadn't kept you in the loop?"

"You don't know how big a mistake you've made," she said, holding her voice steady. "Just give me your card and I can get back to my coffee."

Valley patted the pockets of his camouflage gear. "Well, hell. Isn't that always the way? You never have what you want when you want it. I wasn't expectin' to do any business. Why don't I drop a card by here next time? You can pick it up when you're in again."

"I don't think so," Leigh said. Blood banged through the veins in her temples. "I need to deal with this right away. You can write it down for me—including your office address. And while you're about it, please give me the number you were told to call with your findings."

Her anger was out of control and out of proportion and she knew it. But John Valley didn't even know the painful thing he had done to her, and she was pretty sure there was no way he would care. He wanted to make a buck and if ingratiating himself with her would line his pockets, he would be Mr. Silk—Mr. Silk with a snake in his mouth.

"That's why I spoke to you." His face brightened like a man who just found the escape he never thought would come. "I can't find a call back number. Anyway, I can't stop now," he said. His buddies were trailing toward the door, trying to appear deaf to anything John Valley and Leigh were saying. "Look, I'll stop on my way home. How's that?"

"It's not good," she said, hating the way her voice rose. "How long can it take to write down your name and address, and a phone number? Especially if you'd quit wasting time arguing with me."

"I'm sorry if I've added to a bad day for you," Valley said, condescendingly. He patted Leigh's upper arm as if dismissing her. She had never put up with being brushed off, not since she was a child and couldn't stand up for herself, and she wasn't about to slip backward now. She planted her feet apart and held her ground.

"I asked you for something," she said. "Don't touch me again."

That's when John Valley made his big mistake. He closed his fingers around her arm and his formerly flirtatious smile turned into a malicious sneer as he gave her a small shake. She felt heat wash into her face.

Leigh felt as much as heard a whining, spinning whirl of air. Or it seemed like air. Her hair blew over her face and she stumbled, caught herself on the back of a chair— and felt a large hand steady her.

She brushed back her hair in time to see Gabriel drop a towel in the sink and start around the bar toward Valley.

Too late.

There was one movement at her shoulder, a forceful passing shadow, and John Valley yelled, "No!" His feet left the floor. He landed on his back on top of the bar, slid the length of the polished sheet of wood, shot off the end, and only stopped when his head cracked into a cedar pillar.

Unable to speak, Leigh looked up at Niles, who stood beside her, his blue eyes turned black like polished onyx. Rigid, the muscles in his neck distended, his big hands were balled into fists, and his breath expelled like a long, low growl. There was only one word for his starkly compelling face: predatory.

The breakfast crowd had been ebbing and flowing. A rapid ebb emptied most of the tables.

"My God," Leigh said. "How did you do that?"

"Do what?"

He drew himself up to his full height and she had to crane her neck to see his face.

"The counter's slippery," he muttered as the room

emptied of the last couple of customers. "Doesn't take much momentum to slide on something like that."

"You threw him there. I saw you. Niles, you picked up a grown man and threw him!"

"I had the right angle to get enough leverage." He kept his voice low.

Sean Black stood behind Niles, yet Leigh had not seen him come into the bar again. He, too, had hands curled into fists resembling lethal weapons and his face was completely colorless, the lips clamped tightly shut. His eyes were almost the same pitiless black as Niles's.

Niles and Sean glanced at each other. Only a second passed but Leigh saw what seemed like a message pass between them. With one hand, Niles hauled John Valley to his feet. He shoved him into Sean's waiting arms, one of which hooked around the man's throat.

"Got a pen, Gabriel?" Niles's voice hit an even lower note, laced with danger.

"Got it," Gabriel said.

"This is John Valley," Niles said. "Write that down."

"I'm gonna call the cops," Valley whined. Spittle clung to the corners of his mouth. "Unprovoked attack, that's what this is. I'll sue your ass."

"Office address," Niles said while Sean gave John Valley's throat an extra squeeze.

"I work out of my place," Valley croaked and gave the address followed by the phone number. "You're not getting away with this. I'm an innocent private citizen."

"Innocent?" Niles said. "Treating a woman you don't know like she's yours to handle?"

The sound Valley made resembled a high note from a choirboy whose voice was breaking.

"Ease up, there, Sean," Gabriel said. "A death on the premises would be bad for business."

"If I catch you anywhere near Ms. Kelly, you won't walk for a long time," Niles said. "Got it?"

"Yeah," Valley croaked. "Lemme go."

Leigh's attention suddenly got stuck on Sean. He didn't seem the same as he had. His lips were pulled back to show amazing teeth. Very white, sharp, and with incisors longer than the rest. He looked . . . feral. And he had bowed his head over Valley's shoulder close enough to bring his mouth within an inch of the man's shirt.

Sean began to open his mouth wider. Leigh heard a click.

She came close to screaming but Niles hauled her against him and whispered, "Everything is cool," before he said, "Let him go, Sean. We've done our part. He won't bother Leigh again."

Instantly, Sean released the man and stepped away. John Valley fell in a clumsy bundle on the floor where he lay, panting, for a whole lot of seconds. When he stood up his complexion was putty-colored.

"What if all the customers hadn't left before the final show?" Leigh said under her breath.

"We would have made allowances," Niles said, his arm still feeling like a length of iron around her shoulders. "Get out," he told Valley. "You'd better hotfoot it down to the cops. They'll want to hear all about how Sean and I threw you around and made a bar rag out of you. Get going."

Valley scuttled outside and engines leaped to life as he left with his cronies.

"You were going to bite him," Leigh told Sean. She felt weak and unreal. "Why would you do that?"

Sean laughed. "You're imagining things, Ms. Kelly. It's never a good idea to let your imagination run away."

"Call me Leigh." She felt shaky. Was this what passed for normal out here? Everyone else seemed to think so.

"Sally," Gabriel yelled, and the woman put in an appearance looking, Leigh thought, inexplicably pleased. "Molly get here yet?"

"Nope." Sally shook her head. "She's havin' her hair done. The twins are in, though."

"If word doesn't get out that we're runnin' fights here, lunch is going to be on us shortly," Gabriel said. "Get everyone in gear. Tell Molly to come and see me when she gets here."

"Sorry about all that," he told Leigh. Leigh nodded and gave Gabriel a weak smile. "I'll be in the office."

Niles dropped his arm from her shoulders, but he spread a hand on her back and turned her toward him. "You understand what I meant now?"

"About what?" Leigh turned cold.

"Being careful. Not assuming because it seems peaceful around here that everything's safe." He dug the tips of his fingers into her side. "Valley's no problem. But we get some odd ones from time to time. Best make sure one of us is around if you have to go far on your own, particularly after dark."

Leigh nodded, but she was considering whether she should pack up and leave the area at once.

"You'll be just fine," Sean said. "Won't she, Niles? No need to get scared off and run away."

Niles raised his brows at Sean, who turned away at once and walked outside.

Leigh frowned at his back. Either her thoughts were

written on her face—in detail—or some of these people could read them.

She got a soft, memorable smile from Niles, who followed Sean.

Gabriel hovered, looking around as if expecting something.

"What?" Leigh said.

"Er, I gotta go outside a while, talk to Niles and Sean. I don't think we'll get anyone in but just in case, do you think you can mind the bar?"

She had tended bar for a few months while she was going through school. "Sure. I'll be fine. Go on."

Gabriel left and Leigh went behind the bar. Her only company was country and western music played quietly over numerous speakers, and the distant sound of pots banging in the kitchen.

Two white-haired men with matching paunches pushed through the doors and scuffed up to the bar. They took side-by-side stools and the taller one said, "Who're you?"

"Excuse me?"

"Name?" the other man said. "You're new."

"Leigh," she told them quickly.

They grunted their order and she served two pints of beer, pleased she managed without sending foam all over the floor—that or poured glasses with beer that looked flat and lifeless.

Bringing the smell of grilled onions with her, Sally rocked rapidly up beside Leigh. "You okay?" she said.

"Great. I used to do this when I was in school."

Sally nodded. "From the looks of you that would have been about last week."

She made Leigh laugh. "Thanks."

"You want some coffee?" Sally asked.

"No thanks."

The men at the bar drained their glasses and Leigh refilled them.

"You see the drift this morning?" Sally asked.

With no idea what Sally meant, Leigh said, "Can't say I did. Oh, you mean the tide coming in?"

Sally looked her hard in the eyes. "Watch out to where the rocks are. Sooner or later you'll see what I mean. That's what it's all about, what makes you feel so good here."

"Chimney Rocks, you mean?" Leigh tipped her head on one side. "They don't show above the water, even at low tide. What will I see?"

"Being under the water doesn't stop them from making a difference," Sally said. "Just keep your eyes open and it'll happen. There's not many like you. Can't remember the last one—not that I know."

"The last one what?" Despite Sally's cryptic tone, Leigh didn't feel nervous, just intensely curious.

"I've said too much." Sally gave a secretive smile and left again. Lunch patrons were dribbling in and she went to pour coffee and take orders.

The two men at the bar slid off their stools and turned to leave, but before they could Leigh told them what they owed in an overly cheery voice.

Both of them swung back, amazement in their eyes. "You're new," one said at last. "Just put it on a tab— Jerry's or mine. Don't make no difference."

"Can't do that." It took Leigh all the courage she had to keep a smile on her face. She had looked up the prices on a list and was ready. "Wouldn't look good if I messed up on my first morning."

"Gabriel carries it in his head," Jerry said. "You let him know later."

"Just a minute." She wrote the amount on a sheet in a receipt book, tore off the top copy and passed it to them, still smiling brightly. "I hear we're thinking about putting in a regular customer discount. Kind of like an ice cream store where you get a punch card toward a free something eventually."

At some point the two men saw they weren't getting around Leigh. They each pulled money from their pockets and slapped it down on the counter. "Have one yourself," the man called Jerry said grudgingly, but he didn't give her enough money. They turned and left, grunting and grumbling all the way.

"Don't mind if I do," Leigh laughed to herself as she put the payments in the cash drawer and the coins supposedly for her drink in a glass behind the front bottles of whiskey.

Making a difference to the business, helping to turn it into a financial success, was what she was setting out to do, and it looked as if she would have to do more than stay in her office to get that done.

She was still feeling warm from her triumph with the reluctant payers when two boys of about twenty appeared and started setting tables. They nodded at Leigh and she noted at once that they were almost identical. These would be the twins.

"I'm Leigh," she said in a loud voice.

One boy nodded, the other inclined his head to let long, straight brown hair slide away from one eye. "We know," he said. "He's Cuss and I'm Jim. We're twins."

"Ah-hah," Leigh said. "Nice to meet you, Cuss and Jim. I've got a twin, too, a sister. I like it, how about you?"

They both shrugged but tipped up the corners of their mouths.

She served three more customers before she got another set of tab masters and followed the same routine as the first time. Fortunately, the two men and one woman were too busy arguing to notice the hilarity among several nearby customers who were listening in.

A few minutes later she prevailed, although this time she didn't get a tip. But she did when a man came in on his own and showed signs of leaving without paying. Once more she put the extra money in the glass.

She began to glance at the doors, watching for Gabriel to return, but it was another hour before she saw him and by then the cash register was looking healthy and her "glass for extras," as she called it to herself, was half full.

Unfortunately, when Gabriel returned he didn't look like a man on the hunt for cheerful news. He joined her behind the bar, planted his hands on his hips, and stared off into space.

He served the next couple who came in and didn't say a word when they started to leave without paying.

Leigh caught the expectant eyes of two women who had watched her for a very long time, their delight evident.

Right, she thought, now or never. "Excuse me," she called after the couple. She had heard Gabriel call the woman Merna. "Merna, can I have a word before you go?"

Apparently irritated, Merna turned back and her companion came with her. They both had the florid faces of perpetual barflies.

"You forgot this," Leigh said, passing over the bill she had hurriedly prepared. She waited for Gabriel to say something but he kept quiet.

Merna glared, first at Gabriel, then at Leigh. Without another word, her friend forked over the money and off they went.

The two-woman audience laughed until they almost fell out of their chairs. "Got yourself a shark there, Gabriel. About time, too, from what I hear."

One evil stare from Gabriel and the women decided it was time to go. They left, chuckling all the way out.

"What are you doing?" Gabriel said to Leigh.

She threw up her hands. "Oh, my, I forgot Jazzy. I've got to take him out, then I'll get back to the office."

"If you keep pushing people around like that, we'll lose customers," Gabriel said.

Leigh took her glass from behind the whiskey bottles and emptied the money on the counter. "Tips," she said. "Give them to the rest of the staff. And what's the point of customers who don't pay?"

chapter SIX

Niles was cruising from Gabriel's Place to Sean's cabin on his motorcycle when he got a general alert from Island Emergency Services on his radio. A man called Cody Willet had gone missing from Langley in midafternoon.

The missing persons report had been made by one of Cody's fellow workers at a local government office.

Within minutes another announcement said that Cody's wife called off the alert because, she claimed, Cody was only having a tantrum following a "domestic."

Three definite kidnap victims so far, and all had been women. Niles had started to wonder if Cody was the first male, but with his return they were back to female victims. Gabriel's Molly had been missing for three days and then turned up with no recollection of what had happened to her. Violet, another missing woman, had also returned with some infuriating amnesia, but she seemed happy enough to be back driving her small aluminum trailer from which she sold sandwiches, coffee, and whatever her imagination came up with.

Only Rose, who worked for a used book store on Gulliver Lane and as a relief school bus driver, was still missing.

A short communication from Sean wiped out all thoughts of the kidnappings. A forceful "scramble" warning was his message. Scramble was their no-questions-answered alert code. It wasn't a question of whether Niles was needed by his brother werehounds, but of how fast he could get where they wanted him to be. A bad day was turning into a worse night.

Sean had already left his cabin when Niles arrived. Niles quickly stripped off his clothes. This was the first time he had gone hound in many weeks, but he changed easily and rapidly, and there was little pain.

Shaking his russet brown fur and stretching his back, he leaped out of the open cabin door and immediately took cover in dense trees. "Sean," he called mentally. "Which way?"

No immediate response came, leaving Niles to prowl back and forth, raising his head to catch shifts in atmospheric mood from miles around. What drifted to him was a nerve-scrubbing odor of roiling fury.

"Niles," Sean finally slammed into Niles's mind. "Fully engaged here. Three of Brande's pack. They're guarding something they aren't letting us see, but they drew us here."

Niles focused intently. Brande, leader of the renegade werewolf pack on the island, and the hounds' sworn enemy, usually worked out of sight. For him to emerge, or to have members of the pack emerge, signaled inevitable violent action ahead.

"I'm coming now," Niles said, pounding a zigzag track through the trees. "Is Brande with them?"

"No. There's Booker, Seven, and Mark. They're looking for a fight."

"Don't engage them. Stand off."

Niles scaled a giant fir and threw himself from tree to tree, staring down, searching for signs that would tell him where his hounds had first encountered Brande's wolves. With the steady shrinking of safe territory and gradual loss of pack members, inbreeding had weakened the werewolves, but they remained sly and deadly.

"They're trying to keep us distracted while they move something," Sean said. "Innes and Ethan are with me. Should we alert the others?"

"No. We'll call them if we need them. Can you make out what they're hiding? Anything about it at all?" Speeding up, he hurtled his sinuous body in the direction of the others.

Rain began to fall and quickly turned into a torrent.

"Niles..."

His body prickled. Horror was something he didn't expect to hear from Sean. "Still coming your way," Niles said.

"I'm sure they've got a human," Sean said, very low.

"Can you see who it is?"

"No," Sean said. "But I think they're using her to pull us into their territory."

Her? It took all Niles had not to check his stride. Who was it? He couldn't allow the possible answer to get in his way.

His fear from the moment he had decided to pursue a mate was that Brande would find out and try to stop him.

If the wolves knew about Leigh—and it could only be a matter of time before they found out—they would do anything to stop a mating. Anything that made the hounds stronger, or even worse, put them on the road to complete human acceptance, was a deadly threat to Brande's kind and their plans to control the island.

"If they're trying to get us onto their land, they won't move away unless we follow," Niles told Sean.

For a werehound to trespass on werewolf territory was to risk the temporary paralysis the pack could cast on intruders. The wolves routinely used it to capture human prey and make them submit to pack rule.

Niles felt the proximity of both hound and wolf. "I'm here," he told Sean. "Innes, Ethan, do whatever I tell Sean to do."

Congested, constant movement showed up ahead. Niles scaled a taller tree, launched himself to the next one, and looked down. At least he knew his hounds would do as he told them. In the Middle East they had learned the perils of breaking protocol—the hard way—when they lost Gary.

All three of Brande's wolves were visible. Booker's distinctive white ruff shone in the darkness and the others crowded in beside him. The hounds, always smarter, had ranged themselves behind several big, jagged trunks of fallen trees.

"Hold it where you are," Niles ordered and backed down to take a closer look at a twisted little heap behind the wolves. It was obviously a body—a body with light hair.

His control chipped. Leaping as a hound could and a wolf could not, he flew, clawing his way through the air to land yards from his enemies. "Innes, show yourself but keep your distance from me. All of you; I will attack Booker to draw the other two closer to him. You know the drill. Back of the neck and hang on. Expose the spine."

"No," Sean yelled. "Wait. We've got to think. What if the others come?"

Even as Sean argued, Innes moved into Niles's peripheral vision. "I'm going in now," was all Niles said before exploding onto the scene and throwing himself on top of Booker.

Both of the other wolves went for Innes, leaving Sean and Ethan the seconds of advantage they had to have. Sean's blue-black coat glinted in the night. He took off and landed on one of the wolves. Niles was too engrossed to see which one but he heard a bellow and the crack of an opening jaw. He could only hope it was Sean's jaw and not that of the wolf he had attacked.

Booker convulsed beneath Niles, folded himself into a ball, then flung out his limbs with mighty force. Niles feared he would be dislodged, but his teeth had found muscle and pierced deep enough to drag a scream from Booker.

Niles bit deeper and felt when he passed through muscle to the softer tissue beneath. There was the scrape of bone on bone... his incisors on Booker's spine.

Blood spurted, momentarily filming Niles's eyes, but he blinked his vision clear and the battle raged all around him. He did see the moment when one of Sean's back legs dislocated and hung, useless, but there was nothing he could do to help. Sean fought on, attacking with more viciousness than ever despite the crushing agony he must feel.

Niles felt the seconds and minutes passing. He heard

only panting, rasping breath and cries of pain. This was taking too long. At any moment more wolves could appear, and the longer the woman lay on the ground without help, the less likely it was that they could save her.

Suddenly, from the darkest depths of the forest, a tall, winged creature burst through the dense trees.

A hoarse female voice called out, "Take the wolves," and Niles was knocked aside by the anonymous being.

Closer now, Niles could see that it wasn't wings, but an all-enveloping hooded cloak that streamed behind the newcomer. He threw the hounds away from the fray and took on all three wolves.

Snarling shredded the night. Again and again, a wolf lunged at the figure in black, great teeth glittering, eyes red with rage. A geyser of blood spurted from the tall creature, the newcomer. But it diminished and stopped almost at once.

There was a moment of utter motionlessness when the wolves, their sides heaving and jaws loosened in readiness for the death strike, faced the thing they must kill before it wiped them out.

Seven broke the deadlock first, snarling, gray fur on end, extending claws like scythes and blasting himself into the air.

He exposed his belly, and in a flash Niles soared to tear him open from neck to groin, shaking him, all but turning him inside out, while the dark one whipped to face Booker.

The third wolf grabbed the back of Seven's neck and dragged him after Booker, who was already backing away toward the pack compound at the north boundary of the forest.

For a moment, silence fell like an impenetrable layer from the skies.

The creature moved again, started after the wolves.

"Let 'em go." The hoarse voice, the same female voice they had heard before, came from the cover of thick bushes. "You've done your bit."

In a sweep of flowing garb, the creature turned and Niles saw what he had expected—fangs withdrawing beneath the hood. What else had such strength, but a vampire?

He seemed to dissolve.

"Vampire," Innes muttered. "When did vampires start siding with werehounds?"

Niles didn't answer. He went directly to the woman the wolves had left behind. From the corner of his eye he noticed a movement in the bushes, but it gave him no sense of threat, nor did the appearance of a plump female figure swathed in purple.

He sniffed the fallen woman and gently caught at her shoulder to turn her over. Relief gladdened and shamed him. It wasn't Leigh. Slowly, Sean walked over to Niles, his injury already mending.

"It's Rose," Sean said, "they've killed her." He shook his head as he spoke to Niles. "This is part of a bigger plot. Brande wants something we haven't even guessed at and it's deadly."

"I believe they want to control us, all of us, including the humans," Niles answered. "They want to have this island all to themselves."

Without warning a tiny silver-gray cat streaked toward Rose's body and prepared to attack Niles. It rose to its hind legs and spread long claws like curved needles. Niles looked into violet eyes that radiated a warning. He wasn't fool enough to dismiss this cat because it was little bigger than a guinea pig.

"Skillywidden! Stop!" Sally called from where she stood near the bushes.

This was only the second time Sally, who worked with Cliff at Gabriel's, had acknowledged her fae identity to Niles. The first was when she told him about Leigh's existence.

Leaning against Niles's immovable shoulder, Sally knelt beside Rose and lifted matted hair out of the woman's discolored face. Bending over the dead body, Sally sniffed Rose's mouth. "It's a poison," she said. "A poison of the blood."

The cat's eyes narrowed to slits and it backed off, looking from one to the other of the hounds. She sidled up to Sean and rubbed against his legs. "She's looking for a sympathetic friend," he said, laughing, and the cat instantly slunk away to hide herself in the folds of Sally's purple robes.

"What kind of poison?" Niles asked. He could communicate with the fae while he was a hound, something impossible with humans other than those with paranormal gifts.

"A poison of incompatibility," the woman said. "Rose was given blood she couldn't tolerate. This will happen again—the wolves are using humans to experiment."

"We've got to warn everyone," Ethan said.

"We've got to be smarter than Brande," Sally said. "Panic would play into his hands. Those who have returned without harm must be watched but not yet alerted to what we know. Am I right, Niles?"

He nodded. "Yes, absolutely right. But Rose's body should be found, to make people more cautious."

"That depends," Sally said, and there was no mistaking the sadness in her eyes. She stood and produced a sheet of sparkling gossamer, which she spread over Rose's body. Sally bowed her head. "Go away now, all of you. You're finished here. Don't say anything unless someone else tells you Rose is dead. Now go, and protect the vulnerable. There could be more like Rose before this is over."

Niles wanted to ask about the vampire but Sally and Rose had disappeared.

chapter SEVEN

Yesterday had been rough. Leigh had hoped Niles would come by last night, or call to ask her how she had made out the rest of the day at Gabriel's maybe. He had done neither and there had been no sign of him this morning.

It shouldn't matter whether he came by or called.

One of the twins, she thought it was Cuss, knocked and put himself halfway into the office. "Molly says you're wanted out front," he said, looking edgy.

"Did she say why?"

He swallowed. "Nope. But she's in one of her...moods."

Leigh didn't like being ordered to do anything but she disliked confrontation more. "I'll be right there," she said.

When Molly saw Leigh coming she pointed to a table in the bar as if she were giving an order to a dog.

Leigh muttered, "Down, boy...Over there, boy—" under her breath as she followed the other women.

Molly and Gabriel were close. They couldn't get any

closer. Leigh knew this because Molly had told her—
several times.

And now it looked as if Molly, who implied by her
behavior that she was the joint owner and boss at Gabriel's
Place, had decided it was time to put Leigh in her place.

"It's best not to let Gabe know we've talked," Molly
said. "He gets upset easily and he doesn't need it." Her dark
hair, pulled into a tail that cascaded from the top of her
head, also fell in ringlets around her pretty face and neck.

"You're right," Leigh said, walking behind Molly to a
table in a far corner of the bar. By this time, early afternoon on a Sunday, the place was supposed to hit a quiet
time but not today. Things were hopping.

Molly sat, wriggled herself into a comfy position, and
locked her hands behind her head. She took a very deep,
flexing breath. *My, oh, my* was Leigh's immediate thought.

She was tall, even taller in very high-heeled, Christian
Laboutin shoes, maneuvered to showcase their red under-
sides. If there had been anything but Molly under her
stretchy white blouse and pants, Leigh would have seen
it. Molly was, as someone had written somewhere: broad
where a broad should be broad. But with a tiny waist and
long, shapely legs.

Molly snapped her fingers and Twin Cuss hurried to
her side. "Yes, Molly."

The boy didn't seem to know which bit of Molly to
concentrate on and Leigh smiled.

"Coffee," Molly said. "A shot of Bookers in mine."

Waste of a good bourbon. "I'll take my coffee
straight," Leigh said, but the boy was too diverted to
acknowledge her.

"Now," Molly said when Cuss had left. "I was off when

you started or we'd have had this talk earlier. You need to understand I make all the decisions when Gabriel's not around. And he defers to me if he is."

"Mmm." Leigh nodded and managed her best, wide-eyed look of respect. Gabriel needed protection from this one, not that it was Leigh's responsibility.

"Sunday's fairly quiet so I thought this would be a good time for us to talk."

"Mmm." Leigh looked pointedly around the rowdy room but Molly didn't seem to notice.

"I've been getting complaints," she said.

Leigh managed to brighten up a few more watts in her eyes. "Really? Gabriel's not happy with my work? I've straightened a lot out already. You've only got to look at the office—"

Music suddenly blared from the multiple speakers hidden in the rafters and within minutes people leaped to the small floor in the bar to dance.

"I'm not talking about the office," Molly said loudly, her full lips tight with annoyance. "It's when you take over out here for a few minutes or deal with the vendors that's the problem."

"Really?"

"Yeah, *really*. We're building a tight community here with Gabe and Molly at the center. That means we're all friends. Friends don't make friends feel like shit."

Leigh was really starting to enjoy her job. Offbeat situations suited her. But she wouldn't be taking any crap from Ms. Molly.

"Would you amplify that?" Leigh said.

Molly screwed up her eyes. "Friends treat friends like friends," she yelled.

Wincing, Leigh shook a hand in front of her face. "Sorry, I should have said, *clarify*. I meant I need you to explain this in simpler terms." She made an arc in the air. "Be more obvious. You won't hurt my feelings."

"You've been demanding payment from some of our oldest customers. If they're used to running a tab, that's the way it's going to be. Got it?"

Leigh managed her best "I'm stupid" face.

"You are not to make people feel bad if they don't have the money to pay," Molly said slowly, dragging out each word.

"Oh! Oh, I never would. It's only the ones *with* the money and who don't want to pay," she said. "Have you noticed some folks never want to pay and we're a bit tight on funds around here?"

Molly played with a ringlet. "I don't have to worry myself with things like that. You know we do a good business. But we'll lose it if you make people stay away."

"I'm rarely in the restaurant or bar," Leigh said carefully. She was at war. On one hand she wanted to say she didn't need this job, then walk out. On the other hand she struggled with a sense of loyalty to Gabriel, who had been so nice to her.

Then there was Niles, who was pinning his hopes on Leigh changing things for Gabriel. Leigh liked the idea of Niles being happy—and of her being part of the reason.

And she was making friends. After keeping to herself for so long, she was starting to live again.

Leigh thought about Niles, not that he was being anything other than a good neighbor to her. But he had made her feel different, as if a little spark she never expected to know again had been struck.

Her breath caught. There was more than a neighborly feeling. Maybe for him as well—she had seen it in the way he looked at her.

"Then there's the vendors," Molly snapped. "Simon's been providing wine and incidentals since we opened. He gives us good deals already—"

"Simon seems like a very accommodating vendor, but as part of my job I checked the comps with other dealers and—"

"You told him you want a better deal. We won't get our supplies cheaper from anyone else. They'll promise anything to get the business but when the bills come in there'll be this and that added afterward."

"How do you know?"

"Simon told me and I trust him."

Leigh nodded. She couldn't figure out if Molly was an airhead or being deliberately obtuse because it made her life easier. This conversation would go nowhere. Twin Cuss had delivered the coffee and Leigh could smell the spirits in Molly's mug.

The music got suddenly ear-splitting and even more people poured onto the minuscule floor to squish into the crush. Whoops went up and Leigh smiled. It sounded as if they were holding an indoor rodeo.

"You see what I mean?" Molly shouted. "We've got ways of doing things around here and people like to know what to expect."

"Oh, yes, they do. That works the best for everyone." Leigh started to look around, somewhat desperately, for Gabriel.

Molly took several long gulps from her mug.

Leigh's prayer was answered. Gabriel walked through

the front doors with Niles—Niles and the gigantic blue-black dog.

"Ugh," Molly said. "Gabriel shouldn't let that thing in here."

"Niles is a nice man," Leigh said.

"He's a hunk. But I meant the dog. Nasty piece of work if you ask me. Just sits there and stares. Shouldn't be allowed."

"Dogs always come into the bar," Leigh pointed out. "My Jazzy's in the back."

Molly looked as if she would like to say something unpleasant about poor little Jazzy. Instead she plastered on a prim smile. "Jazzy's different. That's the size a dog should be and he doesn't come out here."

Leigh made no comment.

Niles saw Leigh and came to her side with Blue at his heel. "Hi, lady," he said. His Adam's apple jerked when he spoke and Leigh had the extraordinary impression that he might be nervous around her. Or just very aware? He didn't even glance at Molly, who gave off waves of petulance.

"Hey," Leigh said. "How's everything going?"

"Good," he said. "Good. I thought it was time I introduced my dog properly since he likes to hang out around your place." He went down on one knee with the dog between them.

Niles had talked about looking out for Blue but not about the dog belonging to him, but she was glad. Any dog-friend of Niles could be a dog-friend of hers.

"He's a love," Leigh said diplomatically and managed to scratch Blue between the ears without flinching. With her sitting down, the dog was as tall as she was.

Blue turned his big head to look into her face. Then, without warning, he licked her from chin to forehead and rested his head on her arm.

"That's enough," Niles snapped, glaring into the dog's face.

"Leave him," Leigh said. Dogs always had an inside track with her. "He's a sweetheart." She felt as if Niles was physically very close to her—which he was. "You'd better watch out or I'll steal Blue from you." Even kneeling the man was so much taller than she.

That appealed to her.

"He'd probably eat Jazzy," Molly said, scowling at Niles, who still had not spoken to her.

"Blue likes Jazzy," Leigh said, goaded on by Molly's obvious dislike of animals. "They hang out together." She tightened the muscles in her jaw and draped an arm as far across Blue's neck as it would go.

That's when she glanced up at Niles, who was giving his dog an interesting stare. He seemed annoyed, but she must be wrong.

He caught Leigh's eyes briefly and rested an arm on hers to tweak one of Blue's ears.

Awkwardness made her want to withdraw her arm. Niles's weight and warmth kept her right where she was.

Molly got up and plastered herself against Gabriel, who kissed her forehead and gave her an appreciative once over.

"I made arrangements for you to go up into Langley about the sign, Leigh," Gabriel said, pecking Molly on the lips but avoiding what promised to be a long, passionate smooch. "Do you think you could do that this afternoon? Niles said he'll drive you."

"I'll be able to find it myself," she said at once and without thinking. "I mean, I don't want to put Niles out like that."

"I'm going up that way on business," Niles said, looking at her again. "We're pretty green around here. We save resources where we can."

Short of telling him she was into gas guzzling and waste, there wasn't much she could say. "When are you going?" she asked. "Jazzy's due for an outing first."

"Bring him with us and he can play on the beach up there. Blue loves it, too."

Leigh couldn't find an excuse to refuse. "Okay, give me a call when you're ready," she said. Confession was a good thing—she wanted to go with him.

"We might as well head out now," Niles said. "Get Jazzy and I'll meet you outside." He took Blue by the collar and led him to the door.

Leigh didn't miss the longing stare Molly aimed at Niles. That, at least, gave Leigh some wicked pleasure— even if it did make her worry more about Gabriel's feelings.

She let Jazzy out of the office. He leaped around like a lifer suddenly released from the pen and headed back to the bar, by which time Molly was nowhere in sight.

Gabriel took Leigh aside to one end of the bar. "Cliff recommended this place for making signs," he said, slipping a card into her hand. "Did Molly give you a hard time? From what she just said, I think she might have. The only one you have to take any notice of is me and I haven't seen anything I needed to talk about. You're a gem, my girl."

"Molly's protective of you, is all." Leigh thought about

it. "But we do have to collect accounts from customers—something I'm good at—and after I finish finding out the going rates for the stuff we use, I'll negotiate better prices where it's appropriate. No one has to worry about things like that. People who make their living selling things are used to negotiation."

Gabriel gave her one of his charming smiles and nodded. "You will remember what we discussed about the sign?"

"You bet." She hesitated. "What would you think about holding a dance once a month?"

"People already dance here."

"We could hire a live band. Have prizes and special theme food on the menu."

Gabriel thought about it. "You might have something there. We'd have to plan it with Cliff."

Smiling, Leigh headed for the door. "Niles will wonder where I am," she said.

chapter EIGHT

LEIGH HAD NOT BEEN prepared for what she found outside. A gigantic black motorcycle stood there and Blue had just put himself into the largest sidecar Leigh had ever seen.

Jazzy had to visit some of his favorite territory among the thick screen of firs that framed the gravel car park.

Niles got tired of waiting and clapped his hands. "C'mon Jazzy, boy. Quit checking your pee-mail." He swept up Leigh's dog and stuffed him between Blue's front feet.

Blue gave Jazzy a lick and got an adoring stare in response.

Niles closed down the sidecar and handed Leigh a crash helmet. When she didn't seem to know what to do with it, he put it on her head and carefully fastened and checked it for fit.

He lifted her from the ground and placed her on the pillion, then slid a leg over and sat in front of her.

Her heart did jumping jacks and she thought her blood might have heated up several degrees. The leather-covered back in front of her was impossibly broad and black wavy hair escaped the bottom of Niles's helmet. She couldn't take in everything she'd like to from her current position but flexed thighs filling out his jeans would be hard to miss, and when he leaned forward to kick off the stand a quick downward glance gave a perfect view of hard buns.

She looked at the sky. This was outrageous. What was she doing here with this man? On a motorcycle? Leigh had never been on a motorcycle before.

He smiled at her over his shoulder. "Off we go. Feel free to hang on to anything that appeals to you. Everything about this bike is absolutely safe."

She nodded and thought, *including you?*

The bike roared off, leaving Leigh's stomach in Gabriel's parking lot. A glance at the sidecar showed Jazzy standing between Blue's front legs, body fully extended to reach the window rim, so he could look out with a doggy laugh at the passing scenery. So much for the dog who didn't like riding in cars—evidently motorbikes were different.

Wind grabbed at Leigh's hair, lifting it on either side of the helmet. The air smelled good, of pine and the coldest part of the winter that was almost upon them.

They leaned into a corner and Leigh's tummy went the wrong way again. She filled her hands with the two pleats where Niles's leather jacket expanded for movement. Her own coat, though down, was not thick enough to keep out the biting air.

They shot past several cars and made another turn, in the opposite direction.

Leigh closed her eyes, slid her arms as far as they

would go around Niles, and pressed her visored face into his back. She clung on, letting herself go with the moves until she was almost lulled.

From time to time she looked to see where they were but she was more comfortable with her eyes shut. Once Niles patted her hand against his side and the simple gesture made her smile.

"Fun, huh?" he said loudly.

She opened her eyes and realized they had stopped at a curb and there were a few buildings on either side of a gravel-strewn road on the outskirts of Langley. The ride had only taken about twenty minutes.

With a jerk, she sat straight and pulled her arms back to rest her hands on her thighs.

Niles kicked down the stand and looked back at her again. "You okay?"

"Oh, yes. That was great."

"See those two," he said, pointing at the sidecar. "They want more."

The dogs did look as if they were drunk on pleasure and panting for more of the same.

When Leigh climbed off the cycle she had a shock. Her legs felt like water. They seemed to have no substance and she could scarcely stop herself from falling.

"Hey," Niles said, laughing. "Your first time? That can happen." He put an arm around her waist and took off the helmet for her before removing his own. He hung one on each handlebar, keeping an eye on Leigh at the same time.

Her apparent inability to walk shocked her. She tried to take a step and laughed nervously when Niles swung back and caught her by the shoulders.

This time he didn't laugh.

She couldn't look away from his face. He frowned a little, searching her eyes as if he thought he could see inside her.

"Just stay still for a few moments," he said, his voice quietly, deeply penetrating. "We all need to get our sea legs sometimes."

His lips parted and he passed the tip of his tongue along the top of his teeth. And when she glanced up, his whole attention was on her mouth.

He spread his fingers, holding her with the palms of his hands only, and there was a moment when he started to tip her toward him.

Leigh let out the breath she had been holding. "I'm fine now," she said, smiling brightly. "A ninny, but fine, thanks."

Niles's hands fell to his sides and he gave her a lazy grin. "I guess I'll let you get on, then. Just don't fall and skin your knees."

In the cramped front yard beside them colored plastic and aluminum figures bloomed like the flowers that might have been there. Addams Family birdhouses topped rusty poles, animals made from cast-off pieces of almost anything crowded together. A stream of water slithered down the body of a twelve-foot, aluminum and red glass snake.

"Like it?" Niles said. There was tension in his voice.

Shaken by her reaction to him, Leigh closed her mouth and listened. The water made a hissing sound. She glanced into his face and now he seemed to be struggling to stay serious, or at least not to crack up at what must be the very strange expression on her face.

"This can't be the right place," she said, searching for the card Gabriel had given her. "I'm supposed to go to a sign shop."

Niles pointed to a board on one side of open double front doors. The board resembled a menu. *Come And Get It If You Dare* appeared to be the name of the establishment. The list of wares read: Costumes for any event. Wands to suit you. Hats to make you memorable. Masks to make you memorable but unrecognizable. Shoes to move you faster. Boots to keep you where you are. Robes and what-have-you. Signs guaranteed to be noticed. If it isn't listed—we have it.

Leigh found the card: Come And Get It, and in tiny letters beneath, If You Dare, followed by the address.

"It's got to be a joke," she said.

He nodded, "Of course it is, but apparently Cliff knows they make good signs and they're fast. Some people really get off on this kind of wacky stuff."

"Have you been inside?"

Niles shook his head, no.

She remembered where she was and what she was supposed to be doing. "I'll just get Jazzy out and let you go about your business. Thank you for bringing me. That was quite a ride." She smiled at him. "I've been leading a sheltered life. I had no idea what it felt like to be on one of these things."

"Did you like it?" Niles went around to open the sidecar and lift Jazzy out. The little traitor snuggled up to him, burying his face in his neck. "You kind of have to get used to it. That's why you were shaky getting off. You'll be better next time."

Next time?

"Here." He gave her a piece of paper with a phone number on it.

"Just call when you're ready to go home and I'll take

you back. You sure you don't want to leave Jazzy with
me?" Frowning, Leigh removed her dog from Niles's hold
and set him down. She put on his leash and gave it a firm
pull. "Thanks for bringing us. If you're sure you don't
mind, I will call." After all, she did need a way back.

"I don't mind at all."

He was still at the curb when she and Jazzy went inside
the building.

chapter NINE

Leigh looked at the card again. The shop address was the same, the name on the outside of the shop was the same, but this could *not* be the right place.

She had dropped into a leafy bower, or so it seemed. Surrounded by walls and a ceiling smothered with vines, Leigh resisted an urge to flee. Jazzy sniffed happily at the foliage sprouting all around him. Realistic trees crowded the big room, their branches and twigs used to hang hats, capes, robes in myriad colors, and masks in shapes that quickly got Leigh bending this way and that to see them properly. She assumed the profusion of sturdy sticks, many of them oddly shaped, that stood in buckets were the wands advertised.

On one side of the shop stood several large tables with products in various stages of completion. Thin shiny leather, pigskin, suede, heavy silk, feathers, spools of gold chain. There was too much to take in.

Leigh slapped a hand over her heart—little twinkling

purple lights had popped on among the vines and branches, probably thousands of them. And they twinkled to the accompaniment of what sounded like chipmunks singing in Latin. Or was it "Greensleeves," but distorted by the nuts in their cheeks?

She shook her head and turned to walk out.

Jazzy wasn't leaving. He sat, transfixed, his chin raised to stare at a doll-sized four-poster bed heaped with small, soft blankets.

"C'mon, Jazzy," she said. "Let's go."

The dog's response was to loll his tongue from his mouth and pant happily. He stood up and whined.

From the nest of little blankets, a head appeared, a silvery-gray head with long whiskers and pointed ears with small tufts on the ends. In a smooth movement the smallest cat Leigh had ever seen emerged and sat with its paws in a precise row and a tail twice as long as its body curled in a tight circle around it. Silver all over with violet eyes, it transfixed Leigh. She got a prickling sensation up her spine. The cat was irresistible. Leigh had to reach out a hand.

The cat closed its eyes and purred gently while allowing herself to be stroked.

Jazzy whined louder and the cat jumped down to sniff him thoroughly. Jazzy grinned while the cat scooted to settle on top of his front paws.

"That's weird," Leigh muttered, the spine prickles intensifying.

"Leigh! I thought you might be coming but then I wasn't sure I didn't have my days all muddled up."

She would have recognized that hoarse voice anywhere and swung around. "Sally? What are you doing here?" The second half of Gabriel's kitchen staff slid from an opening in the vines.

"And Skillywidden," Sally cooed to the cat, ignoring Leigh's question. "Jazzy is every bit as special as we know he is. Skillywidden is a perfect judge of character—unless she's protecting the weak. Everyone should keep their distance then. She has adopted Jazzy and he knows he is blessed. She will always look after him."

"That's nice," Leigh said. "She's still a kitten, isn't she?"

Fluttering her hands, Sally said, "I've had her for years. I have no idea how old she is."

"I see." *Whoa, she and Jazzy had gone through the looking glass.*

"Gabriel didn't tell me it was you who ran this shop."

"He doesn't know," Sally said, fixing Leigh with a penetrating stare. "It would be better if he didn't find out. Would that be all right?"

"I guess. But Cliff knows?"

Sally's gaze didn't waver. "No. I gave him that card you have there and said I'd make sure you were expected here. I'm sure you understand it's a good idea to keep two very different sides of my life separate. Most people don't understand any of this." She raised her hands to indicate the shop. "Do you?"

Hesitating, Leigh looked around again. "Probably not, but I really like it. And I believe people have a right to privacy when they want it."

"Oh, good," Sally said, her voice rasping excitedly. "I own the place. Live upstairs. I never see someone I know from Gabriel's because this wouldn't be their cup of tea. Apart from my regulars, only a few tourists come in—and they go right back out most of the time."

Leigh swallowed. "It's lovely."

Sally's figure wasn't shown to advantage by a floor-length pleated red robe with butterfly sleeves—and tiny white butterflies stamped all over. The gauzy fabric clung to all sorts of places probably better not clung to.

She let out a great sigh. "I know it's lovely. But it's working for Gabriel that lets me keep my home," she said. "Every amateur theater, children's play class, May Day Parade, Solstice celebration, fairy gathering, or what have you comes to me for their costumes. Masks and hats are my real love."

"Do you need me to help you collect your bills?" Leigh said, threading her fingers tightly together. People would take advantage of good hearts. "I'm doing that at Gabriel's and it's working already. Some people will put off paying if you let them."

"No, no, no." When Sally shook her head, bells jingled in her red feather turban. "Everyone pays but I have to charge according to what I know they can afford and that's not much when they don't have much."

Leigh managed not to groan.

Sally smiled. "I see your expression. You think I'm another pushover. Perhaps I am but for different reasons. I like to encourage imagination to flourish.

"What you're doing to help Gabriel is wonderful. We all want him to succeed and the fates haven't been with him. He needed you to organize him and give him some new ideas."

The compliments brought more pleasure to Leigh than she supposed they should. "I'm having fun," she said. "I used to design games for a living. Now I feel as if I'm playing games—productive ones—for a living."

"I'm so glad you're at Chimney Rock Cove," Sally said. Without warning, she flung her arms around Leigh and hugged her. "You are special and you've come to a special place. It's where you're meant to be. Just trust that. No matter what happens, believe it's supposed to. And all you have to do if you don't understand something, is ask me. I'll make you feel better about it. I already know that you have the capacity to be what you need to be and do what you need to do. Above all, do not ever be afraid."

"Thank you," Leigh said, feeling wobbly again.

Jazzy yipped and Sally laughed. "Look at that. I heard they liked each other."

As if his legs had become springs, Jazzy jumped to meet Blue, whose feet thumped across the wooden floor. He sat beside Leigh and looked up at her. If a dog could look pleased with himself, then he did. His golden eyes crinkled up and a great many really large and very white fangs—no, teeth—showed all the way around an impressive jaw.

"Blue," Sally said. "Well, I'll be, if it isn't Blue. What have you done with Niles?"

The miniature cat, who looked slightly cross-eyed, so intense was her concentration on the new arrival, strolled slowly closer to Niles's dog.

"I reckon someone's going to be in trouble," Sally said. "No, I reckon someone's already in trouble. Who's a naughty boy? Who's doing what he's not supposed to do?"

Frowning, Leigh turned, expecting to see a child.

"It's Blue I'm talking to," Sally said. "He shouldn't be running around on his own so far from—" She blinked fast.

"Niles?" Leigh suggested helpfully. "You're right. He

drove me to Langley and went to do some errands. I bet
Blue got away and ran off. Wait till Niles finds out."

"Leave Blue be," Sally said, sounding irritated. "Why
interfering people can't mind their own business, I don't
know. You just sit over there, Blue. I'll decide what to do
with you later."

Chastised—and confused—Leigh cleared her throat.
"Signs?" she said. "Did anyone talk to you about a sign for
Gabriel's Place?"

Sally wrinkled her nose. "Maybe they did and maybe
they didn't. If you and I come up with something special it
will probably be because we've both forgotten what anyone else thinks they want. Take a look at this."

She moved scissors and brown paper pattern pieces
from the top of a table, knelt down and struggled, and
puffed, and wriggled a piece of sheet metal from beneath
the bottom shelf of the table. It kept coming until Leigh
got down to help and they wrestled the plastic-edged sign
completely free.

"This will change the feeling people get when they
drive near Gabriel's. It'll make them smile and they'll
want to stop."

With one of them at each end, they hoisted it onto the
table.

"Wow," Leigh said. "It's huge." It had to be twenty feet
long and twelve feet high. "How did you get it in here?"

"I had help," Sally said airily. "I've been expecting a
request for this, you know. But I knew it wouldn't happen
until you came. What do you think?"

To analyze every comment Sally made would be a big
mistake, but Leigh couldn't ignore the little references
to knowing what she would be doing before she knew

herself. Leigh had to step back to try reading oversized three-dimensional letters. The metal board was polished to a sheen but the letters were clear plastic like the rim of the board. She couldn't make out a word, and didn't know what to say. "Um," was all she could manage.

"Silly me," Sally said. "You can't see it like that." She grabbed a plug hanging from a cord on one side and stuck it into a socket strip.

The effect was dizzying. The sign itself appeared more pewter than steel or aluminum, and blood red light ran through the letters in an endless stream that stopped for a few seconds then flashed each time the entire sign was illuminated.

> *Stop!*
> *Turn In Here For Gabriel's Place*
> *Eat Drink And Be Merry*
> *For Tomorrow We Die(T)*

chapter TEN

Niles looked at his cell for a long minute then slammed it back to his ear. "You do know there's a woman missing, VanDoren?" Niles said, pacing back and forth near the trees that shielded the doctor's house from Gulliver Lane.

"Rose," VanDoren said, still sounding as if he would rather be taking a nap. "I'm aware of that."

"Look, are you sure I can't come in? I'd really like to talk to you about this."

"We are talking about it. I try to save a few hours in every twenty-four for myself."

Saul VanDoren hadn't answered his door, even though his medical offices were right there in his house. Niles tried calling him on a whim and the guy had refused to see him.

"Okay." Damn the man's attitude. "No progress has been made in finding Rose. The search parties are still going out from the cops in Langley. I only want to know if you've heard anything about her, any talk of someone hit by a car...anything." Niles knew he was grasping at straws. Not one comment had been made about Rose since Sally disappeared with the body the night before.

His hounds had joined the search today, and they had been looking for the woman's body on their own for days. He could keep the secret of her murder to avoid starting a panic, but he couldn't allow her body to simply be lost.

"I would have reported anything of the kind to the police," VanDoren said.

"Did Rose come to you for any reason recently?"

VanDoren didn't comment.

"You still there?" Niles said.

"Uh huh. And no, she didn't."

Niles's eyes smarted and he blinked. He was sweating along his hairline and the feeling he hated had started in the pit of his stomach. Anger mixing everything up. This still happened sometimes, intense irritation set him on the track back to when he'd lost Gary in that hellhole of a desert. He almost felt as if his dead brother hound were riding on his back.

He took a deep breath. "Okay, Doc. Thanks. By the way, I understand you were real good to Innes when he got hurt. It's nice for all of us around here to know we have a good man to come to."

"I'm always here for an emergency," the other man said, sounding less uninterested.

Niles wanted to ask about the blood sample the doctor had taken from Innes. All Innes had been told was that there was no sign of abnormality, yet it shouldn't be possible to examine a werehound's blood and not find something *really* abnormal. VanDoren's silence on the subject was almost worse than if he'd asked awkward questions.

"Are we done?"

Niles gritted his teeth and wiped a finger along his brow. "Thanks, Doc." *For nothing.* "So long."

The phone went dead and Niles walked slowly through the trees to the street. VanDoren was a convenient target for the anger but he wasn't the right one. Niles knew he owned all of his rage.

The sight of his bike lifted his spirits—for an instant. He'd planned to unload on Sean, who could usually say some of the right things.

"Shit," Niles said. "You goddamn sneaky bastard."

Sean had taken the opportunity to desert the scene. He wouldn't show up till he felt like it.

chapter **ELEVEN**

Niles rode back through Langley to pick up Leigh and parked in front of the shop where he had left her.

The doorway was as far as he got before stopping to take in the scene inside. One look at Sean, giving one of his inscrutable hound stares, began to wind up Niles's temper again. There was too much unanswered for him to have patience with his second-in-command's unpredictable adventures.

A jolt of anger caught him off-guard. He hadn't actually snapped since the time with Leigh at Gabriel's and he didn't want to lose control again. A couple of deep breaths calmed him but cold sweat popped between his shoulder blades.

Sean saw him standing outside and read his thoughts at once. *"Back off, friend,"* he communicated into Niles's mind.

"Why the hell did you take off like that?" Niles responded in kind, grateful that the two women were

too busy poring over a big board on top of a table to have noticed his arrival.

"I wasn't comfortable leaving Leigh alone here," Sean said.

"Did you lose your memory?" Niles asked. *"Have you forgotten I'm the one with the longest sight? I could see Leigh here whenever I wanted to."*

"Did you think to take a look?" Sean asked. *"Did you see who it is who runs this place? Leigh shouldn't be here alone when we don't know what the woman's angle is."*

The second woman, dressed in a lot of red, half turned toward him but Niles could already recognize Sally. He was furious with himself for not knowing more about this place before leaving Leigh. Finding out when and how to expect the bombshell about Rose to drop had distracted him, and getting distracted was something he couldn't afford.

"Welcome, Niles," Sally said, meeting his eyes. "Leigh told me you had brought her. Now, don't you be angry with Blue. You aren't as pretty as she is and he's obviously smitten with her."

"Right," Niles said, forcing a laugh and smiling at Leigh when she turned toward him. "Hi," he said, warmed in all the right places by her obvious pleasure at the sight of him. She turned a little pink and looked away. And Niles knew they were both thinking of those moments before he had left her outside the shop.

He hadn't forgotten his carelessness in not making sure everything was okay with Leigh while she was here. *"I should have looked,"* Niles admitted to Sean.

"Be grateful they're both still here," Sean said. *"We don't know for sure this Sally isn't demonic. If she is, she is too dangerous to take any chances with."*

"Yeah, but she found Leigh for us. And she managed to get her back on the island and working for Gabriel so I have a chance to . . . get to know her."

Leigh was staring at him, and frowning. He tried to relax his face.

"You okay?" she said. "I didn't expect you back so quickly."

"Couldn't be better. There's nothing like a windy blow on my bike to clear the head. I got through with my business faster than I expected. Don't let me interrupt you and Sally. There's plenty to amuse me here."

He could have sworn she was reluctant to return to whatever they were working on.

"We owe this fae woman a favor," Sean said, inclining his big head. *"She hasn't asked for anything yet, but she will. That's part of their lore."*

"I don't need a fae lecture from you," Niles shot back. *"You shouldn't have left without making sure we both thought it was a good idea."*

"C'mon." Sean made a snorting sound. *"Like you didn't expect me to take off from that darn sidecar? I can't wait till I have a chance to make you ride in that thing like an overgrown kid."*

"When Leigh's finished here I'm going to suggest we go to the beach for Jazzy to get a run." The little mutt watched him with adoration. *"I told her I would. If you want to sit on the steps down to the beach, fine, but I don't want you dogging us."*

Sean laughed, the noise sounding more like a snort from his large hound's mouth.

"You know what I mean." Niles smiled. *"There's more than something casual between Leigh and me and it's time to start finding out just how much is there."*

"*Whoa*," Sean said. "*Don't forget the Team rules. She's got to accept you first—all of you.*"

Anger ruffled Niles's nerves again. Niles breathed hard through his nose and did what he was loath to do. He issued an order, blasting it into Sean's mind: "*I am your alpha. We will have this discussion later. You should not have left without talking to me. Times may be changing, that's all I will say now.*"

"*But—*"

"*Not now, captain.*"

At the instant when the hound lowered his gaze, dropped his head, his front quarters, and finally his hind quarters, Niles heard Sally say, "I want you to meet Dr. Saul VanDoren now that he's getting back, Leigh." Sally's eyes met Niles's briefly, then moved on. She said nothing to him and continued speaking to Leigh. "He's someone you can trust with anything. I'll introduce you. He comes into Gabriel's most days."

Sally's sleek little cat strolled, tail undulating, to Niles and jumped effortlessly all the way to his shoulder where she sat staring at him. When Niles looked into her face she blinked slowly and wrapped her tail around his neck. She was weightless.

"Skillywidden really likes you, Niles," Sally said brightly. "Blue, too. You're two of very few. I guess she knows kindred spirits—familiars, perhaps." She laughed.

Niles looked sideways at the cat. Another of the area's shapeshifters, no doubt.

Leigh looked over her shoulder at him and they stared at each other. Niles swallowed several times. In the odd light, her hair shone more red than gold and her dark eyes looked not just at him, but into him. He wasn't the only one who felt they were starting to touch—without having to touch. They didn't need skin on skin to sense the absorption of one into the other.

He wanted to smile, to offer her the welcome he felt throughout his body and being, but he couldn't move.

She had taken off her green down coat. A little woman, really, but shapely in her high-necked black sweater and those tight pants that ended just above the ankle where they tucked inside her short boots. She needed to be more warmly dressed.

Leigh smiled before he did. For an instant her eyes glistened as if she might cry.

"Hi," he finally mouthed, a lump in his throat and something strong and all male flowing through him, hardening him.

The pucker between her brows, her steady stare directly into his eyes stole his breath and his ability to do anything but look back.

"Can you all excuse me for a few minutes," Sally said. "I'm slow-cooking something and I need to make sure it's progressing the way I want it to."

She slipped away without waiting for a response.

"That's convenient," Leigh said. "I was just going to ask you if we could sit on one of those benches outside. I could use some air."

Skillywidden jumped down and nuzzled Blue.

Niles didn't need one of the shop's neon signs to let him know Leigh was tuning in to him much more acutely than she should be. He put a hand on her shoulder and with a warning glare to keep Blue where he was, guided Leigh through the front door.

They sat on a crooked hunk of tree trunk, balanced on its side and highly polished on top.

"Something's wrong," Leigh said without preamble. "I can feel it. And I've felt it before. You want to do things for me all the time. Let me help you. I don't like to take without giving."

"Thanks for caring," he said. "But there's nothing, really."

She turned toward him and wiped her fingertips along his brow. She showed him how wet they were then rubbed her hands together. Then, with the gentlest of touches, she rubbed between his eyes, and then the rigid corners of his mouth. "I don't believe you," she said. "But I understand if you'd rather not talk about it."

Crossing his arms, he struggled with the iron will he had learned, and his own need to feel closer to this woman than he had to anyone. If he wanted Leigh to accept him, he had to begin to share the truth. "I thought I was over it all. I used to wake up from dreams, drenched in sweat. Most of the time I didn't sleep. But I've been better."

"And something has slipped backward for you." She rested a hand on the side of his face and he could hardly breathe.

"Something like that," he managed to say. "Years working with the contract special operations team in the Middle East had showed me the worst there was to see. I thought there'd never be anything worth getting angry about again. That had lasted until I lost a man, Gary. He was bringing up the rear. When we didn't see him we went back but he was gone. There wasn't any sign of him. I kept hoping that meant he was still alive but we never found him. He was a member of our team—a brother."

"That's horrible," Leigh said. "But you weren't there alone. You must all have depended on each other."

"I was in charge," Niles snapped. "The buck stopped with me. A split second of carelessness cost Gary his life."

He thought Leigh trembled and hated himself for scaring her like that.

"If you didn't find him, he might still come back. These things happen. Was there blood? Anything?"

The same questions haunted Niles. "Nothing." He shook his head.

"I'm not much use, I'm sure," Leigh said. "But I know something about loss. Please come to me if you need someone. We don't even have to talk."

"I—" her empathy amazed him. "Thanks. Just stomp on my feet or something if you see me getting nasty." He laughed. "We'd better go in or we'll start people talking."

Leigh stood up and led the way.

Sally appeared at almost the same time. "You'll have to see what we have here later," she told Niles. "It's a surprise for Gabriel."

Smoothly, she unrolled brown paper across the board she and Leigh had been looking at and taped the paper down. Evidently whatever she had covered was not for him to see, at least not yet. He felt curious, but not enough to do anything about it.

How much of an act was Sally's innocuous manner? What would she demand from him?

"*Don't worry, Leader.*" Sean's words came into Niles's mind, muffled and edged with something different. "*Whatever happens, we will all stand together and deal with it. I apologize for forgetting my place sometimes and that's wrong. This all means so much to us. And of all of us, you are the first to walk the line between what we became and what we want to be again. It isn't easy."*

Niles relaxed. He kept on looking at Leigh but told Sean, *"Your apology is accepted but not necessary. We all came together as alpha hounds. The rest of you made me head of the Team but perhaps some areas—when we are not on a mission—some areas need to be revisited. Battle demands a chain of command but we are not in battle now."*

"Aren't we?" Sean asked. *"No one's said a thing about Rose's body being found so I guess it hasn't been."*

"We will discuss more later. We should have thought this far and expected issues. I didn't. Now let me deal with this."

"Remember Dr. Saul VanDoren, Niles?" Sally said. "He'll be back in Chimney Rock at any time now. He'll be his usual helpful self. You can always rely on him to work out any problems."

The message wasn't lost on Niles. "Useful man," he said, not happy the doctor was to be involved with their issues any further. After VanDoren's brushoff earlier, Niles would rather steer clear of him.

But given the continuing worry about what he did or did not think about his examination of Innes, VanDoren remained a potential problem. Innes was convinced Van-Doren was something other than a maverick general practitioner who had to do his own thing—on his own.

It was not possible for a knowledgeable technician to look at a werehound's blood and not know he was seeing something that wasn't purely human. VanDoren had his own little lab and did his own simple tests.

Sean, who was a volunteer fireman and medic, had been out on a call when Innes got hurt but still he blamed himself for not being around at the time.

A phone rang and it was Leigh who grabbed for her coat and took a cell out of her pocket. "Leigh Kelly," she said.

Niles barely stopped himself from trying to listen to her thoughts. He had automatically picked up something when she'd been confronted by John Valley at Gabriel's, but they could not build trust on trickery and that's how she would see it.

For a werehound to read a human's mind was rare but it did happen occasionally, usually when the human had suppressed talents of some kind.

"Hey, Jan," she said, smiling. "You're back...at the Camano house? That's great. Is everything okay there?"

Curiosity came even closer to getting the better of Niles. Camano was the island immediately across Saratoga Passage from Whidbey.

For minutes Leigh only nodded, more and more slowly, and an expression of resignation gradually replaced her smile. "Of course," she said finally. "Will seven be too late, though? My job—"

She pressed her lips together and waited, listening.

"That isn't up for discussion," she said. "Would you and Gib like to come around seven or should we do it another day?"

More listening.

She looked at the floor. "Cheer up. You know I want to see you. Seven then and tell Gib not to drive too fast. There isn't a lot of light down by my house."

Her attention gradually came back to Niles and Sally and she gave another smile, this one much stiffer, as she put the phone away.

"My sister and her husband have a vacation house over

on Camano. They just got back there. It'll be nice to see them." Her discomfort was evident. "Thank you, Sally. I'll talk to you about that"—she nodded toward the table—"and how we should get it installed." Her grin turned very real. "Should be fun."

Sally looked equally pleased. She picked up Jazzy while Leigh put her coat on. The fae woman puzzled Niles. He had not asked her to help him find a potential human mate; she had offered. But the rules remained the same. A favor granted was a favor earned, and the delivery of Leigh so that he had a chance to see if the two of them could become Forever Mates was, indeed, a favor. An even more baffling question was how Sally had known about either the Team and its gradual loss—over a hundred or so years—of all females of their own kind, or the single incredibly rare element in a tiny number of humans' blood that could allow compatibility with werehounds. She was also familiar with Brande and his surly pack of werewolves, and had shown distaste for them.

"Thank you," Leigh told Sally. She hesitated, then hugged the woman. "It's wonderful to discover I have a real friend here. If I can do anything for you, just let me know."

"I am your channel to help," an unknown voice whispered in his mind. "Our connection will always be open. And you can rely on me to be your eyes when your own are not enough. Leigh is important to all of us."

A glance into violet eyes very close to his own made the hair on the back of his neck stand up. This was no ordinary cat standing on his shoulder.

chapter TWELVE

THE ODD LITTLE CAT slithered fearlessly into Niles's big hands. He held her gently while she kept her eyes on his.

Leigh watched them watch each other and she took a deep breath. He was a rugged man who appealed to her in ways she had almost forgotten. Rugged yet...tender? Would he be tender with a woman he cared for?

She quickly took Skillywidden from him, kissed the top of the creature's head, which earned her a cross-eyed look, and gave him to Sally.

Jazzy took his opportunity to leap at Niles and take the cat's place.

Leigh followed Niles from Sally's shop to the broken sidewalk. Blue loped beside her.

She looked aside, embarrassed. Had he aroused her? Was that it? A sexual reaction to a man when she had not ever expected to feel such a thing again after Chris's death. She stopped walking.

"We can get down to the beach over there," Niles said, preparing to cross the road. "We won't stay long but at least we can give Jazzy a little playtime. He's been so good."

Leigh went to the bike. She fingered the nearest handlebar. "That was my sister on the phone," she said. "But I already told you that. They want to see me and it's going to be time for dinner when they get here. I'd better not go to the beach now. I've got to get back to work, then figure out something for dinner."

Her tummy turned and turned. Jan and Gib were coming to check up on her. They felt responsible for making sure she wasn't falling apart at Two Chimneys and wallowing in sadness over Chris.

"What is it?" Niles took hold of her arm and turned her gently to face him. "You look so sad."

"I'm not." And she wasn't. Not really. She was muddled up and trying to sort things out. She would mourn Chris forever. How could she not? But people mourned and learned to love again at the same time.

The thought startled her. She took in a sharp breath and stared up at Niles's very blue eyes, filled with question now.

She owed him some sort of explanation for her mood. "Jan and Gib are sweet, but every time they see me they fuss about how bad it is for me to be alone."

Niles looked thoughtful. "Maybe they've got some reason to believe that."

"But they don't," Leigh insisted. "I'm doing so well. It's almost as if they can't accept—forget I started to say that. It was mean, but they do upset me. I almost feel as if I *should* be falling apart."

"I probably don't have any right to an opinion," Niles said. "But for what it's worth, you have to live your own life and you seem pretty sure of how you want to do that."

She rubbed his arm and had a wild urge to kiss him. Unfortunately that wouldn't be a good idea. "Thank you. Jan and Gib will get the picture eventually. Up till now they're still trying to get me to live with them, which would be a horrible idea. Married couples need their own space. Besides, I'm a private person."

She glanced at Niles, wondering what he would think about that statement—if anything.

"It's natural for your sister to worry about you being okay," he said, but he frowned at the same time. Jazzy crawled up his chest and put his head on the man's shoulder. Niles stroked him.

"Thanks for saying that about Gib and Jan," she told Niles. "I'm too touchy."

"You're thoughtful, that's all. And there's nothing wrong with being private. Beats the hell out of turning all clingy and needy."

Blue went purposefully to stand near the sidecar. Evidently he also wanted to get back.

What Leigh wanted most was to keep on being with Niles. "You could give courses in how to say the right things," she told him.

"Think so?" He looked as if he were trying not to laugh. "I know people who wouldn't agree with you—not at all."

"You are so easy to talk to," Leigh blurted out. "I mean..."

He waited for her to finish. When she didn't, he said, "Ditto," and rubbed a thumb quickly across her chin.

"I need a favor," Leigh said rapidly before she could change her mind. "Would you please come to dinner this evening? I understand if you already have other plans. Or if you just don't want to come. But I thought I'd ask—"

"Thank you," Niles said simply. "I'd really like that." His smile was one she would remember forever.

chapter THIRTEEN

IT WAS ALREADY DARK when Leigh got back from work and the grocery store and parked in front of Two Chimneys.

She got out of the car and poked around in her pockets for the front door key.

"Leigh?"

"What?" She jumped, spun around, and came face to face with Niles outside the cottage. "Oh, you don't know how much you scared me. I wasn't expecting to see anyone."

She needed to get into the habit of leaving the outside light on for when she got home late.

Niles looked chagrined. "I'm an idiot. I'm so used to moving around in the silence here, I never think about it. I'm sorry."

It would be too easy to let him off the hook and tell him that now that she knew who had startled her she was thrilled to see him.

And right after she had spent the drive home giving herself a lecture about going very slowly with Niles—if she went at all.

She opened the trunk of her car but before she could lift out the bags of groceries, Niles had already swept them up. He wore a worried frown that made him look younger somehow.

"Thanks," she said, locking the car, then sorting through her pockets again for the key to the house.

"Sean got called out to a fire and I was just fiddling around in my shop," Niles said. "I need him for the job I'm on now. So I thought I'd come over and see if I could go to the store for you or help with something for dinner."

She let him in. Jazzy rushed along beside him, his tongue hanging out the side of his mouth, panting blissfully.

Jazzy had never cared much for men. Who knew he would get to Whidbey and change personalities?

"Just dump the stuff in the kitchen," Leigh said. "Thank you for coming to my aid—it was heavy."

They stood in the kitchen, looking at each other, both of them clearly trying to come up with something to say.

"Give me your keys," Niles said.

She frowned and he took both the car keys and the separate key for the door from her.

Gentle hands that could crush if he wanted them to. Once again she was too aware of how attracted she was to his power—and to how careful he was to use it wisely.

With a quick flick he slid the door key onto the same ring with those for the car and gave back the bunch. "Should be easier," he said. "But I'll take it off again if that's not the way you want it."

She grinned. "I'm still disorganized. Thanks for the help."

Quiet fell between them again.

"I'm in the way," Niles said hurriedly. "If you still want me to come, I'll be back later. I thought about you and wandered right on over. That was pushy of me."

Leigh smiled slowly. "You and I could do with a crash course in saying what we mean when we mean it. I'm just going to be fiddling around, too. I'm making lasagna, garlic bread, and a salad. Are you any good at washing salad stuff and chopping it up?"

His smile turned her heart as it had outside Sally's shop.

"I'm the most accomplished salad stuff washer for miles around," he said. "Wait till you see me chop. You'll be jealous."

She started unpacking and he took things from the other bag. That's when she noticed a bottle sticking out of each of his large jacket pockets.

"You'll break those against the table," Leigh said, nodding. "Are you a closet boozer?"

Immediately, he hauled a bottle of red wine from one pocket and a bottle of white from the other. "I wasn't sure what to get so I got one of each. I've got a couple more down at my place in case we need them but I didn't want to give the wrong impression."

"Red with lasagna," Leigh said. "But how about we have a glass of white while we work?"

Immediately he took the bottle of white and Leigh found two glasses. She set them on the table and looked at them with a sad little squeeze of the heart. Whatever happened, she must not think of the last time she and Chris did each thing here. There were a million last times to get through and she had to be strong.

"Bottle opener?" Niles said.

"Drawer to the left of the sink."

She set to work, making a meat sauce from a recipe she and Jan had concocted when they were little more than kids growing up in New Orleans. They both loved it. While the sauce simmered, she sliced mozzarella cheese and opened a carton of ricotta.

Niles, she noticed, didn't do more than sip his wine now and again, but he chopped a mean tomato and washed lettuce until it squeaked.

"We didn't say a toast," she said, glancing at Niles over her shoulder. He had shed his coat, hung it on the back of the cleaning cupboard door on top of Chris's old flight jacket. A dark gray cotton shirt with a black turtleneck underneath suited him. Probably, anything would suit him, but his eyes looked even more blue tonight.

"What shall we drink to?" he asked, handing over her glass.

She said, "New beginnings," without thinking, and felt a faint heat in her face. "That's for me because I'm starting over. What about you?"

The quizzical way he returned her gaze made Leigh sense he knew she had tried to cover because she thought he might take the toast wrong. Or right. She looked into her glass.

"New beginnings will do for a start," he said, clinking his glass against hers. "And possibilities, good starts, the unexpected...hope."

Leigh had to take a breath before she said, "I second that and I'll drink to it."

Tension crimped her shoulders and her movements felt jerky. When she looked at Niles, he was watching her mouth. She rested the rim of her glass against her bottom lip.

His next smile was quick and as fleeting as the way he ran the tips of his fingers down the side of her face.

She put down her glass and started putting lasagna noodles into boiling water. While her back was to him, she heard him start to chop again, chop and whistle.

Leigh closed her eyes. Chris used to whistle.

"Can I use one of these wooden bowls?" Niles had taken a big salad bowl from a shelf and she nodded.

While she finished making the lasagna and getting it into the oven, Niles lighted both fireplaces. He had offered to light a fire and she had asked him to do the second one, too.

Chris had often insisted on having both fires alight when it was really cold, and he delighted in watching people's reactions when they first came into the house.

The kitchen grew too warm.

Leigh opened a window an inch or so. The table there was the only one she had and she didn't want her guests sweating over dinner.

A green checked tablecloth, washed enough times to make it soft, matching napkins, and the white plates with blue stripes around the rim didn't make for an elegant setting, but everything was cozy.

She found a vase a little larger than the circus glass with room for several stems and went through the door to the side of the house. A nearby holly bush was loaded with berries and if she could make it there without falling on her face, a few sprigs would be perfect.

Careful to be quiet—she didn't want Niles rushing to do the job for her—she closed the kitchen door again and picked her way toward the woodpile. The holly she had in mind was behind the lean-to. Pungent scents of pine, earth, and cedar filled her nose, and cold snapped at her ears.

When would she learn not to come out here without a flashlight? At least she had thought to put the long kitchen shears in her pocket and wear gloves so her hands wouldn't get torn to shreds.

The berries seemed shiny black in the near complete darkness. A faint moon hovered behind slinking layers of cloud in mottled grays. The best pieces of any bush were always high up. She thought of gathering blackberries in summer and how the fattest, most ripe berries inevitably left her with a multitude of long, often bloody scratches.

She edged around the bush, stood on tiptoe, and reached up with her shears. It took three attempts to cut a laden twig and let it fall. Breathless, she paused before rising to her toes again and brandishing the shears.

Leigh concentrated on snagging what she wanted but couldn't help noticing how her form threw a tall, wide shadow, and how the shears seemed at least a foot and a half long.

Still on her toes, she opened her mouth without knowing why. The shadow shears pointed down, toward her; the ones she held were straight up, the blades closed on the branch she wanted.

The moon wasn't strong enough to throw shadows, and even if it were, it was in front of her, not behind.

Keeping very, very still, and choking silently, Leigh fought to order her thoughts. If she screamed, Niles would probably hear and come. But there would be time for whoever was behind her to make a killing strike, then attack Niles as he came from the house.

The slightest move detached the shears from the bush. Leigh changed her grip to hold them like a knife and swung around with her arm raised.

She tried to scream but no sound came.

Between her and the lean-to, and a vast tree at the opposite end of the little building, a figure hovered. Without substance, rippling like misty white water, it curved high in the air and bent over her. Leigh could see the tree through the figure as if it and the tree were one.

A shrieking laugh tore through her head, growing higher and higher until it floated away like discordant notes played on a flute.

She dropped the shears.

With no warning, no perceptible change of position, the figure shrank and became barely taller than Leigh. Where there had been no features at all, great yellow eyes blinked at her and a mouth as wide as the big tree's trunk stretched as if in a grin, turned up at the corners, and revealed pointed teeth.

The mouth came closer, and closer, opening wider until she knew its intention.

A thick, fleshy tongue protruded to lap her face, slither around her neck, and suck her head into the gaping jaws.

chapter FOURTEEN

Niles felt a breeze, sensed its prickling cold, smelled scents from the forest.

And he felt danger, heard Leigh thinking his name.

He put the fire tongs down quietly and strode to the kitchen on soft feet. As he entered, the breeze became a blast of wind through the open door. It carried the odor of decay, the stench of death. Outside there was a death slave; zombie, werewolf, fae, even werehound, the dead creature's animated carcass had been kept to do dirty work for some malevolent force.

Fighting his own instinct to change and take advantage of the anonymous cover of his hound form, Niles flipped off the light. Darkness was his friend. He saw better in the dark than most people did in daylight.

Slipping rapidly outside, he stared out among the trees. To call for Leigh could work against them. And if she discovered he could talk into her mind, the shock might kill her.

Summoning the skill he rarely used, he flew straight up without the aid of trees to boost him. To fly unaided in the open made him too likely to be seen, but all he cared about now was getting to Leigh. From high above the ground where he could have a wider view of the area, he scanned carefully, tree to tree, space to space. He picked out wild animals, small and large, scurrying or slinking on their way, and he looked into the eyes of an owl wise enough to remain silent.

There it was. Fading into the trunk of a tree, the ghostly form of a decaying woodsman fae.

There was no time to puzzle out the first appearance of such a thing on this island—as far as he knew. But Sally must be questioned without angering her.

He hovered, made a half turn, and saw Leigh—in a huddled heap on the ground.

Niles tried but failed to stifle his fear, his anger, and landed a few feet from her. "Leigh?" he said, running to kneel beside her. He felt her shiver and relief fueled fresh rage. "Leigh. What happened?"

He started to turn her over but she resisted, whimpering and struggling against him.

"It's Niles," he said. "You're okay. Hey, you're with me and you're okay."

She remained bent over, her face buried in her hands.

Gently, holding back the inhuman potential of his strength, he scooped her into his arms, turning her as he did so. And she rolled to press herself against him, still covering her face.

A wide mark circled her neck. Wide and red with darker specks of blood just beneath the skin.

And her hair was damp.

The woodsman had put his mark on her—to please his master no doubt. And to warn Niles not to get in the way of the fae. By nature the woodsmen were not violent, but death could change everything and here it had.

Niles carried Leigh to the cottage, into the living room, and started to set her down in an armchair. She threw an arm around his neck and hung on.

"Tell me about it, Leigh." Brushing back her hair, stroking the side of her face, he willed her to be calm.

She held him tighter, buried her face in his chest. Niles's heart slammed. His arousal was instant and insistent. He spread his hands on her back and rubbed softly back and forth.

"It was huge, tall, with a knife in its hands. When I turned around it was milky, misty—formless. Then it shrank until it was no bigger than me—"

The words tumbled out and Niles's fury grew. Was the zombie woodsman Brande's? Did he and his wolves want to plant more seeds of trouble in the community and cause people to panic, in addition to getting rid of Leigh and the nuisance she could be to the wolves if she mated with Niles?

Why try to force confrontation?

He hushed Leigh and kept on holding her firmly. She weighed very little. These humans were fragile creatures. He wanted to make her his, to keep her with him forever.

This fierce protective urge, this possessiveness...was this how love began? He thought back to his days in Wyoming, to the woman he had known there, his fiancée.

No, this wasn't exactly like that, but then his life had been predictable, the future warm, filled with the promise of home, a loving wife, and children. That had been before the winter of destruction, before the mad hound had come.

"I didn't imagine it," Leigh said in a small voice.

Of course she would not expect to be believed. "Of course you didn't." He took her to the bathroom and set her feet on the floor, turned her to face the mirror, but kept an arm around her waist.

"Look at your neck," he told her, holding back her hair.

Leigh looked and horror darkened her eyes. "What was that thing? Niles, I don't want to leave this place, but when my sister and her husband see this, they will pry and insist I go with them."

He could not let that happen, but . . .

With one finger, he subtly traced the line on her neck, at the back, beneath her hair. "Perhaps you should leave," he said, frowning at her in the mirror.

She met his eyes. "I'm afraid to stay, but I don't want to go," she said. "In Seattle I felt as if I was slowly fading. I didn't care about anything anymore. I've started to live again here. Chris would have wanted that and he always wanted me to be strong."

Her expression was stricken and he wondered how often she had spoken aloud about her husband. He also wondered when she would realize how quickly she was bonding with him. She must be responding to the chemistry they shared. Niles had barely dared to hope this would happen.

The red slash was gradually healing and disappearing. Niles touched it again and the repair worked even faster. Leigh had not noticed.

With absolute certainty that he was right, Niles held her shoulders and told her, "This happened to drive you away." Away from him, away from the hope she brought to his kind. He continued, bending the truth this time, "There are some who love to play tricks on those they think are weak. We've had trouble with some serious pranks and it's causing argument among those who know about it." She was not ready to learn the depths of depravity already at work.

Color slowly seeped back into her cheeks. She never took her gaze from his. "Could rubber do this?" She reached her fingertips to her neck. "Thrown quickly around, then pulled away again? It would break the capillaries and scrape the skin."

He smiled, attempting to lighten the tension. "I shall have to watch out for you, ma'am. I believe you would make quite the practical joker."

Her smile was a poor effort but it was a start. "Should I try to reach my sister and ask her to come tomorrow instead of tonight?"

That was an idea with possibilities. They would undoubtedly stay together, alone, and that could only hasten whatever was to happen between them. "It's too late," he said regretfully. "They'll be here in half an hour or less. Can you handle it?"

She twisted in his arms and surprised him with a quick but convulsive hug. "Thank you. With you here I can do it. But I warn you—they can be, well, difficult. Gib is overbearing sometimes."

"Sounds entertaining." He inclined his head to look down at her. "You think I'd miss a chance to watch your family dynamics?"

"Niles!" She pretended disgust.

"What can I tell you? I'm a voyeur. Probably repressed."

She kissed him quickly on the cheek.

And he had a tough time not kissing her back—on the mouth and elsewhere. Instead he ducked as if he were peering at her neck. "Will you look at that, it's just about gone."

Leigh took another look in the mirror. "How can it be? It is. If I put on a scarf they won't see."

They won't see if you don't put a scarf on. But it was better not to make her think too deeply. "It must have been more a rub than anything else and it's fading fast. Go get a scarf. I'll check the food to make sure it's not burning." Like he knew anything about cooking! "And I'll throw more wood on the fires. It looks great in here."

Her smile was genuine this time, warm and almost happy, although she glanced anxiously at the window. "Thank you. You're . . . you're something."

She sped up to the loft, and he went into the kitchen. There were no evident burned parts on the lasagna so he assumed it was okay. Then he remembered something he'd heard Sean mention and turned the dial down to lower the heat. Cooking had become Sean's unlikely hobby and he considered himself a budding gourmet chef.

A log on each fire and they were as ready as they would be. For what, Niles wondered. Why would a woman like Leigh care so much about these other people?

She ran back down the stairs. As usual she wore black, plain, slim pants, a round-necked top with long sleeves, and flat shoes. But she had added a chartreuse scarf.

"You look great," he told her. She looked better than great. Soft, sexy, a coat of gloss on her full lips catching the light and making him swallow hard. "How long will they stay?"

Leigh skidded to a halt and laughed aloud. "You are so funny. Whatever is on your mind, you say—no pretense. I like that. You don't hide anything."

His own face felt like stone. If only she knew how much he hid. At the same time as he imagined feeling her naked in his arms, he had a gut-punching image of her looking at him with revulsion and he swallowed. She must learn to love him before she found out the rest.

That was another new realization. "I'm a mystery really," he said, raising one brow. "You just haven't figured that out." If it was going to happen at all, the sooner they became sealed together, the better.

Not that he had any certainty she would want to accept him once he let her see his hound.

Leigh looked at the floor and put a hand on his chest.

"What?" He was determined not to invade her mind.

"I think you and I are going to make a good team—at least tonight," she said.

chapter FIFTEEN

Niles HAD NOT CONSIDERED what Gib and Jan Hill would be like but if he had, he would have been wrong.

There was a lot of silence around the table in Leigh's warm little kitchen. "More salad?" she asked Jan, who smiled but shook her head, no. "How about you, Gib, you were always a salad man?" Leigh talked enough for all of them, trying to fill in the silence. Niles figured the shock she had been through made her chatter.

"Not for me," Gib said.

Gib had a narrow but good-looking face with guile-less brown eyes. Niles didn't think the eyes mirrored the man's nature. Despite a crew cut, his black hair showed a lot of gray. His wife didn't look like her sister but she was appealing in a different way. Small but not as thin, Jan's expression gave a lot away, or it did to Niles. This was not a happy or relaxed woman. Dark shiny hair and green eyes should have been arresting but anxiety dulled her.

"How about lasagna, then?" Leigh suggested.

Both of the Hills shook their heads.

"Well, more for me, please," Niles said, smiling all around. He served himself and continued to eat, although it took determination.

Leigh popped up from the table and cleared empty plates. When she caught Niles's eye, she smiled and he hoped it wasn't only because she was grateful to him.

Coffee had finished brewing and she put a plate of pastries in the middle of the table before bringing mugs and clean plates. "Sorry the dessert isn't homemade—or at least not by me—but I didn't have much time after I left work."

The Hills' silence grated on Niles. "Are these some of Cliff's?" he asked about the pastries. "He makes the best." He tried a smile on Gib. "Cliff's the chef at Gabriel's, where Leigh works."

Gib shrugged.

Niles disliked sweet foods but he would eat the entire plateful if necessary.

"Don't you worry about any of that," Jan said to Leigh. She sighed and the breath she let out came in little spurts. What was making her so uptight?

"You look tired, Leigh," Gib said. He pushed his chair back, tucked the ends of his fingers into his pants pockets, and glanced at Niles.

That was a *you're in the way here* look if Niles had ever seen one.

"I never felt better," Leigh said. "I've always loved Whidbey."

Niles read exactly what was happening between him and this man who was accustomed to being in charge. Gib felt threatened. At some unreachable level he sensed he was not the alpha male around here and he chafed against that.

"Of course you love Whidbey. You met Chris here," Gib said to Leigh. "The two of you were crazy about each other and about being here."

"That's true," Leigh said tonelessly.

"You don't get over that kind of attachment easily. Takes years."

Gib gave Niles another of those looks. The guy wanted him to leave.

"I'm glad you can feel good coming back here," Jan said abruptly, her voice breaking. She patted her sister's hand on the table. "It shows you're healing."

Gib gave a harsh laugh.

"Well, doesn't it?" Jan asked. Tears shone in her eyes and Niles had an urge to plant a fist in the middle of Gib's sneering face. "When you can go back to a place you thought you'd have to stay away from—and enjoy it—it's healthy."

"If you say so, Dr. Hill. I guess there are two of us in the family, now." Gib said.

"My husband's a psychologist," Jan said to Niles. "I must have gotten into the habit of analyzing why people do things, I guess. But Leigh and I—"

"Think the same way," Gib finished for her. "We know, darling, but you have a habit of being too close to Leigh, and too protective for her own good."

"Twins are often extra close," Jan said defensively.

That was the first Niles had heard about Leigh and Jan being twins. He looked at Jan with fresh interest.

"The days of matching dresses and hair bows are over," Gib said.

"Oh, Gib, you know we never had matching—"

"We don't have to get into your deprived childhood," her husband said, patting her cheek as if to soften the nastiness.

"This conversation isn't really a good idea," Leigh said, and rather than appearing crushed, irritation tightened her features. "Jan and I don't talk about when we were kids in front of other people. We never have."

"Couldn't agree more," Gib said. "I'm very glad you have a friend here, but perhaps we need some family time alone, just the three of us. You don't have far to go, you said, Niles?"

"Niles isn't going anywhere," Leigh said. "He is my friend and my guest—and you can say what you need to say with him here."

A little thing like that, a comment thrown out in anger, shouldn't bring a man so much pleasure. But it did. "Whatever you want," Niles told her and only her.

"I want you here. Let's go sit by the fire and unwind. How about a brandy, just a little one since you have to drive, Gib?"

Predictably a chorus of "not for me" came from the Hills.

Niles spied the bottle in question and headed for it. "Go settle in," he said and waited until they had straggled out before pouring two glasses.

Did it go over ice?

Damn, he thought he had all these little things down years ago.

The refrigerator was old and rattled. He found ice trays in a little metal box fixed to the inside at the top.

It would be better to forget the ice than to risk raised

eyebrows if it wasn't used. Niles noticed several pieces of raw steak on a plate with plastic wrap over the top. He glanced over his shoulder, then touched it. Leigh wouldn't care about a little bit of meat.

He shook himself. *She's got a dog, fool. It's for Jazzy.*

With a glass in each hand, Niles joined the others. The scent of burning cedar, the flames, the sparks from the logs, pleased him, and he wished it were an outdoor fire with just him and Leigh sitting close beside it.

"Where's Jazzy?" he asked suddenly, giving Leigh one of the glasses.

Leigh turned that interesting splotchy pink of hers. "With Gabriel," she said. "Thanks for pouring the brandy."

"Who is Jazzy?" Gib asked.

When Leigh didn't answer, Niles decided she didn't like having her dog brushed off like a nonentity—a sentiment he wholly agreed with. "He's the same dog he always was," he said lightly and added a little chuckle. "A dog is a girl's best friend."

"You don't have a dog," Gib told her.

The way Jan's laced fingers turned white bothered Niles.

"I do," Leigh said. "He's a sweetie. But I know you don't like dogs so I got my boss to keep him overnight."

Niles wanted to laugh. This guy didn't know real dogs—big, powerful dogs who could snap him in half.

"When did you get a dog?" Gib said.

"I've had Jazzy a year," Leigh said. "And before you ask why you haven't seen him, it's for the same reason he isn't here tonight. He's a cute guy, Jan, you'd love him. Remember—"

"Toughy?" Jan said before Leigh could finish. The

woman's sudden wide smile transformed her. For the first time Niles could see the likenesses between the sisters. "You know I do. Our buddy."

"She wasn't very big but she was lionhearted," Leigh told Niles. "And she was the best company. She came everywhere with us."

"I'd love to meet your Jazzy," Jan said. "Please keep him home next time we come."

"Or better yet," Gib said, not meeting anyone's eyes, "bring him on over to Camano. We're going to be there for a few months and that's something we came to talk about, isn't it, Jan?"

With an anxious giggle, Jan said, "Yes. Come to Camano with us and stay there. Gib has his patients in Seattle so he's busy all the time and—"

"Just spit it out," Gib said, shaking his head. He picked at the thick, comfortable covering on his chair and his distaste showed. "We want you to come to us. Forget all this stupidity about being on your own over here. You don't have anything to prove. We know you're strong and there isn't anyone else to impress."

Ass. The brandy wasn't so bad. Niles had grown quite accustomed to the taste of beer—even liked it since they got the occasional bottle in Iraq—but he hadn't tried much other alcohol since he had been changed.

Leigh was taking a long time to respond. Her mouth was in a rigid line.

"It's lonely over here and we don't want to be worrying about you all the time," Gib said, all gentle sympathy. "You need your own things around you. You need a safe place with people who love you, a safe place to grieve."

This time Leigh looked straight at Gib and said, "I've

got all my things around me. Chris left this house and everything in it to me, remember? He made sure I would be comfortable until I was on my feet again. I'm here for my own sake, to find my own feet and get on with my life. The way Chris would have wanted. I'll always miss him and in a way he'll always be with me. But I'm moving on. And in case you've forgotten, I've got a job here."

Niles got up and put logs on both fires.

"That would irritate the hell out of me," Gib said. "Two fires."

"Two fires for Two Chimneys," Jan said and laughed a little nervously. "I've always thought it was cute, whimsical. I love whimsical things."

"Insecure people often do," her husband said. He shook his head and held a hand toward her. "I don't mean you're insecure, darling. That was a general comment."

Gib patted his wife's hand but turned to Leigh. "You don't need a job. As you just said, Chris left you very well off and you've done great for yourself. This move makes no sense. Come to us."

"You're kind, Gib, but, no."

Forcing himself up with his hands on the arms of the chair, Gib stood and went closer to Leigh. "We'd like to take you back with us tonight."

Leigh's lips parted and she stared at her brother-in-law.

"I expect you need time to think about it," Jan said. She swallowed repeatedly, her throat jerking. "See how it goes, huh?"

"That's not what we both know is right," Gib said. "This woman is a mess and she's doing this stupid thing to try to get a hold of herself. I'll—"

"What did you just say?" Niles asked. He heard his

own voice, dropped dangerously low and took a breath. "Leigh? A mess? She is one of the most in-control people I've ever met. Ask Gabriel—her boss. She's already running that place of his like it was never run before."

"Some sleazy little bar in the back of beyond," Gib said. "Do you have any idea what a good mind Leigh has? She can't be allowed to waste herself up here."

"I guess she'll do what she decides to do," Niles said. He shouldn't be interfering but Leigh didn't have her own cheering squad, which she deserved. He could do a pretty good job of filling in.

"Thank you for the lovely dinner," Jan said, checking her watch. "I haven't even unpacked my suitcase so we'd better get back. I was in California . . . on retreat."

An understanding glance passed between Leigh and Jan.

"Anyway, I want to get unpacked and sleep before I'm so tired I can't sleep at all. I'll call you tomorrow." She got up and put a hand under her husband's arm.

He reached forward with the same arm, severing the contact, and picked up a wrapped package on the bentwood table between the chairs. "Maybe Jan's right. She usually is. We shouldn't rush you, Leigh. But I do know what's best for you, just as I do for Jan. You know that. This is for you."

"What is it?" Leigh asked.

"Open it."

She did, pulling off a red ribbon and peeling away white tissue. It was a framed photo but Niles couldn't see who was in it.

Leigh swallowed and her stare at Gib was accusatory. "How did you get this? It was in my apartment."

With no sign of embarrassment, he said, "Of course

it was. As soon as I heard you'd left I decided I should go by and check from time to time to make sure everything's okay. When I saw that I figured you forgot to take it with you."

Scratching at the door annoyed Niles. He tried to ignore it but automatically opened his channel of communication to Sean. *"This isn't a good time,"* he told his friend. *"We've got big trouble. Company we weren't expecting. Someone's using a zombie woodsman to make a point."*

"How do you know?"

"I saw it, for God's sake. It attacked Leigh."

Niles felt Sean's mind race around. *"Let's go deal with it."*

"Not now. We'll talk tomorrow," Niles told him.

"I've been around since Leigh's guests arrived," Sean said. *"The guy's an ass. You sure you don't need a little backup?"*

"No, I—" Niles rethought what he'd been about to say. *"I'm going to let you in. Behave."* He went and opened the door.

"Oh, my god," Gib said, and took a step backward. "Don't let that in here."

"This is my dog," Niles said.

Leigh held the picture against her chest with her arms crossed over it but when she saw Blue her eyes sparkled. The girl had more than a little mischief in her soul.

"Blue, come on in and meet Leigh's family. Be on your best behavior now."

Blue slid into the room, glancing from side to side with narrowed eyes. When he did that he looked more werewolf than werehound.

"Look at him," Jan said. She stood in front of Blue and

looked into his face. "You are so beautiful. I've never seen such a beautiful dog, have you, Leigh?"

He's going to be insufferable, Niles thought.

"Who, me?" Sean gave a doggy grin.

"Lie in the corner over there," Niles said aloud, considering ways to get back at Sean. "And not a sound out of you."

Blue let out a low, pitiful whimper and Jan wrapped her arms around his neck. Niles couldn't believe it, and the way Blue rested his big head on the woman's shoulder ensured there would be a lot of conversation about this stunt later.

"Let's go," Gib said. He snatched up his jacket from the arm of a couch and tossed Jan her raincoat. "Get away from that thing. He looks wild to me."

Jan kissed the top of Blue's head and the dog managed to look blissful. He licked Jan's hand.

Gib already had the front door open and he hurried Jan onto the porch. "We'll be in touch," he told Leigh. "Think about all of this and you'll know what you have to do," he said significantly.

The door closed and they were gone, just like that. Only a couple of minutes passed before the engine of the Hills' car sprang to life and their tires spurted gravel on the way up the hill and away from the house.

"I am so sorry," Leigh said. She frowned miserably. "Gib can be difficult but I didn't expect that."

Diplomacy demanded he say little or nothing. Niles opted for nothing, just a sympathetic downward tilt of the lips.

"Could you stay and let us drink this brandy finally?" she said. "Or is it too late?"

Nine-thirty was early but he didn't say that. "Maybe

you need to be alone. You've just been through a lot." He wanted to ask to see the photo but restrained himself.

"So has my sister," she said quietly. "But there's only so much I can do about that now."

He nodded.

"Forget I said that. It's none of my business. Jan surely thinks you're something, Blue." She rubbed between his ears. "So do I. You make me feel safe. I guess to know you is to love you."

Great. "Are you having a good time, Sean?"

"You should be glad she feels good around me, boss. That could be really good for you. Her sister's cute."

"She's married."

"Yup. Dammit. She's Leigh's twin. How much do you bet she's got the same blood?"

"Blue and I should get out of here," Niles said to Leigh. "I've got an early job tomorrow." That was true.

The disappointment in her expression didn't hurt his feelings. Before he considered what he was doing, he had touched her temple and let his fingertips travel down the side of her face. "You handled everything really well tonight. Thanks for dinner."

"It was a horrible evening." She touched her face where he had stroked it. "I won't blame you for never speaking to me again."

"I'd blame me." There were things a man didn't forget, including the way it felt to kiss a woman with soft, full lips. He wanted to kiss Leigh. "Now lock this door."

"Thanks," she said, and he herded Blue out into the cold night.

He felt and heard her come after him and turned back. "What is it? You okay?" Before he had time to take a second step in her direction, Leigh barreled into him. Niles caught her against him. "Are you frightened?"

"This feels strange, but it feels right, too," Leigh said. "We haven't known each other long but you make me sure I'm safe, and I know I've got a friend who'll be there for me."

Standing on tiptoe, she kissed his jaw and wrapped her arms as tightly as she could around his neck.

This was as close to walking a tightrope as Niles ever hoped to come. A man could hear what he wanted to hear in a woman's words. Misinterpretation would be a deadly mistake.

"I like being here for you. Remember, all you have to do is call, as the song goes." He laughed but the sound was hollow.

Her upturned face seemed all eyes. She looked at him as if she were taking a picture for her memory. Then she smiled slowly.

He kissed her on those soft, upturned lips; he couldn't help it. And as his tingling skin met hers his own mouth started to open. His arms did their own thing, closing around her tightly, but carefully.

Even through layers of clothing he could feel her breasts against him. Could he risk letting her know he wanted to make love to her?

Not until she knew what he was, dammit.

It was too soon.

He took his mouth from hers, then landed a small, hard, rapid kiss, a severing kiss, and he spun her away from him. "I want to hear you lock that door."

chapter SIXTEEN

Confusion shouldn't feel so good.

The door was locked according to orders but Leigh couldn't move away yet. She settled her hands on the wooden panels, cold all the way through from having been open to the weather, and set her mind to sorting out her impressions of Niles. Of Niles and the way he did or didn't feel about her.

The kiss wasn't really over when he drew away.

Leigh's heart beat hard. She hadn't wanted him to stop.

Neither had he. Everything about him had let her know he wanted much more but was holding back. She faced the room. The man was a mystery and although she didn't like playing games, she thought she could get addicted to sorting out the puzzle that was Niles Latimer.

He was trying to give her more time to decide what she wanted, she was almost sure of it. The big question was, how did she let him know without pushing? They seemed to have a lot in common, one thing being that they were super-sensitive about other people's feelings.

The photograph was on a table near one of the chairs. Gib hadn't stumbled across it, because she hadn't left it in an obvious place in the condo. He had gone through her closet and found it in a box on a top shelf where she had put it for safety.

In the morning she would make a call to the building manager and get the locks changed. That would keep Gib from "checking" on her place again.

She looked at Chris's face, and saw only his smile while he held her hand to his lips. The satin flowers in her own hair made her chuckle a little. Those had been purely for Chris. Leigh wasn't a flowers-in-the-hair girl. She had loved the slim white Vera Wang dress she had worn, though.

A wedding day to remember.

How could she ever forget even a second of that Wednesday.

Okay, the best way to be sure no one thought she was hiding from the past was to pull it into the light. Front and center. On tiptoe to reach the high wooden mantel on her favorite of the two fireplaces, she put the photo in the middle. The silver frame was at odds with almost everything else in the cottage.

Time for that brandy.

She curled up in a chair with the glass, turned off the one lamp still on, and stared into the fire.

Gib had done the opposite of what he had intended. She was glad to have the only photo from that special day where she could see it easily. It felt right.

A smattering of pops on the roof startled her. But she

knew that sound; fir cones tumbling from overhanging branches. She was allowed to jump at anything tonight. But with a few hours between her and what had happened outside she could almost believe she had imagined the whole thing. After all, she had checked her neck again after dinner and there was no mark to be seen.

Tapping on the window jarred her all over again. *Get it together, Leigh.* When didn't it rain around here? It was a good thing she loved the weather on Whidbey and never felt as good as when she was there.

Leigh looked over her shoulder. Drops hit the window glass and glittered there, but in the weak porch light she saw snow mixed with the rain.

And she saw a shadow appear outside, behind one of the open curtains. Someone...or something...sat down carefully in a chair on the porch and rocked slowly back and forth.

Her heart and stomach went on a collision course. Even breathing through her mouth and closing her eyes didn't slow the pounding in her chest.

Niles would come if she called—and he would come quickly.

But he had early work in the morning.

Jazzy was no attack dog but she still wished he were there with her. His bark could be useful.

Carefully, she slid from her chair to the floor where she lay still, her face tilted to watch for fresh movement outside, for what felt like an hour.

The shadow figure continued to rock in its shadow chair.

Keeping low, Leigh crawled toward the window, pausing only to take her cell phone out of her pocket. At

Niles's suggestion she had put his number on speed dial and now she was grateful.

What did she intend to do when she reached the window? Confirm what she already knew—that someone was hanging around on her porch?

No. If she was immediately beneath the window, tight against the wall, she would be almost impossible to see from outside.

The figure got up again and disappeared from her sight.

The chair continued to rock.

Leigh buried her face on the backs of her hands against the floor. Sweat ran between her shoulder blades. She hated doing it but she had to call the police. The darn "smart" phone was so smart it took several clicks and pokes, while the readout light kept going off, to get to the dial pad and punch in the three numbers. Lousy cell reception out here didn't help.

A male voice asked her what kind of emergency she had.

"Intruder," she whispered. He was out there somewhere.

The emergency operator repeated the question and Leigh whispered, "Intruder," again.

"You'll have to speak up. I can't hear you." The voice wasn't unkind.

A board groaned on the porch. He was back. Leigh put her hand over the phone to hide the glow.

"What's going on?" the man on the phone asked.

Leigh craned her neck to peer up at the window again. At first she saw nothing different. Then she made out the figure again, leaning against the wall of the cottage, so close he would be able to look in ... or reach the front door in a few strides.

"Hello—"

She cut off the guy on the phone and peered closely at the keypad to find 5 and call Niles.

Niles felt himself swim out of unconsciousness but with no recollection of actually going to sleep. He must have hit the bed without finishing undressing and as good as passed out.

Foggy-headed, a little sick to his stomach, and bathed in sweat, he clawed his way from the nightmare that plagued him when he was troubled.

Shit, the banging in his chest was too familiar. He heard a noise like something whistling over his head. The bullets again. And he felt the sand sucking at his boots, slowing him down.

Desperate, he flung himself from his belly to his back and jackknifed his knees. His head came off the pillow and landed hard against his legs. *You took your eye off the ball and it cost Gary his life.*

When he was rational, he could justify that whatever had happened to his friend could have happened no matter what any of the rest of them did.

Shadowy figures slipped unseen along the ridge above their heads. They waited until Niles and the others had gone around the next bend, all but Gary, and then they dropped him so fast he didn't have time to make a sound. Even given his strength, there were too many of them to fight off.

And they had left with him the way they came, leaving no sign of what had happened.

Niles turned his head sideways and opened his eyes. That was the scenario he had dreamed up, or dredged up from his nightmares, and it repeated itself. Less and less often, but no less devastating when it did come.

His head thumped. He heard the shriek of a bullet again and started to fall backward onto the mattress.

It wasn't a bullet. He scrambled from the bed and ran for the living room. His cell phone was in the pocket of his parka and he'd dropped it on the couch.

He found the phone but it had stopped ringing. Probably wasn't important but he didn't avoid calls. He checked and the last one had been made from a number he didn't recognize.

Shrugging, he scuffed back the way he had come, looking at the readout. Someone had left a text, too.

Three words: I'm in trouble.

That was Leigh's number.

Wearing only his jeans, and barefoot, he tore from the house, made it up the bluff in two giant leaps and with the aid of a couple of jutting rocks, and rushed the cottage.

Where was he?

Leigh barely got the three-word text sent when the front door burst open.

She would not throw up, not now. "I've got a gun," she yelled, longing for it to be true. "Stay where you are."

There was no response, no sound at all except for the softly deadened swish of snow-laden wind through the open door.

Leigh ground her mouth into the back of a hand, willing herself to kill even the slightest sound she might make.

She prayed Niles wouldn't call back.

A piece of furniture was moved, its wooden legs scraped across the floor. Cold air kept pushing through the door, biting at Leigh's cheeks. She strained to hear—anything—but there was nothing now.

Except that soft, small beat of a heart she had heard when Niles was still there.

Her eyes stung and she pressed them shut for an instant, clearing her vision. What happened next depended on her and her own wits. She had to do something.

From somewhere out there came the round, echoing hoot of an owl.

Time dragged, second by second. She was hot despite the wind from outside.

She didn't know what she felt or thought but pressure built in her head. Noises crowded her skull.

Run. Her only chance was to get ready, then spring for the door. If she could make it to the forest she could lose him. But she would be target practice as she crossed the snow she was sure covered everything by now.

In one smooth movement, she crouched, ready to explode for the door.

A hand on the back of her neck lifted her into the air by her hair and the back of her sweater.

A second hand crushed her face so tightly she fought for air.

chapter SEVENTEEN

WRONG WAS WRITTEN all over Two Chimneys Cottage. No lights inside, the front door wide open, and the kind of silence that made Niles's nerves hum from what he could not hear.

Inside that cottage someone wanted to scream. He couldn't risk trying to communicate with Leigh in case she did hear him, overreacted, and gave away that he was nearby.

With the doorway near, Niles stared, deepening his dark-sight, seeking the distinctive thickening that would pulse, showing life.

And there it was, a man with his back toward him, dragging something—dragging Leigh. Niles had no doubt of it and he set his teeth, regulated his breathing, made himself wait the seconds it took to be sure he wouldn't cause more damage to the one he cared for by striking too soon.

A man suddenly lifted a body as if it weighed nothing, slung it over his shoulder, and bolted outside.

Leigh.

Niles was on the man, peeling her away, dropping her to the snow and tearing after his moving target. "Don't leave this spot," he told her.

The other man moved with incredible speed but not so fast Niles couldn't catch him easily enough.

Slamming his hands down on the other's shoulders, he threw him facedown and fell on top of him. "Who are you?" he demanded. "Now. Tell me your name or you're a dead man."

Not a word.

"Why Leigh? Did someone send you?"

Beneath Niles, the man curled his knees into his body and tucked his head down. With one hand, Niles picked him up by the back of his coat and shook him like vermin. Somehow the other guy remained curled up.

This one was familiar. The realization blasted through Niles's mind but his senses weren't picking up the signs that usually helped him identify a known foe.

"Boss?" Sean's mind speak was clear. *"Trouble? I'm coming. Do we need others?"*

"Just you but don't interfere unless I ask you."

The next move was expected but so expertly executed, it worked—just.

Rotating his body, head over tucked knees, the enemy smashed his feet under Niles's jaw and knocked him off balance for the second it took to keep on rotating.

Like a solid wheel spinning on a programmed course, away went the man, across the snow toward the forest.

Niles landed on him the instant before he saw the shadowy forms of wolves waiting between the great trunks. He counted five before he felt the sinuous unfurling beneath his hands, heard the cracking open of a man's bones, the flaring of his form into a massive animal with thick fur.

Niles was one of the few who were even stronger as humans than as hounds; nevertheless he knew he must change to protect that secret.

The animal howled and turned to fly at him. From behind Niles soared Sean, or rather Blue, heading for the other one's belly.

And in the precious seconds lost by Sean's well-meaning move, intended to give Niles the time he needed to complete his change, the stranger bounded into the ranks of Brande's wolves, ranged beyond the edge of the forest now. They wheeled in one phalanx and retreated, zigzagging, howling.

Niles swore, but so did Sean. "Bad move on my part, boss. Sorry."

Pulsing in every nerve, Niles sank away from his hound form until he could pull his jeans on again. He pushed his hands through his hair. "If you wanted us to keep on living, you probably just made a great move," he said. "There were enough of them to tear us apart."

"It's too bad I feel worse about them leaving than if they had attacked us. They could have taken us—why didn't they?"

chapter EIGHTEEN

NILES CAME from the side of the cottage and Blue was with him now. Leigh dashed to meet them.

"Where were you? You scared me to death." She snapped her mouth shut. She sounded like a mother who just grabbed her child to safety beside a busy road. "I'm going to call the police now," she added, more subdued.

"I understand," he said, surprising her by hooking an elbow around her neck and pulling her close to his wet, naked chest, resting his cheek on top of her head. "You scared me when I saw that text. But we're both okay. Let's get you inside."

His feet were bare but he didn't seem to notice, or to care that he was soaked. They walked into the cottage together.

Leigh turned to him. "That man—"

"Is a mystery," Niles finished for her. "But I'm going to find out all the stuff he obviously doesn't want me or anyone else to know."

"What do you mean?" She wound her arms around his waist. She really had been terrified he would be...killed.

"First things first. What are you going to tell the police?"

Leigh looked up into his face. "What happened. That someone broke in and was trying to take me away. And you saved me."

"Do you think he intended to assault you?"

She didn't want to think about it at all. "He could have done that without trying to take me somewhere. I don't know what he was going to do—murder me, probably."

"Don't," Niles said, stroking her hair. "And I don't think that's what he wanted to do. Look, I want you to sit down and listen to me. If you still think calling the police is the best thing to do, I'll be right here to back you up."

He steered her to the couch and gave her back the brandy glass. She peered at him through the gloom and noticed he didn't attempt to touch the brandy he had left on a table earlier.

She reached to turn on another lamp. "Suddenly I want lots of light around me," she said, trying a smile.

Niles watched her but she had no idea what he was thinking.

"I feel like that brandy now," Niles said. He got up, drew the curtains—closing out the snow that fell increasingly heavily—and went to the door. "Just going to make sure Blue's comfortable."

"Let him come in."

"He'll be staying right where he is for the night—and probably every night from now on. If he'd been there earlier our friend would have lost parts of his body."

He let himself out and almost immediately returned.

"Blue likes his spot. And he's a working dog so he expects to have an important job, like looking after you for me when I can't."

She was important to him? Or was that a willful bending of what he had said? Leigh looked away. "You need to get dry. I'll fetch a towel."

He didn't say anything when she returned, or make any attempt to take the towel from her.

Leigh blotted his face.

Niles stood still, his hands on his hips.

She went behind him to rub his back then returned to dry his chest. And finally she had to look at his eyes.

Not a flicker. Just intense concentration on her until she managed a smile and he tipped up the corners of his own mouth.

Droplets glittered in his dark hair. "Can I rub the drips out of your hair?" Her voice cracked.

"Anytime you want to," he said, dropping to his knees in front of her.

His hands, settling at her waist, made Leigh jump but she set to work briskly drying those almost black waves—curls at the moment.

He muttered something.

"What did you say?" She stopped for a moment, looking into his upturned face.

"Only that no one ever did this for me before. I wouldn't want anyone else to do it for me but I'll run around in snow and rain every day if I can come back for more from you. I feel comfortable with you."

He spoke so simply, nothing fancy or thought through with care, but every word touched her heart. Leigh caught her bottom lip in her teeth and blinked rapidly. She tapped him on his very nice nose and rubbed his hair with all the energy she could muster. She rubbed until he laughed and stopped her.

"Thank you," he said. "Now let's take off your shoes or whatever those silly little boot things are."

So quickly she just about fell onto the couch, he sat her down, pushed her to lean against one arm, and pulled off her ankle boots. "I like those boots," she told him.

Intimacy spun like a net between them, getting more complicated, more high-stakes, and totally irresistible. What Leigh was starting to feel about this man was a little scary. She was in serious "like" with him.

"Is it okay if I sit beside you?" he asked.

"Of course."

He sat close enough to settle her cold feet on his lap. She wore damp socks and he peeled those off. Unlike her brisk efforts, Niles treated her gently, drying between her toes and the bottoms of her feet until she giggled and jerked. He finished but kept his big, warm hands on her skin. When he leaned his head against the back of the couch, arching his strong throat, opening his muscular torso to the play of shadows from a lamp, Leigh had trouble swallowing. They were quiet for a while.

"I have enemies," Niles said eventually. "I'm pretty sure who they are but I don't have the evidence I need against them. It's too bad that guy got away tonight."

"I don't understand."

"Of course you don't. I've led a life you know nothing about." He paused, making sure she was looking right at him. "I don't want you to know the details of everything that's happened to me except that I've never used violence gratuitously. I hate violence.

"Someone has a score to settle with me and you look like a great way to do that. They can tell you're becoming important to me and they figure that by taking you, they can draw me after them and do whatever they've decided will even the score."

She heard his reasoning. It sounded possible. "You're scared," he said. "You've got to be. What I'm going to tell you is going to sound bizarre but it makes a point."

He looked sideways at her.

"Three women have been snatched in this area over the past couple of months. That's why we're all so anxious for you not to drive around in the dark—alone."

Leigh took deep breaths through her mouth. "Three women have been murdered here recently?"

"No. I didn't say that. Two of them are back, only they don't remember what happened to them. They're fine, though."

"What about the third one?"

"She isn't back yet. She was the most recent one."

Horrified, Leigh shot to her feet. "And you think they were all taken to punish you somehow? And if they got me I'd show up again, so everything would be okay?"

"I don't think what happened to them had anything to do with me. I do believe they were taken by the same people who have a grudge against me. They're troublemakers. They mix things up for the sake of frightening people. I don't think they intend to kill innocent people. They don't want the attention. But if they can cause enough distraction, take enough eyes off the ball, they intend to pick me off.

"They want the cops kept busy with unexplained disappearances."

He set his glass aside and stood up beside her. "So now I sound as if I'm asking you not to tell the police about tonight just to save my hide."

"I don't believe that."

"That is what I'm asking, Leigh." He went to the window and lifted a drape again. The snow was very thick. "I want you to trust me to look after you. And I'm asking right after some joker broke in here and started dragging you out. I don't want you to call the police because this isn't their territory."

"Territory?" she echoed. He seemed to be spilling everything out but she didn't understand some of what he said.

"It's not a job for the police. They're great people here and they're smart, but I've told you what I was involved in overseas and it was different. It is different."

Leigh paced away and back again and went to look out of the window with him. "I trust you." Perhaps a so-called sane person would already be in her car and heading out of here, but Leigh had a conviction about Niles. He would look after her and she would be okay.

"Is it possible they want me to go away?" she asked tentatively.

He turned so quickly, she jumped.

At first she thought he had a lot more to say, but he shook his head and rested a finger on her lips. "Could be," was his only comment.

"Then they'll be disappointed." She poked his chest. "But I'm going to buy a gun."

Once more he seemed ready to snap back some comment. He shook his head, smiling slightly. "I'll help you do it, then," he said.

"How long will it take?" She wanted it now.

"By morning you'll have what you need."

Leigh thought about that. "Don't I have to apply for a permit and wait and stuff?"

"You'll have your gun by morning," Niles said in a tone that meant the discussion was over.

chapter NINETEEN

H<small>E OUGHT TO LEAVE</small>, Niles thought. There was a lot to do setting up round-the-clock surveillance on Leigh— and why not be honest, every minute he spent with her made it tougher to go at all.

"I'm okay now," she said. "Go home to bed. You need your sleep."

"True," he said. "You'll be all right here tonight. You'll be safe. Just keep the cell phone near you so you know you can call. I can be here fast." She didn't know *how* fast.

"Right. I'm sorry for being a pain." She almost sang out her words and for the first time, the smile she gave him was phony.

"I've spent a good deal of my life keeping watch on one thing and another," he told her. "I really am good at it."

"I'm sure you are." Leigh looked quickly away. "This will sound silly. It certainly isn't enough, but thank you for everything. And I'm sorry you had to go through that nonsense with my family tonight. Gib thinks he's the alpha and Jan and I are the runts of his pack or whatever. He certainly doesn't think we're very bright."

He didn't respond for fear of telling her she was saying exactly what he already thought. Instead he went to throw more logs on the nearest fire and stood looking at a photo she had placed on the mantel.

"That's Chris, my husband, and me when we got married."

This had to be the photograph Gib had given her, all wrapped up in tissue and ribbon. *What was the man's game?* Niles wondered. "Does it upset you to have this here?"

"No. I was surprised but when I put it up it felt right. You shouldn't try to forget good things."

These two had been lost in each other. "He really loved you." He shouldn't feel jealous of a dead man.

She cleared her throat behind him. "The feeling was mutual but how do you know?"

Niles gave a short laugh. "I'm no expert on the subject but I can see it in the way he looked at you."

"If you aren't going to leave at once, sit down again. I'll run in the kitchen and get some snacks. I don't think you ate much at dinner."

"I ate loads," he said, looking at her over his shoulder. "You must be mixing me up with your brother-in-law."

When he sighed her expression sharpened. "You're tired, Niles."

She must think he wanted to get away from her. "I'm wide awake, suddenly. That happens. But I'm puzzled and not sure if I should say anything."

"That's not fair," she said. "You know I'm going to tell you to go ahead and ask—whatever it is."

He raised a brow. "Your wedding photo . . . It's unusual. Looks like some sort of artsy effort."

This time it was Leigh who sighed. "The love in the mist look was Chris's choice—mine, too, I guess." A misty haze framed them in the shot. "It's pretty clever. You wouldn't know it was taken in a hospital room if I didn't tell you."

He heard her breathing constrict and she held her throat as if it ached. "The hole Chris's death left won't get filled up—not in the same way—but I'm doing my best to patch it. He would want that. I do, too."

Honor was an old-fashioned word, Niles thought, but Leigh had it. She was honest about her feelings. But he believed her when she said she was ready to move on. Grief took its own time and even when you thought you'd beaten it, back came the memories to punch you in the heart one more time.

"Where did you get married?" he asked.

"In that hospital room," she told Niles. "We were supposed to have the whole church, cake, and flowers routine the following Saturday. Chris didn't want to put the wedding off and neither did I. But he was the one who decided to move it forward a few days. I'll always believe he knew . . ."

Niles waited patiently, making no attempt to prompt her.

She caught his eyes and blinked. "Thanks," she said although he wasn't sure why. "You make me feel safe. You've got an open heart. I can feel it. Chris and I met right here—on the beach below the bluff. He pointed out where Chimney Rock is and we spent a long, long time supposedly watching to catch sight of it. We knew each other for two years before we were married. He died a few days after the ceremony."

"Oh, God, Leigh." He couldn't find any clever words.

"There was an accident," she told him. Apart from the police, she had never willingly discussed this with anyone until now. "We went off a road on ice and a boulder rolled off at the edge. The rock came for the car and Chris threw himself over me. I got a broken ankle and arm, a slew of Chris's bones were smashed, and he had internal injuries. It took a week for him to come out of a coma."

Niles turned a hand, palm out, and held it toward Leigh. She hesitated then put her hand in his and he threaded their fingers together.

She tipped her head back but tears still escaped.

"Let it go," Niles said. "Cry. It's okay."

"You've had more than enough of me for one day." She sniffed and gave him a watery smile. "I'm crying because I remember how I felt then. I thought my world was over, but it wasn't. It isn't. Chris was one of those people who thought everything through. He even thought about taking care of me if something happened to him." She frowned.

"Like he knew something would?" Niles suggested quietly.

"Yes." She glanced past him at the fire. "That's right."

He was very aware of their two hands joined. "This is the right place for you to be."

"How can you know that?" she said.

"Because I'm going to make sure of it." He rested a hand on either side of her face and studied her intently. "I've already asked you to trust me—if you want to. Trust me and let go of any fear. I can make sure you stay safe."

"Why should you do that for me?"

"I lost someone I loved once. Afterward I needed strength around me while I healed, but I was alone. You don't have to be unless you tell me to get lost." He grinned and his stomach swooped when she grinned back. "Are you going to do that—tell me to go away?"

"Er—nope."

"Tell me one thing."

"Depends on what it is," she told him, visibly regaining some of her spirit.

"Do you like me?"

Leigh opened her mouth but no words came out.

"You don't like me," Niles said, beginning to frown.

"Of course I do. You're a really nice, kind man and you're a rock when things go bad. I can't think of anyone who would have gone through my little family drama tonight and still come back because I said I needed them. You're also much more straightforward than I'm used to." Now there was an understatement.

"A really nice, kind man," he repeated as if he were turning the words over and examining each one. "That's a compliment."

"Of course it is."

"Thank you."

"You're welcome." Leigh said. She nibbled her bottom lip—which didn't relax even a cell in his body. Her lips parted and stayed that way for an instant before she said, "Sometimes I don't think you've spent a lot of time talking to women."

He laughed outright at that. "You're perceptive. I'm not smooth—sorry."

"I should have mentioned that I really liked it when we kissed," said Leigh. "And when you hugged me. And rubbed my feet dry." She turned that wonderful bright, patchy red.

"You try to be tough sometimes," he said. "I really am tough."

"Sure you are."

"I wouldn't normally mention that about myself but I think it will help you believe I can take care of you."

Leigh would love to ask him if he had any idea of the tight knots he was tying her in. For a few moments her attention shifted toward the door, and what she could have sworn was a thin film of pink, blue, green, and purple vapor slipping through the cracks. It separated into long, elegant fingers and wrapped around the room. Very faintly, a stream of fine glitter raced through the colored ribbons, then it was all gone.

Leigh turned back to Niles, who continued to study her as if she were something rare. "Did you see that?" she asked.

He looked around. "What?"

"Um." She thought fast. Obviously she was hallucinating and she didn't want to add that to the list of weird stuff happening to her that would cause Niles to worry. "Nothing, just the way the windows and doors aren't quite tight. The curtain floated up. It's stopped now."

His long, steady stare almost suggested he knew she was fibbing.

"I want you to stay at Two Chimneys," Niles said. "I hope you'll make Whidbey your permanent home. But I'll understand if you decide against it."

"I'm staying here. My mind is absolutely made up. I love this cottage, and Gabriel's—and Gabriel—and the island and the beach—and Blue"—she giggled—"but don't tell him or he'll be impossible."

"You are an insightful woman, too," Niles said.

"I like all the people here. Sally is super, and Cliff and the twins and everyone." She spread her arms. "Just call me Pollyanna and let me be happy." The darnedest thing was that she did feel suddenly and deliciously happy and whatever came her way, she was sure she could deal with it.

Niles chuckled, then grew serious. "And do you think you could like me, too?"

"I told you I do—you are the most likable man I know," she said and flung her arms around his neck. "What the world needs is many, many more men like you."

He laughed and gave her a bone-bending hug, and kissed the top of her head.

Leigh closed her eyes. She felt the beating of his heart and heard her own. She heard everything clearly, the sizzle and mumble of the fire, the wind blowing snow outside, birds settling into warmer crevices in the trees, a car passing on the road above her property.

And she thought she heard another, much softer heartbeat.

chapter TWENTY

LEIGH DIDN'T find the cat until after Niles had finally gone home, insisting that Blue was happy on the porch in several inches of snow. She had tried to bring him inside but Niles wouldn't hear of it. Blue, he insisted, didn't feel the cold because he was built to withstand it, including having a denser coat than a polar bear.

So she closed and locked the door, climbed the ladder to the loft, and saw Sally's singular cat sitting on the bottom of the bed.

Once she decided there was nothing to be done about the little feline interloper until she could take it back to its owner in the morning, she curled up under the down covers and tried not to think, even when Skillywidden pressed her slight weight against Leigh's back—and she heard that heartbeat, the same tiny, regular beat as she was now sure she had heard before.

Weird.

Not thinking was impossible and turned into a jumble

of remembering her last days with Chris...and wanting
to feel Niles holding her again.

When Leigh woke up it was still dark, as it should be at
five in the morning. And she was so wide awake she knew
she wouldn't go back to sleep.

She got up and piled on the warmest clothes she could
find.

Next the chains for the car tires, then dealing with the
cat who must somehow have sneaked back this way on
Niles's bike. Sally wouldn't want her kitty at Gabriel's, so
Leigh would just have to take her home before she went
to work.

The cat in question continued to slumber in a cocoon
on the down comforter.

Grateful her boots had dried overnight, Leigh emerged
into the snow's pure crystalline sparkle. It continued to
fall against the darkness and she could scarcely keep a lid
on her excitement. Nothing could be more beautiful and
magical than this.

Blue had already been standing when she emerged, his
tail waving slowly. He was on alert and watching her closely.

Beyond the edge of the bluff, Saratoga Passage was
black and without dimension. Snowflakes seemed to snuff
out in that darkness, like extinguished fireflies.

A muted, multicolored haze rose from the water, rolled
toward the bank, and hung around until a shot of glitter
whipped the colors into a spin that evaporated. Just like
the whirl she had seen come into the cottage when she
was with Niles.

Leigh held very still, waiting to see if more shining
streams would come from the depths.

She smiled. The child within, the one who had clung to the comfort and thrill of imagination when everything else seemed to fail her, was trying to come out and play.

With purposeful strides she went to her car. Anyone who lived on Seattle's hills should become a whiz at putting on tire chains. After a few years in the area, and despite having grown up in New Orleans, Leigh was a super-whiz and accomplished the task in record time. She would get going now and have coffee at Gabriel's Place. That's the habit she had formed anyway—just not quite this early. Still on the porch, Blue watched her, and she could have sworn he looked disapproving.

On her way back she stroked him and held his head into the crook of her neck. Evidently that got rid of any annoyance on his part because he sighed and snuggled closer. His head weighed twice as much as Jazzy's entire body—more than that, probably.

Back into the cottage she went, only allowing herself to savor the warmth for a moment before going after the cat.

"Time for the stowaway to be brought to justice," she said, climbing the ladder.

Fifteen minutes later she still hadn't found Skillywidden. Exasperated, Leigh looked everywhere, but she knew when she was beaten. Cats were like that—they sensed when going to ground was in their best interest, and this one didn't intend to be found until she wanted to be.

Sally would already be baking. Perhaps she hadn't noticed Skillywidden's absence before she left home. Leigh decided not to call but to get there and tell her in person. The cat was safe.

Faintly, so faintly it might not have been a sound at all,

Leigh thought she heard the whisper of a heartbeat, and it wasn't her own.

Either she was losing her mind or she was falling under some sorcerer's spell that gave her superhuman hearing.

The drive was easy, through untouched snow several inches deep and still falling. The chains did their job perfectly, and with the blue-gray glow of dawn rising all around, Leigh reveled in the untouched landscape. It was still too cold for much of the snow to slide from tree branches, but she heard animals slinking in search of food.

Leigh braked and started into a skid. Fortunately she knew what she was doing and steered into the spin-out.

She *heard* animals moving softly, silently even, through the forest. Last night, warm and close to Niles, she hadn't registered that it was weird to hear birds settling in the forest. She had accepted the sound of a car on the highway far from the cottage—moving through the snow.

Her own car slithered to a stop. Good grief, had she really heard Skillywidden's heart last night, and when the cat hid from her today? Seeing shimmering colors slipping through cracks in the door and seeping from Saratoga Passage was something she refused to revisit—she hadn't even told Niles about it, because he would have laughed.

Something very peculiar was going on. Imagining the visitation of a monster aside, her absolute confidence in being here, being safe, being powerful was unusual even for cocky Leigh. Not that she was always cocky, just determined.

Hearing the things she thought she was hearing bordered on . . . what did they call it . . . the other-worldly?

And she hadn't turned a hair at the vapors drifting off Saratoga Passage.

Those vapors, and the ones that crept into the cottage the night before, were paranormal. What else could they be? And their appearance coincided with the bionic hearing...

Setting her jaw, narrowing her eyes on the glaring white scene again, she drove on, this time avoiding the brakes.

A hum of voices unraveled her concentration. There was no one to be seen, anywhere. Onward she went and the hum became a mumbling and an occasional laugh— and an occasional cross exclamation.

She would be a liar if she pretended not to be really rattled by too many questionable events, and by being closed inside her car, with blanketing snow deadening any noise around her, yet hearing people she couldn't see didn't make sense.

The car clock showed 6:30. She had made really good time.

When she reached the turn to Gabriel's Place, the muted hubbub grew louder. Leigh saw a little gaggle of swathed figures standing on the road, some jumping up and down and stamping their feet to stay warm. Then she saw Gabriel, who strode back and forth pounding his hands together.

The new sign was hard to miss. It was mounted on a pole, and the lights raced around the letters, flashed several times when they reached them all, then stayed on. In a few seconds the cycle started again.

Leigh put her forehead on the steering wheel while she composed herself. Laughter wouldn't endear her to

Gabriel, and if she got right out of the car she might leap around like a demented kangaroo and laugh with pure delight.

No one would miss that fabulous sign. Now she wanted one out by the main road. The thought of suggesting that to Gabriel made her cringe.

Only when she stood, cold striking through her boots—despite thick socks inside—did she gather the general mood of the little crowd. They were excited, blissful, bubbling with enthusiasm.

Gabriel saw her and marched in her direction. This was the moment to attack, not retreat. "I love it," she said as he reached her. "That shop does great work. They really understand what's needed. Congratulations, Gabriel."

He did an imitation of a beached fish, his breath turning to icy clouds like a stream of smoke rings.

Leigh threaded a hand under his elbow. "And it's really cute. Not offensive or anything, just funny. People will want to come in because they'll expect a warm welcome and a smile."

Gabriel pushed out his lips and narrowed his eyes. "If you look too quickly you see 'tomorrow we die,' not diet. And how was it put up without anyone hearing it going into the ground? That pole had better be in a deep hole or the whole thing will come down and kill someone." He sniffed and said, "That's if I don't take it out myself," under his breath.

With purposeful steps, Leigh marched to the sign and pushed on the very solid pole. "It's not going anywhere. And it's an absolute winner, Gabriel. You'll see."

He rocked to his heels. "You really think so?"

"I know so. Look at all of them—they love it."

They were Cliff and Sally, the twins, and a small assortment of men and women who had evidently sought cover from the weather.

"Well, I don't know so," Gabriel said. "Makes the place look like an amusement arcade. I'll have to think on it."

He marched back to the building, gesticulating and muttering about "Poles that go up in the night."

The others straggled after him, all but Sally, who came and put an arm around Leigh. "He'll warm up to it," she said. "But you'd better wait a week or two for results before you go after the one on the highway."

Leigh nodded and they started to go inside.

How did Sally know she was planning a second sign? Had they talked about it? They must have.

Blue appeared at Leigh's side and she jumped, looking around and expecting to see Niles. She didn't. The dog had followed her all the way here. Now she'd have to let Niles know where Blue was. When had she developed these Pied Piper tendencies? Dogs and cats everywhere—well, two dogs and one cat.

She cleared her throat as the doors of Gabriel's closed behind them. "Skillywidden showed up in my bed last night," she told Sally. "I'm so sorry, I thought it was too late to call you. She must have stowed away on Niles's bike at your shop."

Sally looked totally unconcerned. "Cats have minds of their own. If she's taken a shine to you, let her stay until she decides she wants to come back to me. I think you'll find her useful." She had already shed her huge, puffy coat. "Unless you don't want her around."

Jazzy chose that moment to leap gleefully into sight and launch himself at Leigh.

Leigh had only begun to consider Jazzy's reaction to a cat in the house when Sally said, "At least Jazzy thinks Skillywidden's the cat's meow." She laughed at her own little pun and began her stiff, rolling walk toward the kitchen. "Just let me know if you don't want her there."

Now wasn't the time to mention that the cat might already have disappeared. "Of course I want her there."

Blue and Jazzy made straight for the hearth in front of a roaring fire.

"Good," Sally called. "Introduce yourself to Doc Saul VanDoren. I call him Doc Saul. Just call him whatever he tells you to."

Leigh searched around the restaurant and bar and finally noticed a tall, slender figure seated in the darkest corner of the bar. She approached apprehensively. Getting to know all of the customers and making them welcome was part of her job—or so she had decided—but she knew a loner when she saw one.

He looked up from his apparent reverie well before she arrived at his secluded table and she stopped.

Someone should have prepared her.

Doc Saul VanDoren was not a man you would ever pass on the street without a second look—or a third. She couldn't tell the color of his eyes. Black, or as close to black as eyes could be, she supposed. Arching brows and narrow-bridged straight nose, a mouth with completely unexpectedly full, sensual lips. Cheekbones high and prominent.

Most surprising was the thick, black hair that fell past his shoulders.

"Good morning," he said, but the expression remained serious, even though he looked her over carefully enough to make her skin tingle.

"Good morning. I'm Leigh Kelly. I work for Gabriel now."

"Yes." Now she was getting the eye-lock. "Gabriel mentioned you. I'm Saul."

"Sally tells me you're the local doctor." She tried a smile without much hope of cracking any ice.

She was wrong.

The man spread a lazy smile Leigh could only stare at and held out a long-fingered hand. When she took it she noticed a heavy gold ring on his small finger and the unexpected drape of a full, white sleeve.

Sexy elegance. And in the local medico?

"Sally said you've been away."

He stared back at her. "At sea. I like to take a break as a ship's doctor a couple of times a year. Change is good and I have enough time on my hands to carry on my research."

She might wait a long time if she hoped to be invited to sit. "May I ask about your research?"

"Perhaps another day," he told her, rising to tower over her. He was as tall as Niles. "We'll have another chat soon, Miss Kelly."

"It's Mrs. Kelly, but please call me Leigh."

"Leigh," he said courteously and with a slight bow. "Good day to you."

A renaissance man, as in from the Renaissance. That's exactly what Dr. Saul looked like.

He walked fluidly in the direction of the kitchen. Beyond that there was another outside door and she heard it slam.

Before Leigh could hustle off to recover in her office, a woman raced through the front doors. It was still far too early for regular customers—the little band of those who had gotten off the road to seek warmth was an anomaly—but this person, who was young and beautiful, with green eyes and freckles, started talking to the room at large as if her arrival was the most normal thing at this time of day.

She pushed back the fur-lined hood of her heavy, plaid wool coat and curly red hair began to slide out of a topknot. "I've heard from Rose," she announced. She radiated happiness. "Everybody, I got back last night and there's a letter from Rose."

Gabriel came from behind the counter and Sally emerged from the kitchen with Cliff, covered in flour, trailing behind her. The customers looked mildly interested, but probably more in the newcomer than in her announcement.

"Have you told the police, Phoebe?" Gabriel asked.

The woman slapped a hand over her mouth. "I didn't even think about it. I'll call them." She took folded paper from her pocket and shook it out. A single sheet. "See. She's gone back to Alaska to help her dad. He can't do what he used to do without help, so Rose will help. And she thinks she'll stay there for good this time."

"Leaving all her stuff behind," Gabriel said. "Impulsive, if you ask me."

"That's one of the beauties of living in a converted school bus. With the wheels off and the whole thing up on blocks, it wouldn't be easy to steal. Everything's gone from inside. She didn't have much so it would have fit in her truck."

"Her truck is still there."

Phoebe screwed up her face. "No it's not. I went by there as soon as I got this last night. You know I always have problems storing all the books I, er, acquire. Rose says I can store some of them in the bus. It'll be really useful but I know it won't be easy finding a replacement for her at the shop."

Sally had reappeared, wiping her hands on her apron. "Did you introduce yourself?" she asked Phoebe, inclining her head to Leigh.

"Oh, my. Sorry. I'm Phoebe Harris. I own the used book store in Gulliver Lane. Read It Again. Next to Wear It Again, the consignment clothing store. I'm only here on weekends. In the week I work at a boat storage lot in Everett. Rose looked after the place here. She knew everyone and their interests so she often found a home for a book that came in before we even shelved it."

"Leigh Kelly," Leigh said. She hadn't known there was a used book store in the area, or a consignment shop—or a Gulliver Lane. "I work for Gabriel."

"I think I know someone who would be good with books," Sally said. "Give me a few hours to get in touch with him."

Leigh left them to it, decided to let Jazzy enjoy the fire, and went to her office.

Niles sat tipped back in her chair, his feet on her desk. "I've been waiting for you," he said.

He wasn't smiling a welcome.

chapter TWENTY-ONE

W HY?" SHE SAID. "And why hole up in here until you could jump out at me?"

"That's not what I meant to do," Niles said. "But I want you to take this seriously. I didn't want an audience when I gave you this." He put the Sig Sauer P238 on the desk in front of him.

He had more to talk about this morning than guns, but he might as well start with the easy stuff.

"Have you ever used a gun?"

Leigh leaned against the door and crossed her arms. She stared at the weapon but didn't seem to recoil from it, not that he'd thought she would. "I've fired a gun. Chris wanted me to learn."

He got up and went around to stand on the same side of the desk with her. "This model is called 'Lady.'" He reached behind him and brought the gun to hold in front of her. "A Sig Sauer. Except I knew where to get one that didn't have a red frame, like they usually do, and it doesn't have the cute little gold flowers on it. It's light enough for you to handle—especially since you already know how—but it's not a water pistol."

"I'll pay you for it."

"No, you won't. It's a gift, because I care about what happens to you. I care a lot. Do you understand?"

"I . . . I think you do, but you're angry. I can feel it."

Niles took a breath and softened his voice. "I'm not angry. I'm serious. Weapons are serious." Since he left her, early that morning, he had been busy lining up just the right weapon. He hadn't wanted to do it—guns killed more innocent people than guilty ones—but he understood her need to have some control over what happened to her.

He had also dealt with setting up twenty-four-hour surveillance of Leigh—and made himself face his own feelings. This was personal and doing nothing about it wasn't an option. The desperation he felt wasn't for the future of the team anymore, it was for himself and being with her for good. Anything more that came of it, unless she rejected him completely, would be a bonus.

Leigh didn't take her eyes from his face.

He offered her the gun. Leigh hesitated an instant too long before she held out her hand, palm up, as if he was giving her an apple. When the gun lay there, that's where it stayed.

She was trying to look tough and in many ways he thought she was, but she didn't like feeling a gun in her hand.

He wished she would say something.

"Leigh . . . Oh, hell." Niles jammed his hands deep in his pockets and looked at the floor. "I'm an idiot. This is the wrong way to do this."

"Do what? Test me to see if you can scare me? Try to make me show I'm unsure of myself? You're wrong; you've done that really well."

He couldn't stop looking at her stiff palm with the gun balanced on top. "You're frightened of me? You're not sure I'm on your side. Wonderful. Hours of thinking this through and I still make a mess of it."

"Is there something wrong, Niles? Should I be worried about you, or just about me?"

"I admitted this to you last night. You just...I'm not good at this because I haven't had much practice lately."

He heard her long sigh. "Are you going to explain what you aren't good at?"

"Talking to women. The only woman I really want to talk to. Leigh, this hasn't happened to me before, not like this." Now he sounded wet behind the ears. "I mean I haven't wanted to ask anyone what I want to ask you."

The room was too small. He felt as if the walls almost touched his shoulders.

"I've already told you I trust you," Leigh said. "That hasn't changed. Tell me what you came to say."

"Let me take that from you," he said, indicating the gun. "We'll get back to it."

She made no move to stop him from taking the gun and setting it on the desk.

"You told me you liked me. Did you mean that?"

"Yes."

He crossed his arms and vaguely noticed Leigh did the same. "Do you think you could love me—really love me?"

Her freckles got more pronounced as her face grew paler.

"Leigh?" He moved closer to her but not too close.

Her hands went to her face. She pressed her cheeks. "What does love mean to you?" she asked, her eyes very wide open and very dark. She breathed rapidly through her mouth.

"It's a feeling." He put a fist against his chest. "A longing to have one person belong to you. Not like a thing, a car or something. Attached at the head and heart, I guess. Not wanting anyone else the same way. There's something that happens in your throat—tightness that hurts in a good way. It's needing to take care of someone, just one person, to protect them. I have to know you're safe, Leigh. I think about you all the time. I don't know what else to say."

She kept staring at him.

"I'll try again. It's all the stuff I've already said, but there's a feeling when I see you, or think about you even. I tighten up with needing to touch you. I turn into a verbal idiot and nothing I say sounds right."

"We haven't known each other long," she whispered.

"Who says you have to? Will you think about this? Will you think about being with me all the time? My partner—be my partner, Leigh."

"Your partner?"

This wasn't the place to explain everything she would need to know. "You have to think about it. Maybe I'm crazy to come out with this and think you'll even consider me." But she hadn't dismissed him out of hand, or run shrieking from the room. "Take some time. I'll be watching out for you no matter what your answer is. I'll always do that. But if you think you can, or you want to, would you come to my place this evening so we can try to get at what this means?"

She shook her head and his heart dropped.

"I don't know," she told him. "I can't give you an answer till I've thought about it."

Hope was a dangerous thing, but he hoped. "Look. Just come if you want to. Spur of the moment is fine. I'll be there."

"I don't like to think of you waiting for me if I decide not to come."

"Forget it. I won't expect you to come but...I'm a big boy. If you don't want to, I'll suck it up and forget it."

They looked at each other.

"I know last night I said I wanted it, but would you hold on to the gun for me?" she said. "For a little while?"

He waited a couple of minutes after she left the room and made his way out of the building through the back door—with the gun in his pocket.

chapter TWENTY-TWO

So MUCH FOR FLASHY SIGNS," Gabriel said, glaring around at the mostly empty bar.

Leigh wrinkled her nose at him. "So we're having a slow day." She threw out her arms. "Look at the weather—folks are staying off the roads if they can. But when we get the other sign out by the highway even heavy snow won't keep business away."

She held her breath.

Gabriel didn't notice what she'd said. His mind had wandered. He watched Molly get up from a stool at the bar and shrug into a furry parka. The hood was huge and looked good framing her face.

It didn't take second sight to figure out Molly was deliberately ignoring Gabriel. She smoothed her tight jeans over her thighs and turned the fur cuffs at the tops of her boots over her knees.

Out she walked, twinkling her fingernails in the

air—Leigh presumed that was her good-bye to Gabriel, since she obviously knew he was looking at her.

"I'd better get back to it," Leigh said and slipped away to her office.

Jazzy sat up in his bed, a depressed expression turning his mouth down. She picked him up and sat down, settling the dog on her lap.

Get back to it? Gabriel would assume that's what she was doing but Leigh couldn't concentrate. The day was clicking by and she would have to make a decision about Niles. She wanted him, but it was so soon to make the kind of commitment he asked for.

She couldn't stay at Gabriel's, not right now, not when she needed to be alone somewhere to think.

On her way out of the office again she bumped into Sally.

"I was going to make a suggestion," Sally said. "I was going to call someone else, but didn't you say your sister had too much time on her hands?"

Jan did. "I guess." But Leigh didn't recall mentioning Jan to Sally at all.

"The drive around from Camano isn't so long and the road is never that busy. Maybe she could do a couple of days for Phoebe during the week. At the bookstore. That's when Jan's husband goes in to Seattle, isn't it—during the week?"

Niles must have told Sally about Jan and Gib. Sally had a sympathetic ear and trying to work out a solution was just her style. "I don't know if Jan would want to do it," Leigh said.

"You look as if you could use some time away from here," Sally said. "Why not head out early? Stop in at

Gulliver Lane and take a look at the shop. See what you think. If you like it, Jan's bound to, isn't she?"

"We like a lot of the same things." Jazzy strained in her arms, trying to fly free. "You're staying with me now, boy" she told him. "I need your company."

Jazzy rolled his eyes and Sally laughed, unnerving Leigh. No one ever noticed Jazzy did that.

"Take the second turn to the right after the gas station," Sally said. I'll call Phoebe and tell her you're coming."

"Well—"

"What have you got to lose? She serves great hot chocolate and the bookshop's a blast. Look for Read It Again next to Wear It Again. It's a bit run down but the stained-glass windows are great—Phoebe made them herself."

"Well, I guess—"

"Bless my socks, I forgot to give you this." Sally produced a much-folded piece of paper. "A man called John Valley left it for you. Wouldn't wait. He said for you to get in touch with him and all the information's there. He's got a shiner of a black eye. I didn't figure he liked showing it off."

Sally walked away and Leigh unfolded the paper. Valley's name and number were on the top. The brief note underneath said, "You are never going to get another offer like this. The guy wants your place so bad we could maybe push him even higher. Call me." His number was under his name.

The sum of money written there crossed Leigh's eyes. No one would pay that much for a little cottage, even on a really big piece of land—not in a down market. Although she supposed a developer might see big potential. Leigh shook her head—her property wasn't for sale.

She crumpled the paper into a ball and scrunched it into the bottom of her pocket.

Defeated by a puzzling day and tied in knots over Niles, Leigh let Gabriel know she was setting off early and eventually managed to get her car door open while Jazzy leaped around whining about his cold feet.

She swept enough snow off the windshield, front and back, to let her see and crawled inside the car where she sat while trying to let it warm up. Not that it did much good. The heater seemed to be running on cool.

Jazzy kept jumping on her lap and Leigh repeatedly pushed him to the backseat where he at least had a blanket to curl up in.

The little Honda handled surprisingly well in snow. At least, it did with chains on the tires. She made it steadily out of the road in front of Gabriel's to the secondary highway. Snow piled high on either side.

"Damn," she muttered. Fat flakes hit the windshield again, all but obliterating the view ahead. She turned on the wipers and leaned forward, looking for the gas station.

When she saw it, she was relieved. Any sign of civilization was welcome in this weather. And lights inside showed they were available for what business came their way. Snow didn't stop people around here. Remembering that made her feel brave all over again.

The first turn she came to was little more than a lane but she supposed it counted. Another two miles and she reached an unmarked road. Unmarked and unplowed.

She steered carefully around the corner then slowed to a stop. This visit to Phoebe should wait for another day.

The sooner she got home, the sooner she would be

alone to think about the shock Niles had given her that morning.

What did partnership mean to him?

He'd talked about really caring for her—more than caring. Her skin prickled and she felt too jumpy to think straight.

What did she feel for him?

She felt something, a lot. But was she thinking straight or simply reacting to a very attractive man who made her feel wanted and important? What was it about him that acted like a magnet? Maybe it was his having the chutzpah to come right out and say he wanted her. The expression on his face hadn't suggested chutzpah, rather that laying it all out to her was costing everything he had in emotional reserve.

He had talked about love. Leigh swallowed hard.

The headlights of another car turned onto the narrow street behind her and she had to move. The chains weren't gripping as well as they should here. There must have been time for a good freeze and a layer of ice before the freshest snow fell.

Shimmying slightly, she crawled on.

Those headlights were shining in her rear window, reflecting on the fine layer of snow that had drifted down from the top of the car. The rear-window heater was working, but slowly.

The slightest bump against the back of the Honda startled her. Whoever was back there wasn't experienced and had gotten too close.

The next bump was harder.

Leigh tapped her horn but the lights didn't back off.

An avalanche of snow fell from the tall firs all around.

There didn't seem to be any wind but something had dislodged things.

Another bump.

This one jarred Leigh's neck and when she checked on Jazzy he had been thrown forward onto the floor.

That made her mad, but what could she do about it out here? Someone was having his jollies at her expense.

Her stomach turned. When Jazzy climbed shakily between the front seats, she let him sit on her lap—something she never encouraged while she was driving.

The road curved to the left. Leigh didn't see a building anywhere and anything with stained-glass windows and a name like Read It Again ought to be noticeable. She should turn around, but the thought of actually seeing the clown behind her was scary.

He nudged her again and she tried to speed up. The result was several nasty slips, one way and the other.

And the light was failing. It was too early for that. She realized the trees were becoming so dense they almost met overhead and closed out any light that might have filtered down.

Another curve turned to the left sharply enough for her to be surprised when she actually saw lights ahead. Far ahead, it's true, but lights nevertheless.

Dark multicolored lights, as if they were shining through that stained glass Sally had talked about.

Sheesh, what would be the point of trying to run a business back here? No one would ever find it, or at least not by accident.

She hadn't noticed the other car starting to overtake her. It drew level, a big, maroon sedan, although she couldn't tell the make. Windows tinted black gave her the creeps.

The car stayed level, matching her speed exactly. She slowed a little more. He slowed a little more.

Leigh sweated. Her eyes stung and her throat was so tight it hurt.

He's going to sideswipe me.

Who could she call for help out here—wherever out here was? Niles, of course. He'd said he would keep her safe—he wouldn't be happy if she had accidentally slipped his net, but she wasn't about to become a sniveling, wilting flower who leaned on him day after day. Especially not now.

From nowhere, gravel sprayed the windshield. There was a pop and the whole thing was crazed with cracks.

Deciding what to do next wasn't an option. A big branch crashed down, finishing the job the gravel had started, shattering the window and sending sharp twigs and pebbles of glass into Leigh.

She screamed, tried to cover her face, and managed to get a foot on the brake.

For a sickening instant she was back in that other car, careening down an embankment with a boulder crashing on a collision course with Chris's side of the car.

She took several deep breaths and blinked sweat out of her eyes.

The branch that had penetrated the car pinned her to the seat. A few inches closer and it might well have killed her.

Jazzy's pathetic bark was a relief. At least he wasn't dead. But Leigh knew that pray as she might, the other car might not just carry on and leave her, as she wished it would. She didn't want to deal with people who got their kicks from bumping cars in this sort of weather.

"You okay?" A man's voice called out, and she heard another car's door slam shut. "I'm really sorry I hit you. I got caught without my chains and I'm slipping all over the place."

"I'll be okay," she called back. "Someone will come with a tow truck." She couldn't see who she was talking to, but the guy sounded okay and at least he was apologizing.

"You won't get cell reception out here. No one ever does. Doc's house is up the end of here. I reckon you ought to let him have a look at you."

Leigh didn't answer. She felt completely trapped. And she couldn't locate her bag, to say nothing of her cell phone.

"Does anything hurt?" the voice asked. "Your face is bleeding."

She peered, trying but failing to see anyone. Tentatively she felt her way to her face with her fingertips and felt sticky blood at her temple.

"I'll be okay," she said. Relying on strangers was not a pleasing idea right now. If Niles knew about this, he would be furious.

"Could need stitches, though. And it's pretty cold out here. It wouldn't be a good thing if you went into shock.

"Let's get you out of there." He yanked on the door handle. "I think you've still got it locked," he said.

Her heart beat in time with her very shallow breathing. Jazzy growled and she jumped. Jazzy wasn't the type of dog to growl at much unless he was scared or mad.

"You should be able to reach the lock," the guy said. "Release it and I'll take you to Doc Saul."

If she pretended to lose consciousness, would he go for help or just pound away at her car to get in?

She could push the door release but still she hesitated.

"Can you get it? Or shall I go for help? Could get dangerously cold out here, though. Window broken and all."

Leigh clicked the lock and the door opened almost at once. A man bundled up in snow gear with a stocking cap pulled down to his eyes held the branch away from her with one arm and peered at her closely. "Can you move? If anything hurts, you stay still."

"I can move." But she ached, and sliding sideways out into the snow was horrible. She reached back for Jazzy and pushed him inside her coat as best she could. The coat wasn't big enough.

She couldn't tell how old the guy was. Maybe thirties, maybe forties, and with a pointed nose all his other features looked like they wanted to get cozy with. She'd heard of push faces on dogs, but this was a pull face with small, pale eyes set very close together.

When he put an arm around her shoulder it took willpower not to shrug him away. But he had not said anything threatening, and he had admitted he was responsible for the accident.

"You're probably fine," he said. "But you can lean if you need to. I'm Bill, by the way."

"I'm Leigh," she said. "What's your other name?" She might well want to trace this one about her car no matter how honest he seemed.

"Bill Stravinsky," he said with a chuckle. "No relation to the great Stravinsky."

Her temptation was to tell him she would prefer not to talk at all.

Leigh did feel a little woozy. Bill took her by the arm and held tighter than she thought necessary, but he got her up the street okay, steadying her each time her legs got weak enough for her to start slipping.

"You're okay," he said. "Doc Saul's a miracle worker."

"I'll have to get someone out to help with my car."

"Time for that when you're cleaned up. A hot drink will feel good, too."

In the driveway that led from tall, double wrought-iron gates to the front of the house, Bill Stravinsky hesitated.

Leigh looked at him, at his puzzled expression.

"What is it?"

He shrugged. "I could have the wrong house."

Leigh shuddered. Was she concussed? The branch must have hit her head harder than she had thought.

The front door, its black paint curling off in long strips, flew open before they could knock or ring the bell. A huge lamp shaped like an upside-down umbrella and suspended from the roof of the porch was made of colored glass, and that accounted for the spray of colored light.

"Come on in," a short, plump man in a purple tunic and skullcap said. "You can freeze out there in no time, and if you let much more of that air in, we'll all freeze in here. Come along now. Need your head looked at, do you? Well, don't we all." He laughed like a braying donkey and slapped a foot up and down on the floor. "In we go."

The room she entered behind him had steps leading up to a platform along one side. A carved railing at the back of the platform stood as an apparent barrier between an open space below and the room where Leigh stood. She couldn't see anything but white walls beyond the railing.

"Sit, sit, sit," the man in purple said, waving her to a carved wooden chair. "All our honored visitors sit in that. You can call me Percy. That's my name."

"Nice to meet you, Percy." Reluctantly, Leigh sat. "Is Dr. Saul in?" she said.

"Do you want to look at a book while you wait or will you make up your own story?" was all the response she got.

She rubbed her eyes, so scared every breath jammed in her throat. If she was unconscious, this could all be imaginary.

"Where's Bill?" she said suddenly, wanting to see a familiar face, any familiar face.

"Do you want a—"

"Where is Bill?" She stood up, ready to walk out.

"Bill Stravinsky went to find the doctor. This is the wrong street for his house. We'll look after you till Bill gets back. He doesn't know us very well; I expect that's why he took the wrong turn."

Leigh tried to figure out how she could get away from here.

"I told you to sit down," Percy said, his jovial expression never changing. "Do it or you'll get me in trouble."

She remained on her feet and fought down panic. Was she in a coma?

Through the door came the most beautiful man Leigh had ever seen. Percy backed out of the room, bowing repeatedly and leaving her alone with this unreal-looking male.

The man inclined his head at Leigh, allowing silken blond hair that reached his waist to swing to one side. His black and silver body suit fitted every dip, rise, and muscle without as much as a tiny wrinkle—as far as Leigh could see.

The view was pretty amazing. She moved her stare to his face and kept it there.

This creature—"man" was not an adequate word—studied her with unwavering black eyes that winged up at the same angle as his cheekbones and dark brown brows. His upper lip was narrower than the lower one and his mouth parted in the slightest smile.

He held a hand toward her, inviting her to touch him.

Leigh put both of her own hands behind her back.

"I am Colin," he said, the little smile gone. "This is my house. Welcome." And to Leigh's horror he moved closer, much closer, and rested his hands on her shoulders. "You don't need your coat," he said and unzipped her long parka—slowly. Jazzy jumped down and pressed close to her legs.

Leigh couldn't have said anything even had she wanted to.

Colin slid the coat down her arms and tossed it over one of several pieces of plush antique furniture she hadn't noticed until now. He swept up Jazzy and tossed him after the coat.

With one finger he traced the shape of her face to the point of her chin, slid down her throat and continued on over her silk turtleneck all the way to her waist.

"Nice," he said. "I thought it was too much to hope for that I would get you. You must know how rare your kind are now. We shall take great care of you."

Petrified, Leigh felt as if her mind had frozen. She didn't know what he meant and couldn't as much as start an idea to get away from him.

His next move was so fast she didn't see it until his mouth brushed her cheek and he nipped the lobe of her ear.

The blond stream of his hair slid over her face and

across her shoulders. "No response?" he said, not sounding angry. Blowing softly, he rested his mouth on her ear and caressed her neck until he settled his head there, lips and teeth barely touching her, the backs of his fingers slipping back and forth beneath her hair.

"Mmm." He straightened, so much taller than she. "More to come later."

Carefully, he passed his fingertips over the cuts on her temple and jaw. He smiled again as he slowly licked specks of her dried blood from his fingers.

With that he led her up to the balcony and, with a sweeping gesture, showed her the white room below. More white greeted her with a few pieces of white satin furniture. He took one of her hands and curled the fingers around the rail. He gave the lightest of jumps and became airborne. Looking back at her, his hair flipping and floating, every perfect line of his body silhouetted against the white around him, he smiled as he drifted down to stand in the center of the lower room.

Leigh looked over her shoulder at the door. She had no idea how quickly he could return but she knew trying to escape while he watched her wasn't smart.

He made a clicking noise as if calling a horse, pulling Leigh's attention back to him. From nowhere Leigh could identify, a female figure walked toward him. Laughter, high pitched and excited, came from this woman.

Sickened, Leigh realized she was watching a bride approaching as if to join her groom.

Heavy lace covered the woman's face. The same lace clung to her body in an ankle-length dress, and swept behind as a long train. She carried a single lily and its heavy scent rose all the way to Leigh.

The fingers of her right hand would not separate from the railing. They weren't stuck but paralyzed.

Colin took hold of the bride's dress by the neck and tore it open all the way to the hem. A voluptuously perfect body was revealed, the large nipples on oversized breasts the only color to relieve almost blindingly white skin. He swept up the woman, sucked each nipple into his mouth and pulled his head back to show thin streams of blood coursing down from where his teeth, with dual fangs glittering, had broken the skin. He lapped up the blood before shifting to the woman's neck and biting down with a grunt of satisfaction.

The blood that rushed from there seemed darker, and stained the shreds of torn wedding gown.

Colin opened his own suit over his bulging crotch. A single thrust and the woman's feet shot from the floor. He rose with her, copulating in the air while she hung with arms wide, like a willing, bleeding, sacrifice.

Leigh felt faint.

"Look away, Leigh." She heard the loud order in her mind. A glance down proved that it couldn't have been spoken aloud. Colin would have heard.

A great growl erupted through the whole space. A huge animal with thick russet fur and oversized claws on its outstretched paws sprang into view.

Massive, handsome, terrifying, the doglike beast loped closer, its eyes heated as if by fire. She closed her own eyes, waiting to be mauled, praying it would all be short.

Fur brushed across her fixed fingers on the railing and she could move them again. "Climb on my back," a voice in her mind ordered, and she barely hesitated before climbing on and feeling the animal's thick fur beneath her face and body.

"I need you to hold on until velocity and gravity take over," the voice in her head said. And a second later, "Good. Now then. Hold tightly."

She still did not dare look, but she gripped the giant's fur on either side of its neck.

"I'll get the little dog," she heard next. "And your coat."

Leigh cracked her eyes open but closed them again at once. They were in the air, splintering through the front door. The icy blast of outdoors touched her, then made her so cold she felt nothing.

chapter TWENTY-THREE

N<small>ILES STOOD</small> in the middle of his sparsely furnished living room, waiting for Sean to explain himself.

His second in command rested his brow on the fireplace mantel and gripped it with both hands. They had been back, with Leigh in their possession, for more than half an hour.

"Are you going to explain how this near-miss happened?" Niles said when he figured he would be waiting a long time for Sean to start this conversation. "You could have cost me Leigh."

Sean straightened up and jerked his head toward Niles's bedroom. "Shh. You'll wake her up. She's still much too cold. Better off under that pile of quilts."

"She would have been better off if she hadn't been snatched."

Sean stretched out on the couch and turned his head away. "And this could have cost *you* Leigh. What happened to the team needing her?"

Niles wasn't going there, not now. "How could that lousy scourge have moved into the area without our knowing?" he said instead, then answered his own question. "They've been getting help, that's how. And we know from where. Regardless of how much he hates the walking dead, Brande knows they can help him get what he wants. He intends to run this island—with a little help from a lot of friends. And he can only hold control over Whidbey so long as we never get bigger in numbers. That's why he'll do anything to get Leigh."

Sean scooted up until he could rest the back of his head on the couch arm. "What if Colin wants her, too? It would be just like his twisted kind to want her only to stop anyone else from having her. A fight between the pack and the scourge could keep all of them busy for a long time."

Niles wanted to break something. No, smash something, a lot of things. Pulverize them. The old rage was back as strongly as it had been when they lost Gary in the Middle East.

Tonight, with Leigh asleep in his bed, he couldn't afford to give in to one of the nightmarish episodes that left him sweating and drained.

Jazzy went where Niles went as he paced, pumping his hands in and out of fists. Skillywidden sat beside Leigh on the bed, watching her sleep, and Jazzy wasn't happy with that arrangement.

Without Skillywidden leading the way, it would have taken longer to find Leigh at the vamp's house. The cat had to be as fae as Sally was, but it had an easier time slipping in and out of tight spots.

Niles grimaced. He knew that when Leigh woke up

and discovered she was in his cabin she would be confused and maybe angry. And he wouldn't blame her.

He would need one hell of a cover story.

⌒

Hovering by the door now, ready to leave, Sean had his thumbs hooked into his jeans' pockets and the usual inscrutable expression on his face.

Niles wasn't fooled. "You're as puzzled by this as I am."

"Sure I am. I'm also pissed I didn't realize Leigh had left Gabriel's until too late. Are you going to calm down enough to be rational, boss?"

"Hell, no, I'm not calming down. What were you doing when you were supposed to be watching Leigh—sleeping?"

Sean's expression showed nothing. "In a way."

"Meaning?"

"That's none of your damn business. You're not the only one lonely for someone to..."

Niles sighed. He looked at his bare feet. Putting on shoes hadn't occurred to him. "Let's drop this for now. We've got vampires right in the middle of everything."

"We already knew there was one. We saw him the night of the fight."

"Take it from me"—Niles gave a humorless laugh—"Colin wasn't the vampire from the other night. And if we didn't know about either of them, how many more are there? Rough sex and domination are this latest guy's thing. That, and fresh, supposedly innocent blood—preferably in front of an audience."

"You expected a tea-drinking ceremony, or—"

"This is not the time for jokes," Niles snapped, his

voice practically a growl. "We've got to hope Leigh will think she had a bad dream after a bump on the head in the storm." He gritted his teeth. "I hate it that she saw that sick scene at Colin's. He planned to have her next..."

Sean held up both palms. "Okay. You've obviously got it bad for her. But I've got to remind you that boss or not, the rules apply. That woman in there has to want you before you go any further. You cannot seal until she understands what you are."

Niles still wasn't in a mood to discuss his relationship with Leigh with Sean.

"I want to find a way to get Sally to open up with us," Niles said, narrowing his eyes. "My theory is that the woman wants to be part of two worlds, human and fae. Otherwise, why would she be so helpful to us?"

"Try her being a spy for the other side. How does that fit? That, or she's just a sweet thing who wants the best for all of us." He curled his lip.

"Knowing how the fae keep their secrets, we may never find out her angle. But instinct tells me she'd choose us over any of the others—except for her own kind. And she likes Leigh. That doesn't feel like a guess."

"Boss—"

"I got your message," Niles said. "You can quit lecturing."

Sean slipped away leaving Niles and Jazzy to stare at each other. He picked up the dog and got a frantic licking. Jazzy was panicky.

Niles walked quietly to the bedroom door and pushed it open enough for him to see the bed.

Leigh's eyes were open.

He almost turned around and left.

"What's happened?" Leigh asked. "This is your place?"

"Uh huh. Easier to look after you here." He turned on a lamp.

She struggled to sit up but fell back on the pillow. "Why would I need looking after? I'm all twisted up in this quilt."

With her tufted ears twitching, Skillywidden moved even closer to Leigh. The cat's purplish eyes fixed on her face. With one paw, she touched Leigh's forehead, above the cut Sean had already reported.

"Yeah," Niles said, to either Leigh or the cat or both. "Take it easy, Leigh, I'll unwind your feet, but you should stay there for a bit. You probably want something to drink. I don't have brandy but I've got that other wine."

She frowned as if she found him puzzling. Her expression slowly changed. "Something horrible has happened. I know it. What's happened, Niles?"

Niles fluffed up the quilt, feeling awkward even though he liked the idea of making her comfortable in his bed. "You banged your head," he told her, wishing she would go back to sleep and give him time to figure out how to deal with this.

Leigh put a hand to her head and winced when she felt the crusted-over cut.

"You want that wine?" he said.

"Um." The look suggested deep thought. "Why not? This has been quite a day." She stared at him again. "I want you to tell me everything that's going on. Whatever it is. I'm scared." Her face stiffened even more. "I was going to stop by Phoebe's bookstore then go home. I took a wrong turn. Wow." Her eyes got huge and horrified.

"Wow, I'm all muddled up," she whispered and pulled the quilt over her head.

Niles made it to his mostly unused kitchen and gave thanks for having bought wine with a screw top. That might mean the stuff was horrible, but the guy at the store said lots of wine came that way now and it should be good. He poured a healthy measure for Leigh and turned to head back. He changed his mind. If he had a glass, too, it would be an excuse to sit with her while they drank it.

Leigh sat on the edge of the bed, her feet dangling over the side but not touching the floor. The cat had only moved enough to keep her eyes on her charge. "Well," he said to Leigh, plastering on a grin. "You were coming down to see me anyway. I'm glad you made it earlier rather than later."

The look she gave him would have cracked bones. She ruined the effect when she sniffed and wiped away tears.

"Wine," he said brightly and handed over a glass.

There wasn't a chair in the room. Hooking an elbow around a bedpost, he crossed one bare foot over the other. He raised the glass to his mouth.

"For crying out loud, sit down here," she snapped, pointing to the bed beside her. "Your virtue's safe with me."

His virtue? She was what his mother would once have called sassy. But that had been a very long time ago.

A good look at Leigh's strained face and he figured she wasn't sassy, only shocked.

Niles sat, realized he'd cut off the cat's view of Leigh—cats could glare, or this one could—and moved to sit on the other side. "That cat's got a thing for you," he said.

"I think she's pretty cute." Leigh frowned around, caught sight of Jazzy moping in the hallway, and called him. "Why do you go without a shirt in the middle of winter?" she said.

Niles looked down at his chest. Damn, he'd been in too much of a hurry to think about it. But what did she expect from him anyway? "I've got my pants on," he said and winced.

A snort escaped Leigh. "Should I say I'm grateful for small mercies?"

"Depends on how dangerously you want to live." He was grateful for any sign of her spirit returning.

The humor slid away from her features. "How did I get here? And don't keep making excuses not to tell me."

He had known this was coming. "I opened the door and there you were. But you were icy cold and passed out." Not such a stretch. "I put you under the quilt to warm you up. That cat was with you. So was Jazzy." That much was true.

"That's what happened?" She said it as if trying to remember. "How did I get down here? Where's my car?"

"Your car's up at Two Chimneys. You must have gotten a rock through the windshield. Sean's fixing that. But apart from that the car seems fine."

She frowned again. "You left to go check my car? To find it? Why would you think of that?"

He would have to be more careful.

"Sean saw it and called me. You've only got a few superficial scratches on your face. They're clean."

She twisted around to see the whole room. "I don't remember coming here," she said. "I know I was going to the bookshop, but..."

He hoped she didn't totally freak out. "Car accidents can really shock you. You've probably blocked it out."

Leigh didn't look convinced.

"I didn't handle it well with you this morning," he said. He wanted to rush her past any recollection of being in that house and what she saw there. "I thought I'd probably scared you off completely. Thanks for coming anyway and giving me another chance."

Her expression softened. "What you said didn't make much sense. Or maybe I'm scared of my own feelings. I couldn't get you out of my mind. Gabriel didn't get his money's worth out of me today."

Niles didn't care about Gabriel at this moment. He turned sideways and hooked up a knee, leaning so he could see her clearly.

"I'm sure I got everything you said wrong," she told him.

He regarded her for an instant. "Do you hope you did?"

"That's not fair. More questions instead of dealing with the ones we already know about."

If she remembered what had happened to her she wouldn't be even this calm. "Maybe I'm not sure what to say, Leigh. Talking about feelings isn't what I do—not usually."

"Is that because you're out of practice or just too macho for sloppy stuff?"

"It's not sloppy to want someone." He felt as if he had begun to slide and a ravine opened before him. "I told you I won't push it if you aren't interested, but I am in love with you."

She put her glass aside and took his, too. Then she caught hold of the forearm he'd replaced across his middle and pulled his hand free. She held it on the bed between them.

"Niles, how can you be in love with me? You haven't known me long enough. We've never..."

"Made love?" He smoothed her cheek, took one of her hands to his mouth and kissed the palm.

"That's what I was going to say."

"There's something I believe in," he told her. "If we've come together like this, from a long way, then it was meant to be. We didn't know it but we were moving toward each other and now that we're here, it's time."

Leigh played with a piece of her hair. "Time?" she said and sounded shaky.

"Time for us to begin. *Us.*"

Tentatively, she rubbed his knuckles and stroked the tendons in the back of his hand with a forefinger.

He leaned slowly closer, expecting her to push him away. She didn't. Niles opened her mouth under his and sucked her bottom lip gently between his teeth. And she softened against him.

The kiss went on and on, seeking and finding deeper places, neither of them trying to end it until Leigh pulled back a little before resting her brow on his. She closed her eyes and so did he.

"I don't know what you want from me," she whispered.

"I want what you want." He passed the tip of his tongue along her lip. "But it has to be..."

"What I want?"

He actually shook from holding himself back. Muscles all over his body ached and his thighs contracted until they felt like rocks.

But through it all there was a longing for something else, something he couldn't identify.

Leigh buried her face in his shoulder. He felt her breath

sighing over his skin. This was what he had hoped and longed for, wasn't it? She was drawn to him and he could have her.

No. Not just yet.

The females of his kind had started dying when they gave birth. Then they all died—none of them survived. Niles knew he must not forget the truth about his own kind. And that he must share the truth with Leigh.

He stroked Leigh's hair. He massaged her shoulders and wrapped his arms around her as if he could somehow shelter her from all harm. But no one had been able to save those others. He and the team hoped it would be different with Leigh, but they didn't know for sure, he didn't know.

A shudder shook him and he gritted his teeth. Convulsively, he held her even tighter, his face in her neck, kissing her there.

She made a sound and he winced. Carefully, he loosened his grip without letting her go. Her breasts were soft against him but her small body was firm. Firm but so slight. She would not withstand a violent turmoil waged from within her, one that could consume her life.

The risk was too great.

Still holding her, Niles said, "I should get you home. This isn't the right time to discuss any of this." There would never be a right time, and he felt torn apart by the sense of loss.

"I'm not going anywhere without you." She said it, and as if to force him to believe her she dug her fingertips into his naked back. "I don't know why but I have to be with you, Niles. It's meant to be. There is so much I don't understand but I think I will if I trust."

He didn't dare move and all but held his breath.

"Have you seen it, the film of colors that comes and spreads around us?"

And so it began, what he had expected, the revelation of what was not purely human about this woman—apart from her rare blood type. "I'm not sure," he improvised. "Describe it to me."

"Colors, soft, then more intense. Then a shimmering that comes through them like fingers wrapping us inside. The first time it came was after I met you. You were with me at Two Chimneys."

"Do you see it now?"

She raised her head. Niles looked at her face and in her eyes he saw a reflection of a bright sheen. "I see it," she said, so quietly he held her mouth against his ear. "It makes me strong. It lets me know I can believe in you. We will be together."

"Where does the film of colors come from?" he asked, grasping for anything that would give him time to plan what to do next.

She got up and led him by the hand to the window. "Out there, I think," she told him, leaning against his side. "I've thought about it and I think it comes from the water. I thought I saw it when the light was failing one night but then I wasn't sure. And early this morning, when I was leaving for Gabriel's, I saw it whirling up from the Passage."

"Have you seen it anywhere else?"

"Never. And I didn't see it until I came back here to Whidbey."

He almost wished he hadn't encouraged her to talk about this. "It could be a trick of the light."

"When you were at the cottage with me it came through cracks around the door and surrounded us. I didn't tell you then. You think I'm strange, don't you?"

It might be nice to have that luxury. "No, I don't." He had learned not to discard anything as impossible. "You're shivering. Are you still cold?"

"A little."

At least she didn't feel icy anymore.

If he took her, sealed her to him as his life mate, there would always be that difference between them that he could never forget, not for a moment. The team would accept her, respect her, but if she tried to run with them, she would not withstand what they found ordinary in their lives. She could not live wild in the forests when they felt the need to hide. Her humanness would not withstand being moved at the speed they sometimes needed. Today had been too much for her.

He came close to laughing at himself. Did he really think she would stay with him?

"You could wear some of my clothes," he said. This was such unfamiliar territory. "They'll warm you. Unless you'd rather get some of your own."

"I won't leave." She stood away from him with her feet braced apart and her hands on her hips. "I'm stronger when I'm with you, and you can laugh, but you're stronger with me."

He didn't laugh, but he did have to control his amazement at her words.

"Stay then," he said. The night could be filled with revelation and even with rejection if she couldn't adjust to him. That was if he could find a way to explain himself.

He took a wool shirt from the closet, a T-shirt, and

then a pair of heavy sweatpants. "You'll have to hold them together but you'll be fine once you sleep."

She started to pull her thin silk turtleneck over her head and he turned his back.

In minutes she said, "I'm decent now," but when he looked at her, his shirt flapped around her thighs and she held the pants up in front of her with a bemused look on her face.

Her legs were beautiful. Longer than he would have expected, smooth and shapely with narrow ankles. And her feet...he didn't remember ever looking at feet and finding them beautiful but he did now.

"Hmm," she murmured. Then she sat on the floor, pulled the pants over her feet and legs, managed to stand up, and pulled the stretchy waistband all the way beneath her arms. "This must look really lovely, but thank you, I'm starting to warm up again."

Carefully, he picked her up and put her on the bed. Skillywidden leaped, depositing her minuscule weight on Leigh's shoulder, and gave Niles the cross-eyed glare.

He produced socks and pulled them onto Leigh's feet. They reached above her knees and the heels stuck out at the backs of her calves.

She giggled. "Now maybe you should treat yourself to a shirt before you freeze, too."

"I am never cold," he said.

"Hot-blooded American male," Leigh said with a smile. "Lucky you."

"You should probably get some more sleep."

"We're going to go through what you said to me this morning." She got beneath the quilt and looked at him questioningly. "There's plenty of room for both of us."

"You'll sleep better without a stranger taking up most of the bed," he told her without conviction.

"We're not strangers. Have we kissed and held each other—and wanted more? Or did I dream it? Did we hold each other? Did I tell you I won't go anywhere without you? Did you tell me you loved me?"

Niles gently straightened the quilt over the bed and lay on top. Even through the down he could feel her beside him.

She was quiet and he turned his face toward hers.

"You talked to me about love feeling like being attached at the head and the heart," she said after what felt like a very long silence.

"That's how it feels. It's the way I feel about you. I never expected it. Hoped, maybe, but never expected."

"That's a lovely thing to say."

He took in a long breath and said, "It could be if you don't hate the person who says it."

Leigh scooted a little closer. All of the soft armor wasn't stopping his body from reacting to her. "What was the other stuff you said about loving someone—what it's like?" she asked.

He thought back and closed his eyes. "It sounds weird the second time around. I told you it's a feeling. Wanting to have one person belong to you. I believe that only happens once in a lifetime. You never want anyone the same way."

"But I have loved before," she said quietly.

He nodded. "I loved once, too, but we both lost those loves, so we're alone." She would have to know exactly how it had happened to him but he couldn't tell her yet. "Leigh, I told you I need to take care of you and protect you. It's true. But if you want me to stop talking about this, just say so."

"I don't want you to stop. Would there be someone else for you then—if you didn't have me?"

"That sounds as if you're looking for a way out," he said.

"No, I just want to understand. I am constant. I had no lovers before Chris or since. I thought I never would again."

"You have marked me, Leigh. For me, we are all but joined as if we were one."

"But—"

"This is a joining that happens before the bodies come together. It's my way of life. I want you to accept my life and my body as your own and we would be forever joined here"—he took a fist to his brow—"and here." He spread his hand over his heart.

Leigh rolled against him. She pulled a hand free and flattened her hand on his belly. "I don't know what to say. I don't really know what it all means."

"Listen carefully." Her touch was almost more than he could bear. "You have marked me. That means if you agree, you are joined with me and we are forever sealed as one. My mind and my heart move with yours. I hear the beat of your heart—it moves through me."

"You sound different, from a different culture." Her voice cracked and faded.

Careful. He laughed. "Perhaps I sound old-fashioned because I'm explaining something more important to me than anything else."

Her intense silence made him jumpy until she kissed his shoulder. "You are different, Niles, different from any man, I think."

If he couldn't reach her on a level she understood she would eventually be scared away.

"We should be wondering if we need more time together before we get in so deep," Leigh said.

"I knew it was right the day I saw you," he said. "I expected it before you arrived." Even when he tried, he said what came from his heart when he should be thinking first.

Leigh threaded her fingers through the hair below his navel. "I felt something, too. I was glad you were there and I didn't know you at all."

Hating to do it, he pressed his hand over hers, stopping her from driving him mad.

Leigh pulled away from him and he looked toward her. She pushed the covers down and stretched herself across him, her face against his chest, her hands clinging to his shoulders.

He stroked her back, took one of her hands to his mouth and sucked each finger. The T-shirt was no real barrier between them.

Skillywidden left the room in a gray streak with Jazzy running after her.

"I love you, Niles Latimer. I believe I felt I had to come back to Chimney Rock to meet you. I don't know if fate is the right word, but it feels as if it is and I've been thinking it—when I wasn't arguing with myself." She kissed his shoulder again, then his chest, all the way to a flat nipple, which she took between her teeth until he moaned. "Mark me, too. Join with me. Become one with me here, and here." Leigh touched her head and heart.

He wanted her, wanted to be inside her, to take all of her.

Shuddering, he grasped her around the waist and laid her on her back. Leigh reached for him, but he pulled the covers over her again and held her, a rigid, shocked bundle, tightly in his arms. He dare not test his restraint further.

Knowing she had no way to understand, he said, "Be patient, sweetheart. We'll be together—if it's meant to be."

That was the best he could do—for either of them—tonight.

chapter TWENTY-FOUR

Colin absorbed another bursting climax, ran a hand back through his hair, and withdrew from his "bride," yet again. It amused him to leave her longing for release not once, but time and time again. Tossing his head, he gloried in his own beauty.

This time, so magical was the erotic spell he cast with his sexual prowess that the room had become bathed in brilliant color that rotated as if from a faceted ball. It flowed across the walls, hovered a few feet above his head, obliterating everything but his own capsule of pleasure. Even Colin had been amazed at this phenomenon—his first experience of its kind.

He bundled the blood-stained woman, her hands still reaching for him, her mouth uttering hysterical sounds of desire, into the arms of two waiting members of his scourge.

"No," she cried, oblivious to her tattered and bloody gown or her near-nakedness. "I can't leave you now!"

The two vampires who took her from him grinned and one of them, Hubert, raised a dark, questioning brow.

Colin bowed slightly, giving his permission for Hubert and his acolyte, Fireze, to use what he no longer wanted. Blood dripped from the woman's neck, running in rivulets over her body, between her breasts, over her belly and into the cleft of her sex. The two departing vampires hurried, but paused to lap at their prize from time to time.

Colin had feasted on her once before, when she first came as a delightful gift from Brande, Alpha High Werewolf. Today she had returned and Colin thought he should remember to thank Brande again for his generosity.

Colin still waited to find out what the great werewolf wanted from him in return but he was not concerned—fear was not in Colin's DNA. He was more powerful than any wolf—which probably had something to do with Brande's interest in him.

And now Brande had sent him yet another gift, who awaited Colin upstairs. He smiled in the direction of that room and wondered if his little prisoner could see through the haze that surrounded him. Probably not, which was too bad since she had missed a long and spectacular exhibition. An excited partner, whether from anticipation of ecstasy or from fear, offered particularly titillating potential.

"Now," Colin said to the groveling Percy, who awaited his instructions. "Bring the new one to me."

Colin's little servant, Percy, a captured troll, laughed suddenly, nervously, and clenched his hands together. "She decided to leave, master. I couldn't tell you until..."

"Leave?" Colin cried. "How? Where?"

"Colin, pay attention," a voice snapped. As tall as

he, and as dark-haired as he was fair, the female vamp who appeared to clasp Colin's hand tilted her head. Her almond-shaped eyes glowed the color of rust. "Colin, we must ready ourselves for guests. The fae outcast, Sally, has been here for some time waiting for you. I would not interrupt you until you were ready. She tells us Tarhazian is on her way here."

"Hello, Sephire," Colin said, detaching himself from her grasp. He threw himself into a white high-backed chair and settled his cloak about him. He knew he made an impressive picture, but he felt a moment of disquiet at the thought of their expected guest. "The Supreme Fae?" he muttered. "I was told she never visits anyone."

Sephire sat at his feet. "She considers Whidbey Island her kingdom. We are new here. Sally admits Tarhazian knows we are here at Brande's invitation. She suspects we are plotting something with him that would not benefit her. I understand he will join us today, also."

"Fie," Colin spat. "This promises to be tedious. I am not interested in their little arguments. As long as I get what I want, they must stay out of my way."

"There is a rumor that Brande has long wanted to rule the island," Sephire said. "He's using human women, stealing and performing certain experiments on them before setting them free. When they get back they have no memory of what happened, but they are programmed to be ready to act as spies and infiltrators when Brande is ready for that."

Holding out one arm, Colin indicated the cowering Percy. "Sephire, comfort me while this incompetent finds the plaything he has lost."

"I have told you we will soon have guests," she said.

Colin sighed. He leaned forward and rested a white cheek on Sephire's luxuriant black curls. "Do not let them come," he said, pouting. "This is to be a night of indulgence, my sweet. For me alone. You know how fractious I become if I am denied."

She turned her face to receive his kiss. "But they will come, my beautiful brother, and we must be cautious. Let them both believe we sympathize with them. What does it matter if we agree with them in everything? They will go away again and we will accept any token blood gifts Brande sends our way."

⁓

Sally slipped into the large white room and did her best to shrink into obscurity. She should not have worn red. Not that it really mattered—Colin and Sephire were too engrossed in each other to notice her entrance. But when the humming started, Colin finally tore his gaze from the female vamp.

When the humming reached a near deafening level, Tarhazian, Queen of the Fae, appeared in her streaming robes that glittered with every step she took. Her face beneath its crown of black diamonds resembled the Mona Lisa.

"Welcome, Tarhazian," Colin said, "welcome to my home."

He threw his cape wide, revealing the scarlet satin lining. His suit was soaked with the blood of his last victim.

Unimpressed by the display, Tarhazian looked around and smiled, ever so slightly. "I hope that what I've been told is rubbish, Colin. You cannot be plotting with that wolf to make the werehounds his slaves so he can take over Whidbey."

Sally concentrated on trying to send spells to Tarhazian that would stop her from mentioning it was Sally who had shared this story. Not that any spells of Sally's were likely to work on the Queen.

"Where," Tarhazian said, "is that ruffian animal, Brande? He would do better not to keep me waiting."

As if on cue, The Grand Wolf, Brande, entered in human form, standing tall and broad, his brown hair awry and his beard wild. He favored leather and wore a green satin shirt beneath his vest.

"Finally, the stinking dog arrives," Tarhazian said.

Brande announced, "Wolves are not *dogs,* my lady. *That* is the root of our problem: dogs. The loathsome werehounds, grotesque parodies of ourselves that they are. These are our enemies and we are only here to decide how they can be brought under our command."

Tarhazian looked at her pointed fingernails. "As long as you all remember who controls the veil, we should be able to straighten all this out."

"Be assured, my lady," Brande began, only to be cut off by Tarhazian.

"Come here," she said, majestically extending a hand to Sally, beckoning for her to come forward.

Sally did as she was asked, but she didn't like it. She was at great risk here, but she had decided on her path some time ago and she would not shrink from it. She had been banished for helping the Queen's favorite, a girl called Elin, to escape, and for showing tendencies to shy away from doing as she was told. The fact that the Queen had not ordered Sally's death for such a crime still amazed her. That Tarhazian still hoped to get her companion back was the only possible explanation.

Little did the Queen know that Elin remained right under her nose. The Queen was unaware of Elin's shape-shifting abilities, and as long as she was in the form of Skillywidden, she would be safe.

Tarhazian also didn't have any idea how much Sally liked the humans, or that she felt a kinship with the hounds. One day she hoped the hounds would come to trust her completely, but that wouldn't happen until she dared tell them everything about herself.

"You've been a good servant, Sally," Tarhazian said. "We may be able to do something about that banishment soon."

"Thank you, my lady," Sally answered, bowing her head. "I'm pleased to be a well-behaved piece of fae unimportance from now on."

"I hope that's true, as I believe you may be able to help us."

"Let's get on with this," Brande said loudly. "We can finish and be out of here. We have other things to do. The werehounds have to be made useful to me. *Dogs.* Worst of the worst. We have a new and very successful plan. Well under way now, although it is slower than we had hoped. Mutation, changing humans until we control their minds and bodies *and* have them do what we tell them to do, and it's working better than we hoped. Gradually we will enlarge our influence here, and we will not tolerate interference."

Tarhazian narrowed her eyes at Sally, who shrank back until she hit the wall. "And you want help with this plan? Very well, Sally, we've noticed you get along better than you should with these humans. So supply humans for any use one of us may have. It is not your job to decide who to snatch, only how, and as many as possible. You've loafed around playing sweet old granny for too long."

Brande puffed out his chest. "As I have already told you, we have our own sources of recruits. Do what you will among yourselves. That is not why I'm here. You have forgotten our greatest problem."

"Problem?" Tarhazian returned her dark gaze to Brande.

"You control the veil. I want you to share that control with me."

Tarhazian laughed aloud, and very loud. "The veil is ours. Since the Deseron are extinct it will remain that way."

"Deseron?" Colin frowned. "The abandoned females from New Orleans? The castoffs left by their parents because they had no paranormal gifts? They are characters from stories, Tarhazian. I'm surprised to hear you speak of them."

"They most certainly are real," Tarhazian responded icily. "Or at least they were. They were the products of mixed marriages between humans and someone from our world. Some offspring showed they had inherited the gifts of the paranormal parent, but others, these Deseron, revealed nothing of their potential as infants. Such a waste."

Tarhazian was right about the origins of the Deseron but wrong in thinking they no longer existed. And Sally, terrified at the thought of the truth being discovered, felt her responsibility to protect Leigh even more strongly. Though Leigh didn't yet know what she was, Sally knew Leigh was Deseron and she was not the last of her kind. They must be sheltered. The extraordinary blood that allowed them to mate with werehounds also replenished at an unbelievable rate if they fell into the hands of vampires.

Sally had first locked on to Leigh's vibrations when she had been at Gabriel's with her husband, Chris. Since then Sally had kept tabs on her in case there was ever a time when her particular traits would be needed by the werehounds and because Sally wanted to help Leigh if she was in trouble one day.

"Mmm," Colin sighed. "I understand they were a vampire's wet dream. They could not be turned but they could be all but drained, and come back again for more."

"They are more than a mere snack, Colin," Tarhazian snapped. "Deseron have the ability to see the veil—and use its magic. That was a talent their parents never foresaw."

Colin made an impatient sound. "You tease me with such charming possibilities. Brande is correct. Our first concern must be to plan how best to use this island for our benefit and stop the dogs from interfering."

Suddenly Brande flung himself around to face them. "Silence, all of you. You are fools not to realize what has happened. The Deseron had the ability to mate successfully with the werehounds. In doing so they formed partnerships that cleared the way for some werehounds to move freely among humans—they were accepted."

"What is your point?" Tarhazian asked. "It seems that with a good talking to the hounds, and perhaps a lesson or two, we can be secure again."

"The point, your majesty," Brande sneered, his voice dripping with sarcasm, "is that Niles, the leader of the hounds, has found a female with whom he expects to mate successfully."

Another silence fell.

"The blood element is confirmed," Brande continued. "One of my zombies brought me her taste, so I am sure. Leigh Kelly is a Deseron, my friends."

Sally looked at Colin with horror. He drooled, his extended fangs ripping his own flesh, his blood mixing with saliva and oozing from his smiling mouth.

chapter TWENTY-FIVE

LEIGH WAITED UNTIL she could be sure Niles's eyes were closed. Then she sneaked from the bed.

She put her own clothes back on in the bathroom, in the dark, and slipped toward the kitchen, where she hoped to find her coat and boots. Both Jazzy and Skillywidden slunk along behind her as if they, too, were trying not to awaken Niles.

Trying to keep her mind from going over what had happened with him was impossible. He said he loved her and she believed him, but she did not understand why he would reject her physically as he had. The thought embarrassed her too much to ignore. Had she let her heart run away with her? Was it too soon to let another man inside her life?

She loved him, too, but she would not let a hasty decision set her heart back to the dark place she had come from after losing Chris.

A small, round basket, blue, with a sheepskin pillow

inside, rested on the floor near an oak table with two chairs. Jazzy promptly jumped in and curled up. After eyeing the dog for a few seconds, Skillywidden followed with a single, dainty bound and landed directly on top of Jazzy—who rolled his eyes.

If Leigh hadn't been so disturbed she would have laughed, especially when the cat used Jazzy as a mattress and stretched out on top of him.

At least Leigh's clothes were completely dry now, and warm. Her short boots were nearby and she pulled them on.

Her coat was nowhere to be seen.

"Why are you leaving like this?" Niles said behind her.

She spun around so fast she almost lost her balance but stepped out of Niles's reach when he made a move to steady her.

"I'm sorry I woke you up," she said. "I tried hard to get out without making a sound."

"And that's supposed to make me feel better? That you want to escape from me?"

Without meaning to, she touched the cut above her temple. It felt bruised.

"That hurts, doesn't it?" Niles's mouth set in a hard line. "Some ice would help."

She felt deeply sad. They might want the same thing, but Leigh couldn't banish the conviction that Niles was keeping something from her. "I'll put some on it when I get home."

"I've got ice here."

If she knew how, she would just spit out her feelings, tell him she felt rejected and that she thought he was keeping something from her. He watched her, unblinking, until she looked away at the animals.

"Thanks on the ice, but...Blue couldn't get one paw in that pet bed." Tiny Skillywidden was on her back now, all four feet in the air but watching Niles and Leigh with those transparent lavender eyes.

Niles laughed, his blue eyes still watchful.

He wouldn't be thrown off topic by the change of subject, but Leigh would take any bought time she could get.

"You're right," Niles said. "Blue wouldn't fit. I got the bed from Sally. She had an extra one lying around and I said I'd like it for when Jazzy came to visit. I need some coffee. How about you?"

This was even worse than any scenario she could have imagined. She couldn't tell him that what she wanted was a clean, fast getaway, that she wasn't as sure of him as she needed to be, or that it mortified her that he had been the one to put the brakes on sex between them. "I'll put some coffee on for you," she said.

"I won't be able to drink it if you're not with me."

"Oh, come *on*," she said. "That's ridiculous."

"It's true." He put two mugs on the table.

Leigh couldn't think what to say next. She started the pot.

"Are you hungry?" he asked.

"No, thank you."

"But you're mad at me."

Why couldn't she get a break here? "I'm not mad at anyone. It's just time for me to go home."

"Through the dark? In horrible weather? On your own? After all the things that have gone down?"

"I hadn't thought about it," she told him honestly. "But I've got to get over being scared to be in my home."

He had opened the refrigerator to take out cream and

paused. "Yes, you do. But that doesn't mean you have to go running up there now."

Why didn't the man ever wear a shirt, darn it? "I'm not running up..." Yes, she was.

The way he looked at the ceiling reminded her of Jazzy.

He pulled the lid off a container in the refrigerator and extracted several pieces of raw bacon. As soon as he set the cream on the table he began to chomp through one slice after another.

"Ick," Leigh said.

"Ick, what?"

She widened her eyes innocently and said, "I didn't say that."

"Yes you did."

"Okay." After what he'd done to her ego, why should she save his feelings? "Eating raw bacon is awful. Jazzy likes that, but he's a dog."

Niles looked at the final slice, dropped it into the sink and turned on the disposal. While he washed his hands he gave her an odd, sideways glance. "I eat when I'm uptight."

"So do I. Usually fudge or cookies."

The coffee was ready and he filled the two mugs. Pulling out a chair he said, "Sit, please."

"Do you really never get cold?"

"No," he said. "Would you be more comfortable if I got a shirt on?"

Probably. "Of course not. I get cold so easily, that's all. I'm jealous."

They sat side by side, a less comfortable arrangement than Leigh had been ready for. "You were really kind to help me out," she said, both hands wrapped around her mug. "I felt very safe here, and I thank you for that."

"I like having you here." He poured cream in his coffee.

If she were a man she would tell him he sent mixed messages, but that would only make the situation worse. "I'm so sorry I embarrassed you, Niles. In fact, I'm mortified. And I am sorry."

"Embarrassed me?" He screwed up his eyes. If they weren't quite so blue they would be easier to resist—maybe.

"I was too forward. I made you uncomfortable."

For an instant his face lost all expression and her heart thudded. Then she frowned, suspicious he might be trying not to look amused. And then he laughed. With the back of a hand over his mouth, he chuckled.

"Just because you're kind it doesn't mean you're attracted to me—in that way," she said.

Niles stared into his coffee and didn't answer.

Rumbling thunder rolled and rain hit the windows like fine grit. Leigh looked up in time to see narrow strips of rainbowlike colors arch over the area outside and stream toward the ground. Niles was also glancing at the windows but showed no sign of having seen anything unusual.

"You're going to have to stay here," he said. "I need to get the fires going at Two Chimneys. It'll be too cold up there."

Leigh got heated again. Now she didn't want to be diverted. "I'm not a forward person. It's always been hard for me to be intimate, at least at first." *When you're in a hole*... "I don't even like wearing a swimsuit in public." ...*stop digging*.

"That's stupid," he said, then immediately threw his

hands in front of him, palms facing Leigh. "I'm not saying you're stupid. I only meant you should be very comfortable in a swimsuit anywhere."

Leigh looked down and gripped her mug tightly. "You hated it when I got too close to you."

He got up from the table so abruptly he had to catch his chair to stop it falling.

"I'm sorry," Leigh said. "I keep saying the wrong things and making everything worse. I'm going now."

Niles thumped back down into his chair and gripped her forearm. "I didn't hate it when you...I want you close to me all the time." He rubbed his face hard, shaking his head at the same time.

"I think you want that to be true. But I wasn't—*right*—I wasn't what you wanted. I wasn't pleasing—oh, forget it. I'm sorry."

"Damn. If you say you're sorry again, Leigh, I...I'll do something drastic."

She gaped at him. He was furious and, wouldn't you know it, fury suited him.

"You know how I feel about you in every way," he said.

Tears welling in her eyes were less than welcome.

"I covered you up in bed because I was protecting you from me," he said. "You have to be ready, really ready for me first and you're not."

"How do you know?" she asked in a voice that cracked.

"I loved a woman once. Very much. She loved me, too, and we were going to marry. In the end she couldn't do that—she didn't want me anymore."

Leigh's heart started a hard, uncomfortable tattoo. "You haven't told me your story. I didn't want to push you."

"Now you have to know it and I'll understand if you walk straight out of that door."

He tipped up his chin to eye the big, round clock on a wall. It ticked loudly. "It was in Wyoming."

Leigh nodded, "Where you're from."

"Cattle," he said and his eyes lost focus. "My grandfather's ranch was big. He brought me up after my parents died."

She felt sad for him. She and Jan didn't talk about it—although Gib liked to push them for more details—but they had never known their own parents. All they had known was foster homes. "I bet you were close to your grandfather."

"Yes. A storm came in early. We didn't expect it and there weren't enough hands to get things done. We had a couple of feet of snow on the ground almost before we knew it was going to be a problem.

"We did okay with the stock but there were stragglers way out. I couldn't ask the men to go again. My grandfather was sick. I went alone. Never intended to go too far, just wanted to see if I could get to a few of them."

He bowed his head, pushed his mug back and forth on the table. The blue-black hair at his neck curled forward and it shone. His hands were big, long-fingered, and hard. They were capable and Leigh figured they must be very strong.

"It was so cold," he said.

She could only think it must have been arctic, since he didn't seem to feel the cold at all here.

"I got disoriented and dark came in. I went what I thought was the way back but I must have been going the opposite direction. Then I couldn't push my horse anymore. The lantern blew out but I managed to relight it. Then the thing slipped through my fingers and went out again. I couldn't find it."

Leigh had both hands over her mouth. She felt as if she was waiting for a terrible story to end badly. But he was here so he hadn't died.

"The next thing I knew I was flat on my back just seeing shadows and feeling like I'd been hit over the head. Only I hadn't. There was a dog standing over me. Biggest damn dog you ever saw. At first I thought he was a wolf and he'd have been big for that. But the shape was wrong. He was a dog."

"Was it Blue?"

His features twisted. "No, it wasn't Blue. And it was too late by then."

Making words was getting tougher. "Why do you say it was too late? Too late, how?"

"I was torn open by its teeth and claws. Changed forever. The dog stayed with me, half-dragged me all the way back to the ranch. Then, standing in the bitterness of that storm, he showed me what I had become. He *demonstrated* my future."

Niles confused her.

"I tried to explain to Abbey but it was too much for her. I had to leave. I joined up with a band coming West for the Gold Rush."

Leigh's mind was blank for seconds. She blinked and started calculating. "But that was way back in—"

"Yeah."

"But—"

"I was a man and a hound, a werehound. The animal in the snow did that to me—but he also saved my life."

Leigh stood up. "Why are you saying all this?"

The corners of his mouth turned down sharply. "Because it's true."

"I don't understand you."

He turned up his palms on the table. "I'm a werehound, part of a team of werehounds."

Leigh backed up a step. "I don't believe you." She thought about it. "I've never even heard of werehounds."

"But you have heard of werewolves?"

"Of course."

"Of course. And now you've heard about us. We were always much fewer in number and our makeup is different. We are never fighters from choice."

"Okay," she said. "How am I supposed to react to you saying these things? You're human again now?" Even discussing this felt bizarre.

"I hope to be soon." For a moment, they stared at each other in silence. "Do I scare you?"

Leigh's blood drained to her feet. "You don't scare me. You've just got a weird sense of humor."

Niles jumped up and tore the outer seam of his jeans apart over the left thigh. "What d'you think made that? What does it look like?"

If she could have screamed she probably would have. "You are frightening me now. There. Are you satisfied?"

"No, dammit, I'm not. Look at this and tell me what it is."

The corner of the room was at Leigh's back. She had no place to run.

Niles took one step closer and held the destroyed leg of his jeans open.

She made herself look and all the air went out of

her lungs. From the inside to the outside of his heavily muscled thigh stretched big, deep, silvery marks. Old scratches—or gouges.

"What is this, Leigh?"

"A big...animal...scratched you."

"Exactly the way I told you. I should have died from a wound like that but the big dog made sure I healed fast. That's one of our skills. We're not as practiced as werewolves, but we're good. Now, turn around and don't turn back until I tell you."

She did as she was told, and closed her eyes.

Subtle noises, quiet but foreign, came from behind her. Rustling, cracking, a long moan and a series of whines. Leigh wiped sweat from her brow.

Niles poked her between the shoulder blades and she spun around at once.

And looked into the face of a dog almost as tall as she was. Russet in color with a thick, glossy coat, huge feet, alert ears, and eyes that could be black—or very dark blue.

In a vision that was more a flash, she remembered a wolflike dog, russet colored with eyes that seemed dark blue rather than black. That dog had grabbed her, made her climb on his back, and she had held on to his fur while he carried her to safety. He had been enraged, flying across the room, destroying anything in his way. Yes, he had flown with her and she had lost consciousness.

She couldn't look away from Niles. He stared back, inviting questioning but wary. He was that same hound who had snatched her away from that horrible house. How could she have forgotten about it? It was as if her mind had frozen everything out but now the memories were thawing.

She felt wobbly, and weak.

The dog sat and stared at her, assessing her, her reaction. He tilted his head on one side and she knew she saw real sadness in his eyes.

Leigh began to cry, silently. She leaned on the wall and covered her face. "Can you still talk to me?"

"I think I can."

She flung herself toward him. "I heard you in my mind."

"Good. I can't speak aloud in this form. And I couldn't mind-track with you if you weren't a sensitive. You've got special gifts, Leigh. I was pretty sure you did. You're special."

"Will you ever be human? Just human?"

Part of her longed to touch him but she was afraid. He was a magnificent animal.

"Close, I hope," she heard him say. He dropped into a crouch, every line of his body drooping. *"I'm working on it. I never stop working."*

"I can hear you!" She shook convulsively. "What would it take for you to be completely human again?"

"Complete acceptance as I am." He stared into her eyes. *"By a woman who will stand beside me and stand up for me. And love me no matter how hard it is sometimes. That woman would go through a lot and some of it could be terrible. Painful even."*

Leigh touched his head lightly, rested her hand on his neck.

He nuzzled her other hand and she put her face, tentatively, into the thick fur on his head.

She began to cry, tears that streamed from stinging eyes.

Then she walked away from him and out into the night.

chapter TWENTY-SIX

A FLASHLIGHT BEAM came from behind Leigh and illuminated the concrete steps up the bank from Niles's house. He was following her.

Panicking, filled with fury that she was up to her neck in something she couldn't change even if she wanted to, she went faster.

"Wait. Put this on."

Dimly she realized she wasn't hearing Niles's voice but still she scrambled, stumbling on the steps, using her hands to grasp the edges of the treads when she lost her grip on the handrail.

"Leigh, stop it. I'm not going to hurt you."

She couldn't close her mouth and freezing air scraped down her throat. Her face lost all feeling. Pain clawed at her ears. Sleet and rain drove sideways, pushing at her, trying to drive her back.

"You will fall!"

That was Sean. She hadn't heard him speak often but now she recognized the low, penetrating tone.

At the top of the steps she kept running and didn't stop until she stood at the edge of the bluff in front of Two Chimneys. Buffeted this way and that, she braced her feet apart. Tears froze on her eyelashes.

"Your coat," Sean said. He took one of her tightly folded arms and stuffed it into a sleeve, then repeated the process on the other side. "Please look at me."

Leigh shook her head, no, and a sound erupted from her that she didn't recognize, almost her own howl. The wind tore the noise away but it came again.

Sean put up her hood and fastened the front of the coat. He took big work gloves from his pocket and pushed them on her hands. "Go inside, please."

"No!" Her teeth chattered uncontrollably. "Do you see it?" She pointed to where streams of color, dark green, purple, ochre, brown, and navy blue streamed out of the water. "Chimney Rocks are under there. That's where the colors are coming from and I think they do something to me. Niles says I'm something different. I think he's right. I think it's something to do with that out there."

Sean put an arm around her and she didn't pull away. "I can't see it," he said. "But I know it comes from Chimney Rocks and makes the veil that covers this place to separate the two worlds."

She clutched the front of his shirt. His hair wasn't tied back and whipped around his head and across her face. "Two worlds? I don't know what you mean."

"And it isn't my place to tell it all. I don't even know everything yet. But there is the human plane and the so-called paranormal plane. Someone else must explain how you are different from other humans, what gives you the ability to see the veil. I believe you draw strength from out there." He pointed to the sea.

Without warning, her knees buckled. Sean held her up. "You must go inside and get warm."

"I love him!" The words, torn from her, were clear as if a still space had formed in the raging storm.

"I thought you did," Sean said. "He is lucky. But so are you."

"Lucky?" She laughed and found the strength to stand alone. "Lucky to love a man who is a dog, a hound?"

"He can give you everything you need. He can protect you from things you know nothing about."

Pictures, snatches of scenes, flared in her mind. A physically beautiful monster doing unspeakable things to a woman shrouded in white. A car bumping hers from behind, jerking her neck each time.

She heard Jazzy bark and whine. "Poor guy," she said and lifted him up. She undid enough of her coat to stuff the dog inside. "We'll warm each other."

Promptly, Skillywidden landed, almost weightless, on her shoulder and wrapped herself around Leigh's neck.

"May I get Niles to come?" Sean asked.

"No."

"But you love him?"

"Yes."

"He loves you and will never desert you even if you pretend he doesn't exist."

Flinging wide one arm, she yelled incoherently into the roiling wind and wet, the ice spicules that pierced her face.

"Come." Sean pulled, but gently, and he stopped as soon as she resisted.

"I'm not normal, either," she shouted at him. "There's something different about me—you just admitted it—and I have to know what it is. I could hear Niles talking in my mind when he was...wasn't a man."

"You are blessed with special gifts," he said. "That's why you're here."

"I can't go back to the way I was before, can I?"

He shook his head, no. "And once you understand more, you won't want to."

"And Niles knows all this?"

"Of course."

"Has...Was there a spell? I can't believe I'm talking about these things. Was a spell put on me?"

"That isn't for me to know. If I have to pick you up to take you inside, I will. Niles has told me I must."

Trees bent. Branches cracked and moaned. Leigh smelled smoke but saw no fire. And she heard small, rapid footsteps skittering through the forest.

"Niles is talking to you?"

"We're talking to each other. He isn't talking to you because he knows how afraid and shocked you are."

Turning from Sean blindly, Leigh struggled uphill to the cottage. The keys weren't in her pocket and Niles had made her stop keeping one over the door.

Sean reached past her and opened the door.

In the living room, barely warmer than she had been outside, Leigh faced Sean. "And if I don't want any of this? Can I change it?"

He looked away. She knew he was silently telling her she couldn't choose her own path.

"Be patient and you'll learn everything. Niles will help you. We all will, but Niles most of all."

"Vampires," she whispered, moving closer to him. "There are vampires out there. There was one in a house someone took me to...he wanted me."

"You are not alone with this," Sean said.

"Yes, I am. No one can live my life for me, or take this away for me."

Quickly, he threw logs into the fireplace and started a fire. "Only Niles can deal with this. It is his place."

"Why?"

"Because it is between the two of you. You have been marked for each other."

chapter TWENTY-SEVEN

Sean, or Blue as he'd been when Leigh last saw him, had spent the night on her porch. She also thought she had seen a second oversized hound, this one gray and black, blending into the trees at the back of the cottage.

This morning it had still been dark when she had ignored Blue's agitated pacing and gotten into her car. She had figured out that Sean appeared more often as a were-hound than a man because it allowed him to protect her in places where a man would seem strange.

Already in the parking lot at Gabriel's, she still had enough spirit to admire the wonderful flashing neon sign that was becoming the talk of the area.

They were definitely seeing an increase in business, not that Gabriel was willing to admit any connection.

"I'll carry you, Jazz," she said, grateful for even the sound of her own voice. She picked up the dog.

When she reached for her computer bag, the glow of

otherworldly eyes tucked into a dark side recess, next to the computer, made her jump.

She glanced at Jazzy, who rolled his eyes but settled down as if this were all normal. Skillywidden's unspoken message was, "Here I am, make the best of it."

Leigh shook her head. "You two are going to lose me my job." The miniature cat tucked herself down into the computer bag as if to demonstrate that smart people didn't get found out. Skillywidden was smart and she wasn't leaving Leigh.

"You, Ms. Skillywidden, are a manipulator," Leigh said, making a dash through the cold to the building.

With a wave of the hand, she shot through the bar toward her office. Gabriel called, "Hey, there, Leigh. Any trouble getting in? It's too early for you to be here—as usual."

"No trouble," she said without turning around. "I kind of like the challenge of driving in this crud. You need to watch for black ice under the snow, though. Anyway, yesterday was a short day. I've got to catch up."

"You don't need to catch up anything," Gabriel announced in his big, gritty voice, but Leigh only waved at him again.

But she didn't get through the room fast enough to miss seeing Niles sitting alone with a mug of coffee between his hands. He didn't say anything to her and she held her tongue.

Sally walked up to him and set down a huge plate of food.

Leigh heard Gabriel say, "Hey, Blue, come and warm up," behind her.

This time she couldn't manage any surprise that he

had followed her. She had been told she would be guarded at all times and apparently her guardians took their promises seriously.

She had nowhere to go but this place. It wasn't as if she didn't really like being here but she felt trapped nevertheless.

Fifteen minutes passed, then twenty, twenty-five. Leigh went over bills received and checked for payment. They were climbing out of the red, slowly but steadily, not that they didn't have a long way to go.

She made two calls to the East Coast, to upstate New York where the day's work was just starting for most businesses. Each time she hung up feeling satisfied. Her relationship with suppliers was on solid footing. She wasn't above a good deal of haggling but both sides usually walked away happy.

Skillywidden remained in the now empty computer bag beneath the desk but gave Leigh's leg the occasional pat to let her know she was still there. The cat wasn't just a cat—Leigh wasn't so earthbound she hadn't figured that out.

She even had a couple of theories about why the animal was with her, the primary one being that she somehow communicated information about Leigh to someone else. If it hadn't been Sally's cat who moved in on Leigh, she might have been edgy about the deal, but she was starting to really enjoy Skillywidden. In fact, Jazzy and the cat slept together most of the time, always with the tiny one arranged so that Jazzy acted as a mattress. It was an amicable relationship.

The enormity of what she faced crashed in. Leigh folded her arms on the desk and put her head down. There weren't any guidebooks for people who found out they had fallen in love with a werehound and that they, themselves, might have some sort of weird power. Trapped didn't really cover how she felt. Who could she talk to, other than Niles? And even being too physically close to him scrambled her logic.

Someone tapped on the door, waited a little, and came in. Swathed in her kitchen gear and already liberally coated in flour, Sally closed the door behind her. "G'morning, Leigh," she said, much too cheerfully. "How's it going?"

Leigh rubbed her eyes.

"Not so good?" Sally said. "Well, all that's going to change."

"What's going to change?" Leigh gave Sally her full attention. She didn't waver even when the cat appeared and sat on the desk with the look of an intelligent, attentive student about her.

"Your life," Sally said, stroking the cat. "Try to be patient. I mustn't forget to mention that Phoebe's stopping by later. She'll cheer you up. She was disappointed you couldn't make it yesterday but she understands. Maybe Jan could come over and meet her."

The only thing Leigh knew for sure was that she didn't want someone else, least of all her sister, dragged into this. "Let's put that off for a bit. The weather's awful and I'd just as soon Jan didn't drive around in it." She wanted to keep Jan away until she felt it was safer for her to be here—if that ever happened.

As it was, Jan called every day and the conversation always went the same way. Leigh should move in with Jan and Gib.

The calls from Gib were even more disturbing. He never missed an opportunity to tell her it wasn't safe for her to be alone at Two Chimneys and she should get rid of the place.

Sally sat down opposite Leigh, who looked sideways at the floor.

"Can I help you with something?" Sally asked.

Leigh shook her head, no. "Everything's fine," she said.

"That's not a fib?" Sally said. "You aren't only trying to make me feel better? You don't have to do that."

Leigh sighed.

The little office hadn't warmed up yet and Leigh shivered.

"C'mon," Sally said. "You look exhausted and freezing. Hot coffee and hot food for you. Let's go." The woman's husky voice comforted Leigh, maybe because it sounded so familiar.

"I have a little problem," Leigh said.

"Skillywidden? I knew she'd start coming to work with you. Don't worry about her, she won't bother anyone. She likes you, Jazzy, too, so I guess you've got a happy family. Gabriel will be happy to have her around."

Leigh stared at Sally. "Do you know anything about me that I ought to know? I keep feeling as if I'm more of a mystery to myself than to you," she said, not caring whether it was wise to be so open.

Sally got up again. "You and I both know your life is changing. You will have to be very careful as we go forward and that means you can't try to stop Niles from guiding you. Please don't forget you have powerful friends even though you don't know all of them."

Leigh bowed her head. "After we met, you told me I'd come to the right place for me. That this is where I'm supposed to be—here on Whidbey and at Two Chimneys. Why?"

"You should already know that." She leaned forward. "You are different. The vapors of Chimney Rocks are from the realm of your ancestors. You see them because you are Deseron. Later that will be explained to you in more detail. You see the colors of the veil, the veil the fae consider their property. It divides the human from the paranormal and creatures like you and me are the only ones who actually see the substance of that separation. I am fae. You are Deseron, but don't worry about that now. I don't know how many there are like you but there are more. Of that I'm sure. And now you are needed to help restore balance to a world that is out of control. Right here on Whidbey."

Leigh swallowed. "Deseron?" she said softly.

"Let's go," Sally said. "There's a lot to be covered and not much time to do it. We have reached the crisis."

Leigh's heart sank lower. But, at the same time, she wanted to see Niles, to be near him.

She followed Sally, who went straight to Niles's table.

She couldn't look away from him. He stared back, inviting, questioning, but wary. He was the same man she had met and wanted to be with, the man she admired. Niles was the man she loved, but she didn't know what she should do about it.

Dr. Saul VanDoren walked in, the shoulders of his long, black coat dusted with snow. A collection of other local men joined him, including some of the regulars at Gabriel's.

The glance between the doctor and Niles, then the nonverbal communication with Gabriel and the arrival of Cliff Ames from the kitchen, as if he had been given a silent message, all put Leigh on guard.

Sally stood still and so did Leigh.

"Something's happened," Leigh said softly. "It's bad."

"Mmm. You see Saul and Niles? That is unusual. They would not normally speak in confidence to each other like that."

Dr. Saul spoke quietly to Niles, Blue sitting close beside him. They closed Gabriel and Cliff out of the soft conversation.

Leigh frowned at the two men. "I can't see why."

Sally smiled a little. "Now that you have met the type of vampire to be feared—as most of them are—surely you see how it is that most of us like Dr. Saul. He is a good man who hates what he is."

"Dr. Saul is a vampire?" Leigh said. She stared at the man. "Of course, I should have wondered about him. He isn't like anyone else I ever met. Today I might well have asked questions—with everything else that's happened."

"Vampires and werehounds—but even more so, werewolves—do not make relaxed alliances. Werewolves and vampires hate each other. With the hounds it is a more a cautious ambivalence between them."

A small assortment of regulars slammed through the front doors, puffing with exertion and excitement.

"What is it?" Gabriel said loudly.

"There have been more disappearances since last night," one man said. "Violet has gone again. A woman from the new bakery, and a waitress, and a woman who tends bar at Passage Point north of Langley."

Passage Point was one of those places people stayed away from unless they were looking for action, the kind of action that could be more than many were ready to risk.

Sally murmured, "I was afraid of this. I've been waiting for it."

Leigh swallowed, watching Gabriel's face. "Is Molly okay?"

He looked over her head. "Molly's decided she needs a break. She's in Seattle thinking things through." He finished on a note of finality that didn't invite further questions. "At least we know Rose is all right, even if she has run off to Alaska. That's something."

Niles and Dr. Saul kept a definite distance between them but stared at each other. She sensed they were wary of each other. Blue disappeared, and a moment later Sean entered the bar in his place.

Sean cleared his throat. "We don't see Cody Willet in here very often," he said to Niles, who followed the direction of Sean's stare to a nondescript gray-haired man standing a little apart from the group of regulars.

"Yeah," was all Niles commented.

The phone on the bar rang and Gabriel hurried to pick it up.

Sean joined them with another man Leigh would make a bet was a member of the werehound team. This one also had an awesome physique. His face was that of a Scandinavian, open, light blue eyes, regular features, but his hair was a very dark blond and curly all the way past the collar of his crew-necked sweater. He stood like a panther ready to pounce.

Niles held a hand toward Leigh. It was an invitation and the ultimate opportunity to declare herself or deny him. She glanced at Sally, who smiled, rolling in her lips as if she was trying not to laugh.

"You are a puzzle," Leigh whispered, but she went to stand near Niles. She did not take his hand.

She hadn't been prepared for the deep intensity of his gaze, or the inward dip at the corners of his mouth that turned into a soft smile.

Leigh realized the one reaction missing, the one that would have sent her running: triumph. But she felt a flash of triumph herself. She had shown that she was not afraid of Niles. Her stomach dipped. Could she overcome that fear or was she only pretending to herself?

"Meet Innes," Niles said to Leigh, indicating the man with light blue eyes. "He is a close friend."

When she offered him her hand, Innes hesitated before shaking it. His reaction could only be described as wary.

They nodded at each other but Leigh got no smile from the man.

Gabriel hung up the phone and rejoined them. "Lenny from Passage Point." He let out a loud breath. "No one's gone missing. They all took off in Violet's van. Girls' sleepover at some B&B in Port Townsend. They'll be back by tonight. You folks should have checked with Lenny first—he gave his girl the time off and Violet and the woman who owns the bakery can go where they like, when they like."

Leigh saw Sally frown before she hurried off toward the kitchen.

"Finish your breakfast," Leigh told Niles, giving his plate a fleeting glance. A raw egg filled a well in the middle of what looked like a mound of raw ground beef. "What's that?" she asked, wrinkling her nose.

"Steak tartare," Gabriel said. "Niles has elevated tastes. It's his favorite start to the day. Puts hair on your chest, right, Niles?"

Niles nodded, not looking too amused by the comment.

The phone rang again and since Leigh was closer she told Gabriel, "I'll get it. I hope there's hot coffee somewhere. Sally used that to lure me out here."

By the time she picked up the phone a large cinnamon roll dripping frosting and smelling like ambrosia was plopped down on the bar by a smiling Sally, along with a huge mug of coffee with the thick cream Leigh favored still spinning like whipped butter-colored marshmallow on the top.

"Gabriel's Place," Leigh said.

"Hey, there, sis. It's Gib."

"How are you?" she asked stiffly.

"I'll be better when you tell me you aren't mad at me for being a boor."

Leigh thought about Jan and said, "I'm not mad at you, Gib. I am a bit busy now, though."

"I tried your home number. You're at work early."

"I usually am." She captured a little frosting from the bun and licked it off her finger. Talking to Gib was the last thing she wanted to do.

"Did a real estate guy contact you about the property up there?"

Her thoughts raced. "Why do you ask?"

"Because we got a call from someone looking for you. He said he'd left a rough appraisal at that place where you're working. They were supposed to give it to you but he hasn't heard anything."

Yes, she had the paper and it was stuffed in her coat pocket. She had forgotten all about it. "It's around somewhere," she said. "I'll take a look at it. Thanks for reminding me. Gotta go, Gib. Be good."

She hung up and drank some coffee to give herself time to settle down. Why would John Valley call Gib? How would the real estate agent know anything about her relatives or where to find them? She didn't like him.

With the coffee in one hand and the cinnamon roll in the other, she started back to the group, only to have the phone ring again.

Balancing the plate on top of the mug, she picked up the phone once more, said, "Gabriel's Place," and listened to silence.

The line was not dead. She could sense someone also listening.

"Gabriel's Place," she repeated, grateful for the noise in the place that stopped others from looking at her to see what was going on.

"Is this Leigh Kelly?" a man asked.

"Yes." The skin on her face tightened.

"You shouldn't be here on Whidbey. It's not your fault and you must leave."

The plate almost slid off the mug. She set them down without disaster and said, "Who is this, please?"

For seconds she listened to what sounded like wind blowing hard wherever the caller was. "You've been tricked," the nondescript male voice said. "You're being set up. Listen to me carefully."

"I don't think I want to."

"Yes you do. I'm on your side. Nobody else around here wants the best for you. They want to use you."

She turned her back on the room. "Say what you have to say. Fast."

"I think you know what Niles Latimer is."

Leigh's breath caught sharply.

"Yes," the man said. "Of course you do. If you want to live, go to the police and tell them everything about him, then leave. I will come for you later."

"Good-bye."

"You don't want to do that. You need me and I will be there for you—always. We shall be one and rule together."

Leigh looked in the mirror over the bar. Everything seemed distorted. She sought about in her memory for what felt familiar. Something was very familiar.

The hollow sound of this man. She had heard it before.

"If you stay without my protection—" the voice said. "—Once you've served your purpose, they'll get rid of you."

chapter TWENTY-EIGHT

Dr. Saul VanDoren's face showed no emotion. His stillness didn't fool Niles. Tightly harnessed, a potentially disastrous confrontation was only a careless word away.

"We can't talk here," the doctor said, almost under his breath.

Niles gave him a quizzical stare. Saul was a maverick vampire, an apparently honorable man, who, like Niles, preferred his humanness over what he had been somehow forced to become. The entire pack chose to accept Saul, although they kept their distance. They had become agitated when Saul ran a blood test on Innes, but since there had been no ramifications, no attempt to use the knowledge he must have gained against the hounds, it was never mentioned.

"Our feelings about each other are irrelevant; we have mutual business," Saul said. "It is not my wish—I detest dissent—but we're forced to work on the same side against a common enemy."

Sean and Innes moved closer to Niles so that all three of them faced Saul.

Innes said, "We don't take orders from you, blood eater."

Saul laughed his deep, hollow laugh that faded so quickly it might have been imagined. "I see we remain on two sides."

"You can't expect instant acceptance," Niles said. "We have to understand why you want a coalition with us. Outside?"

The doctor turned on his heel at once and walked out with the three werehounds behind him. Innes and Sean didn't look happy but Niles urged them on, knowing they were experiencing their own disturbing reactions to the vampire.

As Niles left the building he caught Sally watching them. She gave a short nod and a smile that suggested approval. He wished he knew what favor she would exact from him in exchange for her finding Leigh.

This was looking bad, Niles decided, in ways only he was considering at the moment.

Leigh had answered two telephone calls and gone straight back to her office without another glance in his direction. But her expression was anything but calm.

When she had come to stand beside him a little earlier, he had started to hope, but he had been too optimistic. He should have known when she ignored his attempt to hold her hand that she was only testing what it felt like to be anywhere near him.

Her decision had not been what he wanted it to be.

With his gliding walk, Saul covered ground quickly and entered the forest, pushing branches aside as he went. He bent low to avoid an arch of brambles.

"Of course," Niles said in a low voice, pulling Sean and Innes to a stop. "He was the vampire with Sally. On the night when Brande's wolves lay in wait. I see it now, in his manner and stature. In his way of moving. Saul was the one who took Rose's body away that night."

Sean stared at Saul's profile as he bent down. "Why didn't we figure that one out? Damn, I wish we knew what all these people really want. Sally has never mentioned a liaison between the two of them, yet he helped her that night. You heard the story they've set up about Rose going to Alaska?"

"I heard it," Niles said.

Innes muttered, "They could be setting us up right now."

"Yes," Niles agreed. "We will need all our skills—natural and learned."

"Too bad we can't shoot all of them," Innes said, apparently hankering to use his special operations training.

"That won't work here." Niles gave him a half smile and carried on after Saul.

"Dr. Saul the vampire is Sally's good buddy," Sean murmured. "They could assume we know. But this feels like standing on a bridge collapsing into quicksand. We'd better hurry."

"We could take him," Innes said. "One less vampire isn't much but I would take it."

He made a growling sound and Niles slapped a hand on his shoulder. "Save it. Whatever happens, do not make the mistake of revealing that we are stronger as men than as hounds—we may have to make use of that secret advantage one day, but not for anything we can deal with otherwise."

They caught up with Saul in a cramped clearing.

"What about Leigh?" Sean said to Niles.

"I haven't forgotten her. Campion is out back of Gabriel's," Niles told him, referring to another member of their team. In truth he had to be cautious not to concentrate on Leigh to the exclusion of everything else. "Sally's there. Go and watch in case Leigh comes into the parking lot. If she does and she wants to see me, send her here."

"That's irrational," Innes said. "She isn't even—"

"I decide what she is," Niles retorted. "She is mine and there's no point in trying to shield her. Her life depends on the decisions she makes."

The quiet lowering of Innes's eyes acknowledged that Niles made final decisions for them. A stirring burned deep in Niles, a shock he absorbed quietly and not without triumph. He longed to lie with Leigh.

Sean was already making his way back through the trees.

"What is it with the Deseron woman?" Saul asked. "Why do you bend rules for her? You would allow her to join us here on team business? You do not establish her position as inferior to you?"

Niles gave himself a second to make sure he didn't look surprised at Saul calling her Deseron. "I don't owe you those answers but as my chosen mate she is not inferior to me." He hated the way the hair on the back of his neck prickled when he was near Saul or any like him. "How do you know what she is? She may not even be exactly what was meant by Deseron. Her kind were supposed to be gone."

Saul smiled. "Another theory suggests the first Deseron lived—and were abandoned—in Belgium where some remain. Others were and are in New Orleans." He shrugged. "Who knows. But evidently your woman is close enough to being a Deseron for you to think she'll be of use to you."

"Don't discuss Leigh." Hearing Saul call her "of use" shamed Niles.

Saul's dark eyes took on a knowing gleam. "Fair enough. I understand. Do *you* understand how much danger she's in? No, I'm sure you don't. There was a meeting at Colin's house. The gathering would have shocked you."

Niles's face took on a look of stony calm.

"If there is something I need to know, tell me." Niles stepped closer to Saul.

Saul didn't retreat. "It's delicate. Your woman is not the only one to be protected."

Niles wanted to take him by the throat.

"You hate me," Saul said. "It's natural. But we are not so different, you and I. We lost our mortality to save our lives. And although it was long ago for me, it's not so long that I forget how it feels to . . . love."

Niles was quiet. He didn't want to feel a kinship with a blood eater but he felt it nonetheless.

"Boss." Sean's communication came urgently to Niles. *"Leigh's coming your way. She wouldn't go back inside Gabriel's and wait. She says she has a right to know what's going on."*

Niles and Innes looked at each other and Innes, who had obviously heard Sean, communicated, *"She will cause trouble."*

"No." Niles could already hear her light tread and he spoke aloud so Saul would hear. "As my marked mate Leigh is part of what we have to deal with and possibly the answer to some of our problems." What he felt when he thought about her had little to do with anything but his wanting her. "She does have a right to be beside me."

"Is this wise?" Saul asked. "Allowing the woman to see us together like this?"

"I am responsible for Leigh."

She came, Sean holding her hand and leading the way. Niles smiled at Sean, grateful for his comforting her even though he didn't approve of what was happening.

Occasional flakes of snow found their way through the dense branches overhead and it might all have been beautiful if an aura of approaching horror hadn't sobered each of them.

"I need to tell you a few things," Saul said to Niles. "You might want to step away from—"

"No," Niles said, determined now.

Leigh left Sean, smiling up at him, and came to Niles. She held out her hand in the same offer he had made her earlier and he folded her small, cool fingers into his warm grasp. He wanted to yell, to rejoice. The acceptance in her upturned face held more love than if she'd told him how she felt. Her gold-blond hair fell back and even in the gloom of the little forest glade her brown eyes were bright and clear.

Niles kissed her lips softly and she reached up to slide her arms around his neck. If only he could carry her away and forget all this.

It was the utter silence that stopped them. They separated, all but their grip on each other's hand. Sean and Innes were examining the trees. Saul watched Niles and Leigh, a slight smile on his lips.

"At the meeting, Brande and Tarhazian sparred," he

said without preamble. "Each wanted the other to give up power. They referred to sharing, but it was obvious each desires to have ultimate control."

Saul laughed before Niles could. "You can imagine how much progress either of them made with those ideas," Saul said.

"Foolishness," Saul continued, turning his face toward Leigh. "Brande is leader of the werewolf pack, Tarhazian is the Supreme Fae who commands armies of the unmentionable inhabitants of her realm—and the veil that separates humans from the reality of what we know exists. This meeting was in Colin's house. I understand you've been there."

She gave a little gasp and Niles narrowed his eyes, unimpressed with Saul's attempt to shock her.

"I'm surprised you were included in the gathering," Niles said. "I thought you were considered a maverick."

"I was not there, but I have my sources. Tarhazian made a deal. She will forgive some of those with whom she is angry if they provide...fresh subjects for the use of them all."

Leigh's fingers squeezed Niles's and she folded her other hand over the top. Perhaps this was too much, too soon for her—but he would only make things worse if he suddenly said she couldn't be there.

"Do I have to tell you what Tarhazian meant?" Saul asked. "Humans will be taken to the scourge."

Niles frowned. "Who? Who will take humans and deliver them to the scourge—that is the vampire community," he added to Leigh. "Who would feed innocents to vampires?"

The harsh lines of Saul's face made it obvious that

he didn't like this any more than Niles did. "There will always be those whose appetites overcome any scruples."

Sean and Innes kept quiet, allowing him to speak for their group, but agitation emanated from them.

"Will you take part in this?" Niles said, taking a step toward him. Saul raised his hands as if to attack.

"Niles," Innes said urgently.

But Niles had already taken Saul by the shoulders and spun him around. He held him in a lock.

Rather than fight back, Saul said, "How interesting. I would not have expected such power from you without the benefit of a change. Would you care to explain that?"

Niles met Sean's and Innes's eyes, but both men looked suitably blank. Leigh, on the other hand, hugged herself and moved back and forth as if deciding on her next move.

"I won't be explaining anything to you, blood eater," Niles said. "Just remember: do not pit yourself against any of us." He gave him a shove that should have landed him on the ground, but Saul kept his footing.

"I am not your enemy," Saul said. "As I told you, I seek an alliance and it would serve all of us well. You asked if I would be any part of the plan to abduct and use humans. Such things are behind me. Being a doctor is not without its benefits for one such as I. Medicine is my chosen profession. Whole blood that is out of date for transfusion is my bread. That is more than you deserve to know about me."

Niles studied the man, the confrontational lift of his striking face. "Very well," he said. "I had no way of knowing. Yours must be a lonely life."

"No. It is a useful life," Saul argued. "But you have things to decide about, perhaps to act upon, but not alone. I can help you and you will need me."

Innes couldn't hold his tongue any longer. "We don't need him," he burst out.

"I think we do," Niles told him. "At least until he proves to be a liar."

Saul's nod showed he accepted and understood the comment.

"Someone is going to take people away to criminals like that man Colin?" Leigh said. "He—he raped a woman. We can't let this go on."

So her memory was returning more clearly. Too bad.

Out of respect for Saul he merely squeezed Leigh's hand but didn't say anything to her.

"It will be more than difficult to stop this," Saul said.

"Why do you care about humans or hounds or any of us?" Sean questioned angrily.

"I have told you all you need to know about me." Saul's pale face became expressionless once more. "We all follow our different paths. "Brande's wolves were offered a portion of the humans Tarhazian's minions collected."

Leigh choked and coughed. Niles pulled her against him.

"Why?" Niles demanded, and his two hounds moved closer to him.

"I don't know. But they said they had no need of them because they are working on mutating humans into creatures they can control without turning them. They apparently don't want more wolves, only humans to perform some service. And the wolves want to dominate the team, but perhaps you guessed that."

Suddenly Saul's demeanor changed, tensed. "I must go," he said. He braced himself against a tree.

"You're ill?" Niles asked.

Saul shook his head. "It's time for me to leave. She is the one most at risk." He indicated Leigh. "They believe she could ruin every plan they've made. There will be a great reward for the one who delivers her."

And with that, Saul left, gone almost before they heard him move.

"I'm going home," Leigh said. She tried to pull her hands away. "I'm not what I thought I was. I'll have to find a way to protect myself and not get anyone else hurt."

"Leigh, you're not alone." Niles kissed her again, hard, and thrust her to the others, who held her fast. They made sure she didn't see him change; there must be time before that happened. But when he wanted to move fast and unseen, his hound body made the most sense.

His pack brothers swung Leigh onto his back, and he felt her clutch at his fur. They took off, dodging obstacles until they flew, skimming the treetops.

chapter TWENTY-NINE

THE BODY BENEATH the russet fur Leigh clung to gave off enough heat to keep her from freezing. They flew through the snow-laden clouds that huddled around the tops of trees. Rushing wind and frozen flakes blasted her ears until she heard nothing at all.

What did she want? To be with this man-creature? She could never think of Niles as any kind of hound.

She knew what she wanted: Niles the man. And in time, perhaps that would overcome the animal he could become.

Could she make that happen for him? He wanted only humanity, he had already made that clear.

Streaming downward, the ground seemed to rise too fast. Suddenly they were on the porch at Two Chimneys. Leigh stayed, pressed against him, rubbed her face and hands as close as she could get to the skin. The fur was too thick to let her in very far. She felt perfectly peaceful.

As he was, he could not speak aloud to her but he

would understand her. He had communicated directly with her mind, and she wished he would talk to her now. "When I'm with you, I feel completely safe," she said. "Nothing can touch me."

Carefully, he settled on his stomach as if he liked the feel of her clinging to him.

Leigh rubbed his neck and he put his head on his paws.

"Will we be allowed to be together?" she said, more musing than asking. "There are so many forces I never thought existed. I still can't believe it all. If they are as strong and evil as they seem, how can we have a life?"

He looked at her over his shoulder, his eyes sharp and more definitely blue than the last time she had seen him like this.

"A man called me at Gabriel's," she said. "I don't think I know him but he knows about you, about us. He asked me to tell the police about you so you and the team would be stopped. I hung up on him. If he calls again, I'll tell you."

Niles stared at her, his eyes narrowed to slits. Then he closed them completely, as if in thought.

Leigh glanced around. "What time is it? It can't be getting dark again." But it was. Light faded early at this time of year.

Niles, of course, didn't answer.

She sat beside him, cross-legged, leaning into the heat of him. "I don't want to leave you." It didn't seem appropriate to take him into the cottage as this massive hound. True, Blue had come many times, but that was different.

Why was it different?

Niles watched her face again.

It was different because she wasn't in love with Sean

the man and she could separate him from Blue. She couldn't, she realized with a shock, completely separate Niles from this beautiful animal.

"Hello?" a tentative voice said.

She jumped but Niles moved his head languidly, almost with disinterest.

The tiny man from that dreadful house, Percy, hopped onto the end of the porch. "Just a little visit," he said, shifting from foot to foot in his agitation. He waited for a response and when he didn't get one, started wringing his hands.

Leigh couldn't make herself speak to him.

"I'm a friend," Percy said. "I know I... well, I didn't do anything to help you when you got to Colin's house. But now you have more information and you understand how oppressed we underlings are by the powerful ones."

Niles sat on his haunches, his muzzle lifted as if he sniffed the air.

Percy really agonized now. He hopped and twisted and wrung his hands. "I have come alone. By my life, there is no one following me and no one knows where I am."

Niles grunted.

"What do you want?" Leigh said, finally finding some voice.

"To apologize." Percy swept off his skullcap and knelt. "I am your servant and I am sorry for my transgressions."

Leigh and Niles waited.

"I want to be your eyes and ears in the enemy camp," Percy said, standing again, his cap held in both hands and a serious frown drawing together the place where his eyebrows would have been if he had any.

Leigh believed in mercy but this miserable little man

had left her to be molested. "Why would you change sides?" she said.

"I'm done with those stinking, selfish...disgusting... Done with them. If I could just stay in your woodshed, I would be eternally grateful and eternally at your service."

Leigh stared at him. "You've been kicked out of that horrible house, haven't you?"

"That doesn't matter." He crossed his arms. "I can take many forms so I can come and go among them without discovery. Then I can report back to you."

Niles side moved and she glanced at him. She thought he might be laughing.

Percy stood as tall as a very short creature could stand. "I chose to leave, but I must belong to someone. If I could live in your woodshed and you could send me out as a scout from time to time?"

Leigh raised a questioning brow.

"And throw me a little food from time to time." Percy kicked at the boards of the porch. "I can get into just about anywhere or anything, you know. I can be useful."

Since she didn't know what to say and Niles wasn't being helpful, Leigh nodded.

"Thank you," Percy cried. "You won't regret this." And he darted away around Two Chimneys.

"We might as well know where he is," Leigh said. "Or he will either become someone else's sneak or constantly get into the cottage and steal."

For longer than she had to, Leigh remained, leaning against Niles and soaking up some peace. She didn't dwell on the weird twists her life had taken, or the strange events that definitely waited ahead.

She got up, found her key, and unlocked the door. Only

then did she remember that she'd left Jazzy and Skilly-widden at Gabriel's.

"Sally will care for them till tomorrow."

For a second time, she jumped. Niles had decided to read her mind and respond.

"I'm going to get changed," she said, not feeling secure enough to try to communicate with him the same way. "You wait here. I won't be long."

Niles sat very still.

Leigh sighed, contented just to run her fingers through his fur. She kissed him between the ears. "You are a beautiful hound, you know. But you're an even more beautiful man. And I worry about you being around like this. Remember how afraid you were of Blue getting shot?"

He watched her face steadily. There were no more messages in her mind.

She scratched his head and neck and realized how fond she was of him like this. "I'll have to be careful or Jazzy will get jealous."

Flopping down once more, Niles rested his great head and closed his eyes. He gave a heavy sigh.

"Okay," she said brightly, and hurried inside, leaving the door ajar.

She soon stepped back outside. "I might have known it. Look at this." Skillywidden had landed on her shoulder, who knew from where?

Niles had left the porch and in no more than seconds was nowhere to be seen.

chapter THIRTY

W<small>HAT'S UP</small> with you?" Sean said. He stood not far from Niles's front door. "You aren't even hearing what I'm saying. We've got an opportunity to strengthen the team with more members."

Niles braced himself in the doorway to the kitchen and let his head drop forward. Why wouldn't Sean go away? Why had he come, tonight of all nights?

"The others are waiting for your opinion," Sean said. "It could be a good thing to accept these two werehounds from Europe. We're interested in their petition. From what we can tell so far it sounds like a good fit and we could use them in our ranks. We would have to examine their histories carefully but we would visit them there first. There would be no added jeopardy brought here."

"Not now," Niles said.

"It's Leigh again, isn't it? She's safe up there. We've got the place covered on all sides and Sally's cat is on telephonic duty."

"Good."

"What should I tell the others? They're eager for the possibility of new blood. We've never needed to pull on all the strength we can find as much as we do now. We all know what Saul told us is going on."

"I don't need you to tell me the obvious. The fae will always be an irritation. Mixing it up is a pastime for them. It's Brande and his ilk we face. They have no conscience, which means they intend to go after what they've decided they want and they don't expect to die in the attempt."

"But we don't have a plan," Sean said, raising one brow.

"This is the plan," Niles said. "Listen, follow the instructions you've been given. Storming Brande would get us nowhere—they'd know we were coming almost before I gave the word, and we'd be fighting our way out of an ambush. And keep it in mind that we don't know how many vamps—of his own kind—Colin could call in. We've got to be smarter than Brande. And the next move is his. We will be ready."

"Are we going to discuss this? Do you want to have the others here while we have this discussion?" Sean said.

"We don't have time. *I* don't have time."

"It's all about Leigh, isn't it?" Sean said. "She's front and center for you and it's not going smoothly. What happened when the two of you came—"

"Get out of my house and make sure that cottage is so tight a tick couldn't get in. If she makes a move, you move with her and you let me know."

He didn't watch Sean leave but he winced when the door slammed. Blood beat hard at his temples. Leigh had told him to wait on the porch—and he'd take any bet she didn't realize what that had felt like for him.

Maybe it would be as well if he and Leigh didn't see each other tonight. The kind of intensity building in him could be too much for either of them to handle.

"Coward," he told himself quietly. "You're afraid she won't come. Maybe never again."

He could go up there and say he'd come to meet her. Or he could call her. If he were honest with himself he'd admit he expected her several hours ago, that he had started for the door at every sound. If she weren't deliberately staying away she'd be here by now. He didn't want to push her more than she had already been pushed.

The dark blue shirt he wore was made of soft cotton. He hadn't put on one of his comfortable old favorites. He had *chosen* this shirt because he wanted Leigh to like it. If he had ever done such a thing before it was too long ago for him to remember.

She wasn't going to come.

Somehow she had sensed he was conflicted and would stay away until he made the next move.

Things needed to be put right with Sean. What had just happened between them was wrong. And they needed to discuss the call Leigh had talked about from some unknown man. Why hadn't he raised that with Sean? Brande's pack was becoming a bigger and bigger threat. Niles had no doubt it had been one of them who telephoned Leigh.

All he could think about for more than two seconds was Leigh. They had issues, big issues, and they wouldn't be dealt with this way.

He rotated his shoulders, trying to loosen himself up, and went to the front door. Listening in to her mind wouldn't be right but he was sure she was up at Two Chimneys thinking about him.

When he opened the door to leave, she stood there with knuckles raised to knock.

Niles caught hold of her wrist reflexively and swung her inside. One look at her wide eyes and he let go. "Sorry. You caught me off balance. I was coming to get you."

"I thought you'd come a long time ago," she said quietly. "But you left so quickly, I wasn't sure what you wanted to do."

"You left me. On the porch, remember?" he said.

"I came back out—it was only a minute or so later—and you'd left."

A dog told to wait on the porch should do as he's told. He was blaming her for nothing. She intended nothing—or had she?

"Let me take your coat," he said.

"Are you sure you want—"

"I want to take off your coat. I want you with me and I never want to be apart from you again, ever." This was not the moment to take her into his arms. He didn't trust himself. "You belong with me. Things aren't the way they must be yet, but we can change that. We don't have any choice but to move forward, but we can't afford to make mistakes."

"Meaning?" she said.

"That call you got. The threatening one. Are you sure you didn't recognize who it was?"

Leigh thought about it. "There was something familiar about the voice, but I don't know who it was."

"You heard what Saul said," Niles told her. "We're in a war—not you—us. You can help the most by not making me wonder what you'll do next."

She pointed her steepled fingers at him. "Niles, I . . .

You change. You say different things and I don't know what to believe."

"I don't change. I'm not always sure about you is all."

Leigh shrugged out of her own coat and handed it to him. "What's happened, Niles? Did I do something you don't like? If I did, I don't know what it was and there's never an excuse to just get mad at someone for no reason."

But he had a reason. "That's true. Sit down by the fire and warm up." He indicated the L-shaped gray couch. It was the most comfortable piece of furniture he owned. Not that he'd ever cared before.

Leigh remained standing, watching him.

"I'm scared," Niles said, surprising himself. He smiled uncomfortably. "Scared of losing you, that is. I can't make myself believe you've accepted me as I am—all of me. I know I'm asking you to do what should be impossible—"

"I love you," Leigh said. "All of you. What do I have to do to make you believe me? If I didn't love you I'd be gone. It's too scary here but I'd fall apart if I was somewhere else without you."

He glanced away. "You know how to destroy a man's tough front," he said. "I wish I could just carry you away and pretend I don't have to keep the wolves from the door."

"How will we stop them?" she asked quietly.

"They're going to make a move and it'll be soon. My people will be ready for them." He looked her over, realized his lips were parted and he was staring. "I think the fire's good," he said, turning away. But he had to look at her again.

"What's the matter?" she said.

"You're so beautiful."

She turned bright red with the patches of white that always formed around her freckles when she blushed. "This isn't pretty," she said, pressing her palms to her cheeks.

"It is to me." He was under control now but it didn't stop his pulsing need for her. "I've never seen you dressed like that before. You shouldn't cover your legs."

Immediately she smoothed the skirt of her green woolen dress. She wore flat, black shoes with some sort of leather flower on the fronts and she crossed one foot over the other as if to hide as much of her legs as possible.

Niles laughed. "Is that a new dress?"

She seemed bemused. "No. I haven't been wearing dresses here because the weather isn't right. And I don't usually do anything that makes me think of wearing one."

The bodice had a round neckline with buttons down the front to a belted waist. Long sleeves ended in narrow cuffs. The slim skirt fitted sweetly curved hips perfectly. "But you felt coming to me was a good time to wear a dress?"

Leigh gritted her teeth a moment. "You are awful. I feel so embarrassed. I took ages to choose this and I thought you might like it."

"I'm crazy about it," he said. "I think you try to pretend you're not feminine. Don't ask me why because you can't hide what you are. I feel like a million dollars knowing you chose the dress for me. How about my shirt? I chose it for you, too."

They both burst out laughing.

Niles sobered first. "What would you do if I threw you over my shoulder and carried you off . . . to do all kinds of things to you?"

He settled his hands at her waist, dropped to one knee, and smoothed all the way to her calves.

Touching her, even through her clothes, made him tremble. "I am going to do all kinds of things to you," he said. "Make you scream for me to make you come, again and again. That'll be before and after I strip you naked—slowly—and lick every inch of you, then suck every inch of you."

"Niles." Her throat sounded dry.

If Niles had known picking up one of her feet would make her grab for him he would have done it ages ago.

"Niles!"

Slowly he massaged her foot, smiling a little when he touched the arch and she jumped.

The sensation as he moved from her foot, to her ankle, to the smooth skin of her calf made him feel anything but smooth or relaxed.

This wasn't what he'd had in mind, seducing her in the entryway, but it felt just fine, at least for a start.

Beneath his hands, the soft skirt of her dress slipped up easily until he felt lace at the top of her stocking, and satin where garter met lace.

He filled his lungs and pressed his face to her belly.

Leigh pushed her fingers into his hair and held him to her tightly. He felt the rapid beat of her heart.

The skin on her thigh was more satin. Niles ran his fingers high between her legs, pressed the tip of his thumb briefly to the hottest, wettest part of her. He told himself over and over that he would not hurt her, he would hold back the force she would find unnatural.

When his hand moved away from her heat, she moaned and he smiled with satisfaction.

He hiked the skirt above the edges of her white lace panties. She made another little sound when he started to unfasten her garters and he paused, looked up at her face. She bit her bottom lip.

"You should look at yourself from where I'm looking," he said. "Sexy lady." He nipped the soft inside of her thigh and kissed a path to her panty leg, and opened his mouth over her mound, using his tongue until the fabric was completely wet and her hips started moving involuntarily.

Niles separated his mouth from her just far enough to allow for his tongue to get under the fabric and continue driving her mad.

Her fingernails dug into his shoulders and the one leg she stood on started to buckle.

"Hold on," he said, keeping her skirt firmly up around her waist but letting her foot slide from his thigh. "Are you ready for me—for us? Once we really get going on the journey I have in mind there won't be any turning back. I don't want to hurt you but I warn you, I'm stronger than a man should be and it's up to you to let me know when something is too much."

She caught him off guard by kissing him. Kicking off her other shoe, she stood on her tiptoes, wound her arms around his neck, and showed him she knew how to use her tongue, too. She nibbled his lips, reached deep inside his mouth, moved her head this way and that searching for more ways to bring them pleasure.

When she had finished they were breathless and her mouth was red and bruised-looking. "Don't take me for some wilting flower," she told him. "I'm a strong woman."

Her little laugh sounded uncertain.

Niles picked her up by the waist and cradled her bottom in his hands, amused by her startled expression. "Why the look?" he asked.

"I'm small but I'm not a feather. You didn't even move a muscle to pick me up like that."

The temptation to show off just how easily he could do a great deal more than she'd seen so far was childish. He nuzzled her neck instead, breathed in the clean sweetness of her.

Leigh had a knot in the pit of her stomach. Lust wasn't foreign to her but it had been a long time. And she wanted to drive Niles wild, to make him feel as insanely sexy as she did. Who had she become? What had she become?

She was to tell him if he was too much for her? Once more she wanted to laugh. Twisting a little and enjoying hearing him groan and grit his teeth, she wrapped her arms around his head and held her face against his neck.

And she pressed her achy breasts to his chest.

With Niles she felt safe and protected, but she knew he could bring danger her way. And she only felt invincible when she could see and touch him.

She couldn't think clearly anymore. Her life had turned upside down. But this man who held her tight, while the world did whatever strange things were planned for tonight beyond the walls of his home, was the only good change she could point to.

She leaned even nearer to him and slid her tongue along his bottom lip.

Niles let her ride lower on his hips and his penis moved against her.

Leigh worked a hand down between them and squeezed him.

"Damn, you like to live dangerously," he said, looking

into her face again, his eyes turned black and unreadable. He kissed her until she had to break the embrace just to breathe.

"All right," he said. "Let me show you some things you don't know about me."

If she wanted to change her mind, it would have to be now. And she knew he would not force her to do anything.

"I want to learn everything there is to know about you," she told him, even while she quaked inside.

He put her on her feet in front of him and ran a hand between her legs until he touched dampness again.

"You are so excited," he told her with a brief, hard kiss and continued rubbing. "You're driving me over the top."

Leigh grabbed his shirt. Holding her with one arm, he rubbed back and forth, never taking his eyes from her face.

Pressure mounted and she started to cry out.

But he stopped, the corners of his mouth tilted down and triumph oozing from him.

Leigh sucked in a great breath. "You tease me. You want to play with me like—"

"Like the most desirable woman I can imagine. That's how. And I want it to last, but not without learning all the little things you might not tell me just because I asked."

Her heart thudded harder and she braced her hands on his shoulders. "You're going to torture them out of me?"

"Something like that. Have I told you I'm crazy about your breasts?"

"Hush." She stood upright. "You can't just say things like that."

"Yes, I can. That and much more. I want to see them. Undo some buttons for me. Just one or two."

So hot she felt slightly faint, she shook her head, no.

And he shot his hands up the backs of her legs to hold and squeeze her bottom. "Just one or two," he repeated, his smile wicked now. "I love your ass, too."

"Niles!"

"Do it."

So he wanted to taunt her. She could play that game, too.

"Buttons?" His fingers slipped over her flesh and into the cleft of her bottom. He stroked her there very softly, letting his little fingers stray under her enough to barely touch the part of her that still throbbed.

Leigh undid a button on her dress. He raised his brows and she pushed another one undone and, without any indication from him, opened a third and a fourth.

The top of the dress was meant to be snug. Unbuttoned, it gaped.

Niles held the tip of his tongue between his teeth.

Leigh spread her dress open wider. She was coming alive in a new way. Pleasing him obsessed her.

"Why do you wear this?" he said, tracing the edges of her bra.

Confused, she looked down. Apart from the dress, the bra was all she wore above the waist, a white piece of lace that didn't quite cover her nipples.

"I like it," she said, wrinkling her nose at him.

"Mmm hmm." Languidly, he reached to flip his tongue beneath the lace of her bra to surround the nipples and leave them exposed. She tried to arch her body and keep him touching and stimulating her there, but he drew back. "It doesn't serve much purpose, this little piece of nothing." He stared at her breasts and his fingers on her behind dug in forcefully.

"Although I like the way it looks," he added.

"What about showing me those things I don't know about you?" Leigh said.

A shadow passed over his features. He stood up, so close she had to arch her neck to look at him.

"You're still sure you want to know?"

"You can't imagine how much."

Niles took her by the hand and led her to the room she had thought must be a second bedroom, or another bathroom. It was neither. Except for boxes that looked dusty enough to have been there forever, the room was empty.

With one hand he moved aside stacks of boxes taller than he. They had hidden bifold doors, gleaming dully as if made of an old metal, but without handles.

"They can't be pushed open. Not by anyone but me, unless I want them to."

She felt sweat on her back. Moment to moment she moved deeper into a dark and enigmatic world.

Niles looked at her, and at her breasts. He bent to makes circles around a nipple with his tongue until she wanted to scream.

"Passion is power," was all he said.

He looked at the door and it swung open. "My initiator was no ordinary werehound. He had come to his state by strange paths that traveled through sorcery. Some of his powers were passed to me."

She slid her hand back into his and straightened her shoulders. "I have powers. One day I'll know about all of them, not just that I am sure I can hear what I shouldn't hear or see what other people can't."

"You're a gutsy woman," he said. "Don't worry. I never

doubted you'd turn out to be a tiger. Now come on. I can't wait any longer."

"This is a passage into the cliffs," he said, nodding ahead where an unearthly green glow showed rough-hewn walls that curved to meet overhead in a tunnel that gradually disappeared out of sight. "It goes all the way beneath Two Chimneys. I was told to build the cabin by Chimney Rock, and my sanctuary in these cliffs. I can't tell you who told me what to do—I don't know."

She swallowed with difficulty. "The glow," she said. "Could this be something to do with the light from Chimney Rock?"

"The light I can't see, you mean? I suppose so. I only know what that looks like because you've told me. Before you came I learned that Chimney Rock was responsible for the veil that separates the natural from the supernatural world, but no details. There was no one to ask. No one I could trust to tell me the truth."

He walked slightly ahead of her, enveloping her hand and leading her.

"This supernatural world," she said. "How extensive is it?"

After some thought he said, "It extends beyond our understanding. But we know it is vast and its members are more numerous than any one of us will ever completely know. And they come in a multitude of forms. Good and evil. And quixotic. It's only through time and experience—and often a lot of trouble—that we learn who we can trust."

He stopped and faced her. "My team is honorable. I'm honorable."

"I believe you." Leigh squeezed his hand. "What about

the Deseron? What do you know about us—if there are such people?"

"Almost nothing. There were never large numbers and you aren't supposed to exist anymore. Thank God you do. There is too much uncertainty for us to pursue it now but when we can we will talk to Sally. I believe she may know more than most."

He kissed her hand but what he had said frightened her. She wanted answers to her questions.

"Come." He smiled at her and they went on until there was a curve in the passage and more metal doors, these so shiny Leigh could see Niles and herself in them. "They look silver," she said.

"They are. Silver doesn't hurt us like it does the wolves."

Once more they opened in front of him, and closed behind them when they were inside. Leigh was speechless. This cave was huge.

"Are you finally frightened?" he asked.

She shook her head, no. Little did he know the truth and he wouldn't learn it from her. One thing she knew for certain. She would not give in to fear.

And in truth, she would not want to live without this man or this moment.

Many lamps in vaguely familiar shapes, all made of silver and inset with colored glass, hung from the ceiling. The cross over a simple white-covered bed was the easiest symbol. Leigh thought another lamp had a masonic shape and several others resembled ancient pagan carvings. There was a circular lamp, amazing in its construction and the way shafts of brilliance seemed to shine inward rather than outward, as if the sun had found it. She realized it looked like a druid circle.

The lights were hung too high to totally penetrate the chamber's shadows.

In the very center of the room water bubbled almost to the brim of a large circular pool.

Stone walls were unadorned and the bed was the only furnishing.

"I can sleep here in complete safety if I ever want to," Niles said. "I can bring my team here also. And if you choose, you can come at any time. You will be my mate. When we are sealed, what is mine is yours, including the loyalty of the team."

He took off his shirt, stripped away his jeans, and stood before her.

Leigh's heart did the strangest things and her knees felt weak.

He was naked.

He was beautiful.

And he was dangerous to love with a capital D.

She wouldn't change a thing.

"You do have to tell me if I'm acceptable—as a man. As your man."

Leigh took in every sexy inch of him. She had no idea how to respond.

"Leigh?"

Bemused, she shook her head.

"You dislike something about me?"

"I think you're the most fantastic male I've ever seen," she blurted out. "You are incredible. You make my legs weak. I want to touch you."

"Then touch me."

He smiled but she noticed there was a hint of relief and almost laughed aloud.

His hips were firm and narrow and she could grip them while she tried to figure out what to do next.

Suddenly she knew. She traced his face from flaring brows to full, sensual lips, his clean-cut jaw, strong neck, and massive shoulders. With her fingertips and palms she made a map of his triceps and biceps, the solid muscles in his chest, the ridges over his midsection. Her fingertips moved down his hair-rough belly to his groins and thighs. Cupping the male weight of him knocked all the air out of her lungs.

Without warning, he dived sideways into the pool, disappearing at first and coming up quickly, slicking his hair away from his face. "I think you enjoyed that, woman. Very much. Now you have to pay for your pleasure."

He rose out of the water, climbing steps she couldn't see. He pulled her toward him too fast for her to react.

He shimmied her dress from her shoulders, tugged her arms free of the sleeves, and swept it down until she had to step out. That dress hit a wall, torn away with such force that it was in shreds.

Two fingers between her breasts made sure she would never wear the bra again and her thong simply disappeared, together with her garter belt.

With another serious look into her eyes, he rolled her stockings down and took them off with care. He held them to his mouth then set them aside. "I shall keep them," he said. "A memento of this night."

Without a hint of a smile, he returned to the water and said, "Jump. I'll catch you."

"I'll knock you off your feet."

His laughter echoed. "Let me worry about that. Just jump to me." As he spoke he took another backward pace.

"What if I can't swim?"

"What does it matter? You're with me."

Leigh drew in a breath. She held it, ran at the side of the pool and jumped toward Niles, closing her eyes as she felt herself suspended in midair and without any support.

His hands closed around her ribs, just below her breasts, and her eyes opened. He grinned up at her, circling slowly, letting her feet and ankles trail in the water. And he kept walking backward, going deeper into the water. Leigh clutched his wrists.

"You're safe!" He tipped her face closer to his. "Kneel on my shoulders."

Scrambling, she managed to get her knees onto his shoulders, which barely cleared the water. Still held only by his hands, the next part of him to touch her was his mouth—between her legs, across her clitoris, curling up and back, up and back—before she cried out and twisted, sensation burning, knifing, exploding until she felt torn in half and never wanted this to stop.

When her head finally cleared a little she was held in his arms, her head on his shoulders. "You planned it," she said, panting. "Every second of it."

"I did, ma'am."

"You started out there." She pointed vaguely toward where she thought the cabin was. "And you knew I'd go right over the edge the instant you touched me again."

"Guilty as charged."

The grin fell away. He let her legs down until they were body to body, facing each other, and he slid her over his penis, making sure she felt exactly what he was able to control.

He made circles over her breasts with his mouth,

working inward until she pressed for him to suck at her nipples. Then he kissed her mouth, wide and wild. Leigh had to wrap her legs around him to hold on.

"Are you ready?" he asked quietly, sounding very strange.

She stared into his mysterious eyes. "I want you."

"This will be a commitment. You and I will be lovers, mates, forever."

"I am ready." She spoke firmly, staring into his face.

Niles lifted her into the air once more. His features toughened. The veins at his temples and in his neck stood out. He climbed with her up the steps again and as they reached the top he brought her down, sheathed himself in her, and moved, they moved together, driven by his strength. Niles lifted and lowered her, never completely leaving her body until, with a harsh yell, he drove himself in so far her body vibrated.

There was bright, hot sensation. Her body might have exploded. She felt as if she were swimming against a rip tide.

The climax broke again, washed over her. And singing pain followed. She must be opened up, torn in half.

She tried to say his name, but she was too far away, and slipping farther. He wouldn't hear her. She was such a long way away now, disappearing into darkness.

chapter THIRTY-ONE

Niles looked down at Leigh stretched across the white bed in the cavern. He had carried her there when she passed out.

He sat beside her and cursed himself for not being more careful, for not searching out better guidance.

Who could he have gone to? He had read what was written in the old books they had carried with them through the years. A reference to "more fragile mates" and the need to be gentle, to hold back the full force of the werehound's strength during "ultimate loving" with a human was all the research he had.

He had thought he was following the instructions flawlessly.

Her hand on his arm startled Niles.

"You look so worried," she said sleepily.

Some color had returned to her face. For the half hour since they made love she had been so pale she scared him. And she slept as if she was deeply unconscious.

Yet her breathing was even, her heartbeat regular.

He smoothed back her hair and smiled. "I was thinking about team business—it always intrudes." A lie could be excused under the circumstances. "We are considering taking new members from Belgium. It's a big decision." He bent to kiss her cheek but she captured his face and made sure the kiss was long and arousing.

"I'm pushy," she said. "Did I tell you that yet?"

"Must have missed it." Many small, seeking kisses resulted in Leigh's pushing aside the sheet and sitting up to wind her arms around his neck.

He drew her naked body to him.

"Mmm." She rested her forehead on his mouth. "Well, I am. And for now it's all about me, wild man. My satisfaction. My pleasure. I don't know how I got so lucky, but you've turned me into an insatiable sex maniac."

Holding her away to see her face, he laughed. "I did that? Maybe you were already. Maybe you're the one who's corrupting me."

"I was only joking about being selfish," she said, dropping a quick kiss low on his abdomen. "It's all about both of us."

Niles's belly tensed painfully. She knelt beside him and he stroked her body. Tenderness and desire made uncomfortable partners for a man already fighting a war with himself. He was ready to make love to her again.

"How do you feel?" He chafed his thumbs up and down at her waist.

"Incredible. How do you feel?"

"Even better than incredible." Holding her to him, he searched for traces of blood and found none. "I have to ask you this, Leigh. You passed out for a while. Did I hurt you?"

Her fine brows drew down and she sucked in her cheeks. "I understand now," she said and moved like quicksilver to sit astride his thighs. Her position meant that it would take very little for him to be inside her again.

"I don't think you should do that." He took uneven breaths. "I really don't."

"I'm staying right here. Unless I'm causing you horrible pain, please stop telling me what to do."

What did you say to a comment like that except, "You're in charge."

"Good thing you realize that." She shifted slightly and half-closed her eyes. "You are, well...I think you are really blessed in some areas. It hardly seems fair to other men, but there you are. You've got it, and I've got you. End of subject."

He couldn't allow her to laugh her way out of every tense moment. "Have I hurt you? A straight answer, please."

Rubbing his chest, she thought before answering. "You shocked me. You made me feel like I've never felt before and I want a lot more of what that was. My body wasn't ready. I thought it was, but how could it have been? When I passed out I felt myself going but it wasn't from pain. I was overcome."

She took his penis in both of her hands and looked at it from several angles.

He didn't know whether to yell or just show her what the object of her interest was for—again. "What are... what are you doing?"

"Admiring this," she said but her smirk slipped and she buried her face in his chest. "I've got a lot on my mind, too, Niles. But I love you and that comes first. I don't think I know how to deal with this happening to me. I never expected to fall in love again."

He bore the word "again," glad in a way that she could speak easily of Chris.

"There's something we should do," he said. "Just you and I alone here. Then it'll be time to call the team together. We have several members who choose to live alone and more distant from the rest of us. They will come later."

"I don't want anyone to come." She looked horrified. "I don't have any clothes."

"I'll lend you some."

"Very nice. Let me introduce you to my mate; she's the one in the flannel shirt and work boots."

Niles stretched her gently on the bed again and lay beside her. He made sure not one inch of her body was covered by anything. "Too bad they don't get to see you like this, but if they did I'd have to kill them afterward."

"Niles!"

"We'll deal with the clothes." He rolled half over her and they kissed, rocking their mouths together, nipping, reaching deep. Niles started touching her, running his hands all over her. And Leigh matched his every move.

With a pillow pulled beneath her back, thrusting her breasts toward him, he took a very long time using his mouth, and the stubble on his jaw, to arouse her to the breaking point.

Leigh arched her back and moaned.

He kissed and licked her nipples until she showed signs of dissolving into a frenzy and he gave her relief.

Her stomach, the insides of her thighs, the still swollen parts of her that had received him, nothing went unattended.

"Off!" With as big a push as she could muster, she shoved at his chest and he drew back with a surprised yelp. "On your stomach."

She moved and he lay prone, his arms spread and his legs relaxed, until she started her own minute torture.

Niles hung on through nips to his neck, full kisses to the sides of his body, and more nips and kisses over his buttocks. He enjoyed the way she started at his ankles and ran her tongue up each leg.

But when she went between his legs to nuzzle beneath his penis, Leigh was no longer in control of anything.

He whipped around to restrain her.

Every nerve, sinew, and muscle in his body was rigid, but the hands he cradled her with revealed none of the fight he was having with his desire to overpower her. And neither did his face reveal anything.

"Make love to me again," she said softly.

"Are you sure you're ready?"

Her smile was dreamy. "I'm ready."

They were so wet this time it was easier to slip in slowly and rotate without pulling at her.

Still he worried, but only until Leigh took charge of the pace and they fused, crying out fulfilled. Niles could have slid against her forever but finally she slowed, gasping, clinging to him.

Soaked in sweat they lay together and he couldn't stay awake.

Leigh's eyes opened slowly at first, then wide when she remembered everything. Niles wasn't beside her. "Niles!"

"I'm here." He came from a far wall of the cavern, a

fairly small box shaped like a leather trunk in his hands. "Are you ready?"

She frowned and inclined her head. Like her, Niles was still naked, but she felt completely comfortable.

"Will you allow yourself to be sealed to me?"

What had that meant? "I guess."

"You guess?" He sat beside her again and opened the box. Inside was a round, black stone burner over which a tiny bowl of the same stone was suspended. He lit a candle beneath the bowl and put a piece of purple material from a silk bag into the bowl itself. Very quickly, the light beneath the bowl melted its contents to a smooth, violet-colored pool.

"Wax?" Leigh asked.

He blinked, thinking. "Not wax, although I suppose the word seal might suggest that. It's a dye, an ancient dye. I would like to use this seal." He lifted a slender black stone stylus, like a fountain pen with a flat end where the tip would be. It had been beside the bowl and burner in the little chest. Niles showed her the blunt end where a round insignia had been worked deep into a gold inset. "See how small this is?" he said. "It will burn you for a moment, but only a moment. If you want to do this, you will let me seal your hand and then you will seal mine. This is the way we have joined with our mates throughout time."

Excitement made her jumpy. She wanted it, but she didn't fool herself that it was likely to be easily undone if she changed her mind.

Leigh held out her left hand.

Without comment, Niles set that hand on her thigh again and took her right hand. He dipped the seal into the hot dye and pressed it into the center of her palm.

She winced but didn't make a sound.

"You are my lifelong mate," he said and gave her the seal.

Leigh cringed at the thought of burning him, but still she repeated his process. "You are my lifelong mate."

He pressed their palms together, entwining their fingers, and closed his eyes. Then he rested his cheek on her shoulder and folded her into a warm embrace.

He sat back and placed their right hands side by side. Their palms held matching circular wounds, tinged the color of gentian violet. Within the circles Leigh saw the simple shape of a knot.

They held each other again and Leigh never wanted to let go.

"We have to see the others," Niles said after a while. "I will call them."

"I have no clothes!" Leigh grappled with a sheet.

He stood up and pulled the sheet away. "With a little help I've made sure you do have clothes." He went to the doors and they opened inward. A bag stood there, and so did Skillywidden, who leaped into the chamber and stretched herself out on the bed. Instantly she closed her eyes.

"Is that because she's tired," Leigh said, "or shocked?"

"That isn't something we're ever going to know. See what you can find in there."

She looked into the bag. "It's not mine. Where did it come from?"

"Will it work?"

An emerald green sweater with buttons at the shoulder and soft silk pants of the same color were her size. The bra and panties lower inside the bag also seemed to have been supplied with only her in mind. Soft green suede boots that ruckled at the ankles, and personal items to make her feel completely comfortable were there, too—nothing had been forgotten.

Since Niles had already pulled on his jeans, she got dressed quickly and held out her arms for his opinion.

"Perfect. No one would know you hadn't tried everything on in a shop."

"I'll have to pay someone for these."

"I already have." He smiled at her.

"Sally got them, didn't she?"

"I have to keep some of my secrets. The team is on its way."

Of course, she had forgotten how fast werehounds could travel. Niles almost laughed at the bemused expression on Leigh's face when they walked into the cabin's living room and four very large men waited there, all standing, all appearing uncomfortable. Sean, Ethan, Campion, and Innes. They were an impressive group.

One by one the men came forward and stood in front of Leigh. Each repeated much the same phrase: "I am happy to meet our leader's mate. I owe you my loyalty always."

When it was Sean's turn he couldn't keep the delight from his face and he actually kissed Leigh's hand. He gave his promise and added, "You've become Niles's echo. All you have to do is ask for something and we will comply just as we would for him."

"Okay, back to your posts," Niles said, but each of the men smiled broadly.

Leigh stood at the window, marveling at the persistence of the snow. It must be very deep in places. But why should she care? She had everything she needed.

"It's dawn," she told Niles. "Just about."

"You must be hungry," he said.

She didn't get to answer before the phone rang. Niles answered then offered it to her with a smile. "It's for you."

"Idiot man," a woman's voice said. "I wanted to talk to him, too. This is Sally. Do you remember the woman at the used book shop—Phoebe Harris?"

"Yes."

"She wants to see you right now and so do I. There was an attempt to snatch her. She has a broken arm and Dr. Saul is on his way to deal with it."

Leigh took a while to respond. "Why me?"

"You'll find out. We're at Gabriel's."

chapter THIRTY-TWO

LEIGH AND NILES had to pound on the doors at Gabriel's to be let in. Once inside, quiet but intense activity met them.

The lights were very low, except for a few lamps shining on a supine body atop two tables that had been pushed together. Paint cans—more than Leigh had ever seen in one place, except a DIY store—littered the floor.

Gabriel paced, pausing to look at the table at each pass. He still had his coat and snow pants on, and a checked wool cap with woolly ear flaps turned up.

Talking in a low voice, Sally hovered over the patient.

With Niles beside her, Leigh made a hurried path through the paint cans to the table. The patient was Phoebe Harris from the bookshop—a very pale, scratched, and bruised Phoebe Harris. Her bright red hair contrasted frighteningly with her white skin, and frothed out around her head in curls that reached the edges of the table.

"What's happened?" Leigh said. She composed herself. "Did you have a fall?" If she showed how shocked she was, it wouldn't help Phoebe.

"She's not saying much," Sally said from the other side of the tables. "She was when I got here but now she's quiet." Movement across the room caught Sally's eye. "Saul! Thank goodness you're here." She looked past Leigh at the doctor, who glided toward them.

Leigh saw an unexpected movement up by the ceiling. A shaft of purple coiled from between the beams and shot toward a table.

Percy.

He looked at Leigh, shook his head, and pointed toward the back of the room. She followed his pointing finger but couldn't see anything different.

When she looked back at Percy, the fae creature disappeared.

Saul pulled off his long coat and covered Phoebe, feeling for her pulse, looking into her eyes. "Light the fire. She's going into shock."

The fire was already laid and Gabriel quickly went to work to get flames shooting up the chimney.

Phoebe's teeth chattered loudly and Sally spread a thick, soft blanket over Saul's coat. Where the blanket came from, Leigh didn't know, but she was learning not to question as much as she once had.

Phoebe moaned and tossed her head from side to side. Her green eyes opened but the lids looked heavy. Saul had his hands on her shoulders and he looked into her face as if he could see inside her somehow.

He moved to check for injuries and knocked over several paint cans. They turned over and rolled around. Saul's expression didn't change from complete absorption in his patient.

"What's with the damn paint?" Niles hissed toward Gabriel.

"I'm going to paint the logs inside," he said.

Leigh caught his arm. "Why? You love the bare wood. We all do."

"Molly doesn't. Never did."

"Molly's gone," Leigh said before she could stop herself.

The sadness on Gabriel's face made her want to kick herself.

"We talk on the phone," he said. "When it's all done I'll surprise her. There's too much of this stuff to store at my place so I brought it here. It was in my truck. Just as well I did. When I went out of here for the last batch of cans, Phoebe was curled up on the doorstep."

Cliff Ames came from the kitchens carefully carrying a steaming cup of something. Silently they watched while the cook, whose eyes darted anxiously about, set down the cup and left.

At the same time, Sean slipped into the bar, apparently from the delivery door at the back. He went at once to Phoebe. The sudden transformation of his expression from just curious to involved puzzled Leigh.

"When?" Niles said. "When did you find Phoebe?"

"An hour ago," Gabriel said, shrugging. "Four, four-thirty."

Niles gave him a disbelieving stare. "That's when you decided to come over with about a thousand cans of paint?"

"I couldn't sleep," Gabriel said.

Leigh looked at her boss and saw the deep purple beneath his eyes.

Gabriel shook his head and heaved a heavy sigh. "I know where Molly is," he said. Leigh expected him to continue, but he only started moving paint cans out of the middle of the bar, shoving them wherever there was a space on the floor no one was likely to use soon.

"Listen to me, Phoebe," Saul said, drawing everyone's attention back to the tables. Without his coat he wore one of the full-sleeved white shirts he favored with black pants. He had wide shoulders and narrow hips, and Leigh decided he was too thin.

Slowly, Phoebe focused on his face and, amazingly, she smiled.

"Keep looking at me," Saul said. "Talk to me when you can."

"What's wrong with her?" Sean said. He touched one of her curls.

Saul glanced up and shook his head at the other man.

"I didn't see them coming," Phoebe said. "They ... it was big. A big animal. It knocked me down and snarled in my face. I thought there were others back where I couldn't quite see them. The one who attacked me got its claws in my hair." She began to reach up with her left hand but cried out and took deep breaths. "My arm really hurts. I expect I've got big scratches on my head," she said through her teeth.

Leigh didn't allow herself to look at Niles, but his hand settled comfortably on the back of her neck.

Sally indicated the cup Cliff had left, looking to Saul for approval. He nodded and she lifted Phoebe's head. The drink looked like tea but Leigh could smell brandy.

"Has she got a broken arm?" Niles asked.

Leigh turned her face up to him and recognized one

of his rare angry outbursts in the making. His lips made a hard, white line. On the back of her neck, his fingers dug in harder.

"No," Saul said, looking hard at Niles. "A pull at the shoulder, I think. Perhaps partial dislocation. She's going to be fine."

"He had eyes that shone in the dark," Phoebe said. "I was in my place at the bookshop. All the lights went off and I was dragged outside. I screamed but no one heard— no one who cared." She gulped more of the spirits-laced tea and color started to return to her cheeks. "He threw me down. Every time I tried to get up, he threw me down again." Her gazed settled on Leigh and didn't move away.

"You aren't alone anymore," Leigh told her. "I'm sorry you were scared."

"I went down to your cottage to see you about contacting your sister," Phoebe all but whispered. "But you weren't there. I waited, then drove back home. That creature came right after I got back."

Saul, Leigh noted, held Phoebe's arm just above the wrist. The look of pain was fading from her face.

"Holy . . . Who the hell is that?" Gabriel said.

A woman Leigh had never seen before stood at the end of the bar. She came forward a few steps, an arrogant curl on her bright red lips. Heavy makeup didn't make her look ugly, just artificial. "Sally," she said. "Where have you been? You don't follow instructions too well, do you, girl? I've looked for you all over. Good thing I've found you now, by the looks of things."

Saul turned to stare at the woman, who took a half-step backward and all but snarled at him. "Saul VanDoren. I should have known you'd be here."

"Who is that?" Gabriel said again, this time more loudly. "Ma'am, do we know you?"

She swayed, moving the long skirts of a dark brown striped Victorian-style traveling dress. "Who cares if you know me—you don't and won't," she told Gabriel. "I'm not here to see you. I could tell the kind of trouble people were getting into and the signs led me here."

The woman looked at Phoebe and frowned. "Who is that creature?"

"You don't need to know," Saul said. His nostrils flared as if he smelled something he didn't like. "Give her more tea, Sally, please."

Sally did as she was told and managed to indicate to Leigh that she should come closer.

Leigh moved but Niles went with her as if they were fused together, and she smiled at him. Fused to Niles was exactly where she preferred to be. His hand clasped her waist possessively.

"Will you hold her shoulders for me?" Sally said.

Saul had moved in closer, too, and between them they more or less closed Phoebe off from this newcomer.

"Have you forgotten who you answer to, Sally?" the woman said, her voice grating. "It's very unwise for you to ignore me. If you ever want to go back—"

"This is my old friend, Ms. Tarhazian," Sally all but bellowed. Then she dropped her voice to a whisper only those gathered at the table could hear. "I want to get her out of here, but I dare not openly offend her."

"Is she the Fae Queen?" Niles asked.

Sally nodded, and her complexion turned a little green.

"Percy was here, too," Leigh said, ignoring the blank faces around her. "I think he wanted to warn us she was coming."

Sean continued to rub Phoebe's legs through the blanket and looked at her with something between fascination and adoration. This night—or morning—was getting too much for Leigh.

"Sally," Tarhazian yelled. "I made myself clear to you, but you couldn't manage to follow my orders. You've managed to mess everything up. Again. For that, you will pay."

As silently as she had appeared, Tarhazian was gone. Leigh couldn't tell if Sally felt relieved by her departure, or even more frightened at the threat. Before she could ask, Phoebe sat up, supported by Saul. "Leigh," Phoebe said quietly but desperately. "Come close. You, too, Sally. All of you.

"I heard something, or I'm pretty sure I did," she said to Leigh, who clutched Niles's arm. "One of those animals called me, Leigh. Can you tell me why he would do that? I worried about you."

Saul rested a hand on Phoebe's cheek, and when he moved it to the other side of her face, Leigh was almost certain the bruises and scratches were fading rapidly.

"No, I don't know," Leigh told her.

"I think I do," Niles muttered.

Abruptly Phoebe burst into tears. "That thing was a great big wolf," she sobbed. "I didn't say before, but he had another animal beside him the whole time, only he was a bit smaller. Kind of like a big dog.

"I think they were going to kidnap me until the smaller one got a good look at me. He made a wailing sound and the other one backed off. They howled in the darkness like there was a lot of them. And then they turned away as if I wasn't there."

"Thank God," Gabriel said.

"I was glad," Phoebe agreed. "But that one who attacked me thought I was someone else, another woman. I'm sure of it. They're out there now looking for some poor woman they want to drag off into the forest. It really could be you, Leigh."

Leigh felt Niles grow as still as a stone statue.

"We will be ready," Saul said to Niles. "We have more power on our side and we will stand together."

"Strange bedfellows," Sean muttered.

chapter THIRTY-THREE

WITH BROADENING dawn, a cold, blue-gray light settled in. The impact of the heavy snowfall was startlingly visible on the laden boughs of trees, the tall white ridges on fences, the mountains of white that lined the road. Hardly a naked twig showed to break the flat, white margins of the world.

Leigh's Honda ground along on chains that didn't completely reach through the icy coating beneath the snow. So few cars had come this way that she and Niles made mostly fresh tracks.

The heater wasn't working well and on the backseat, Skillywidden had curled up on top of Jazzy. Jazzy hated the car even more than he used to and the addition of cold left him shivering and snuffling, and rolling his eyes at Leigh each time he had a chance.

"Sean wasn't leaving Phoebe no matter what anyone else thought," Leigh said. She glanced at Niles.

Niles nodded. "That was one instant case of magnetism—at least on his side."

"Phoebe isn't well and it shows," Leigh said. "But I can understand the attraction. She's vibrant and interesting. I think Sean would be drawn to that. He's reserved but he's on top of everything in that quiet way of his. Sometimes he makes me laugh. He says things I don't expect."

"Are you trying to make me jealous?" Niles stroked her cheek with the backs of his fingers. "I don't know if I can bear having you admire another man."

"Just you, huh?" she said. "How do you plan to make sure I don't admire anyone else? This ought to be good."

"Give me a hint. What kind of answer do I give to that?"

She shrugged, turning on the windshield wipers to sweep aside a small avalanche from the roof of the car. "Feats of strength, maybe. Dancing exhibitions, singing opera. I prefer ballet, by the way. Gourmet meals you cooked yourself." Rolling in her lips, controlling a grin, she gave herself a second before she said, "Mind-bending lovemaking. Luscious, lustful sex in every place in every way, every day—maybe several times a day."

As he watched her, a sly smile parted his lips.

"That should cover it," Leigh said.

"And this is what happens to a nice girl once she's been with me?"

"You're complaining?"

Silence didn't last long before Niles said, "Pull over."

She glanced in his direction, a smug grin in place. "We'll be home soon."

Niles looked very serious. "We've got to get started or I won't manage everything I've got to do in a day."

She removed one hand from the steering wheel and placed it on top of Niles's firm thigh. "I promise to help you. I wouldn't dream of letting you shoulder the whole burden on your own."

He sighed. "Leigh, this feels so good, just to let the tension go for a while and enjoy each other. We know we've got hard times ahead. But I do love you. I don't know if I can ever tell you how much."

"You'll manage," she told him.

Reaching over the console, he kissed her neck and ran the tip of his tongue around the inside of her ear. He slipped his right hand inside her coat, under her shirt, and gently lifted a breast from inside her bra. His thumb ran back and forth over the instantly rigid nipple and Leigh let out a cry.

"Mmm." He bared her breast and bent his head to kiss her there.

"You'll put us in a snowbank," she said. "Oh, God, I want you now. Stop it till we get home."

He continued to run the edges of his teeth over erogenous skin and pull her flesh into his mouth.

"Niles!" She slammed on the shrieking brakes and the car fishtailed into the nearest wall of snow. "Look what's happened."

Reluctantly, Niles looked up. They had almost reached the entrance to the track leading to Two Chimneys. Or the place where the entrance was supposed to be.

What he saw didn't fool Niles. The track hadn't simply been blocked by a fallen tree. Piles of snapped limbs, chunks from the trunks of trees, bushes, shrubs, and foliage of all kinds crammed together in an unholy mess only a supernatural rage could accomplish. Roots, spread wide and black from being under the wet earth, curled above the snow like big, inky spiders.

"Turn off the engine," he said. "*Now*. I'm getting out. You're staying here with the doors locked and if anyone but me comes your way, leave."

Her shock almost immediately turned to a mutinous expression. "Where you go, I go. We're sealed, remember." She held up her palm to show the purple stamp there. The edges were still red.

She didn't understand that there were some things she couldn't do, some things she might do to slow him down. He covered her palm with his own. "I may have to move fast. You know what I mean? I need to know you're safe. Go to Gabriel's if you have to."

"What's the big deal?" she said. "It's just the weight of the snow that's made this mess."

"Perhaps." If she could think that, so much the better.

Out of the car, he waited for Leigh to lock the doors and went into a crouch. He hurried to the first demolished gatepost. The gate itself usually stood open, but he could see pieces of it scattered around.

Working rapidly, he hauled aside branches, jagged pieces of tree trunk, and one wrecked piece of forest and fence after another. He didn't get it, not yet. What reason could there be for this—except rage? He tossed aside a twisted and rusted piece of metal that must have been buried in the undergrowth for years.

Rage with what, or with whom?

Leigh?

The wolves had come here, following Phoebe. That's the only explanation that fit. They had followed her here, then back to her place. They didn't share the werehounds' ability to see in the dark, or not to the same degree.

What Phoebe had mentioned about one of them using

Leigh's name made sense. Once they found out Phoebe "wasn't the one" they had thrown her down and left.

Hell, why play games with the obvious? Brande and his pack were after Leigh. They knew she could be a bridge between the hounds and the humans and they wouldn't want that. They had thought Phoebe was Leigh and followed her. There was no reason they would know what kind of car Leigh drove.

Then, when they hadn't managed to find Leigh back at Two Chimneys, they had trashed the place. Trashing what didn't belong to them was a favorite pastime of Brande and his followers.

They wanted to use Leigh against him—and ultimately against any werehound attempt to bond with the humans.

He cleared part of the track and started dragging larger branches into the forest. They would go back to nature there.

Niles walked backward, pulling the top twenty feet or so of a giant fir with him.

"How can you do that?"

His head jerked up and he glowered across the branches at Leigh. "I told you to stay in the car."

"I'm getting bored. I want to help. This is my place." She pointed to the chunk of tree he held up by a couple of snags. "That's huge, Niles. It's bigger than most trees. You're tossing it around like a matchstick."

"I'm strong," he said. There was no point making up some elaborate story.

She opened her mouth to speak but crossed her arms instead.

"What?" he asked.

"I know how strong you are. Or maybe I don't. I wonder how much I don't know about you."

"Your timing for an inquisition is great," he said. "What don't you think I've told you? Isn't it enough to know I'm a—"

"I'm being stupid," she said, cutting him off. Shrugging and giving him an abashed smile, she picked up several sticks. "Sorry."

"No. You've been through too much, too fast—"

"Niles!" She shrieked his name so suddenly, he jumped. "Someone's under there. I can see a foot." Leigh pointed past him to a tangle of thick vines.

He saw the leg at once. A leg in ripped rain pants with a high-topped black sneaker on the foot.

"My God. Oh, no, Niles. Quick. I'll help."

He had torn aside the vines before she could start and sent a message out to Sean. He was the one to help with injuries, particularly serious ones, which this already looked to be.

"He's dead," Leigh said. She turned aside and he thought she would throw up but she took breaths through her mouth and held on to a tree for support.

Sean erupted into the scene.

Too late Niles saw that no medic, no matter how gifted, could do anything for this man.

"I think you need Saul," Sean said before he got a good look at the corpse. "No, I guess not. He doesn't raise the dead—or not that dead."

"He's broken," Leigh cried. Niles put an arm around her. "He's bent backward so far his spine must be broken...in several places."

Niles caught Sean's eyes and they exchanged thoughts.

"Our special operations method," Niles indicated. *"Neck will be snapped, too. Fastest, most efficient way to kill without a lot of noise and without much to hide."*

"Just a rolled-up bundle of bloody bones and flesh," Sean responded. *"Only we bagged 'em afterward. I thought we were the only ones who did this."*

Niles simmered. *"I thought we invented it and we only used it in extreme situations."*

"On someone who would kill us if we didn't kill them," Sean said. *"In a war zone."*

Niles wrapped Leigh hard against him and kept staring at Sean. *"We left all this behind."*

"You never quite did." Sean shook his head. *"I shouldn't have said that. We have to deal with whatever comes our way and get over it. We've got a chance to start again."*

Niles looked at the heap of human pulp on the ground. *"You wouldn't know it from this. Leigh will expect us to call the police, not get rid of him."*

"Might be the best thing to do." Sean knelt and turned the man's broken neck to the side to show his face. "Shit. We know this one."

Leigh gasped. "It's John Valley."

chapter THIRTY-FOUR

LEIGH CRINGED. She pushed away from Niles and made herself look more closely at the dead man. "That's terrible, but at least it must have been fast." She scuffled around in her coat pockets and found a crumpled piece of paper. "He left this at Gabriel's for me last week. He kept trying to get me to—you know how he asked me about selling this place? He tried again and then there was this offer someone made."

Frowning, Niles took the paper from her, looked at it, and passed it to Sean. "That's a lot of money but it is beautiful land."

"I kept on saying I didn't want to sell but he wouldn't give up."

"There's soot on him," Sean said.

Leigh felt very sick but she made herself stand up straight. "Call 911."

She couldn't miss the nonverbal communication that passed between Niles and Sean.

"What's with the dead birds?" Sean asked. "Don't tell me they died when he fell on them. They would have flown off." Several large, black, dead birds lay around Valley.

Niles gently pushed one of the birds with the toe of his boot so they could get a better look at it.

"Crows," Sean said. His gold brown eyes caught the cold morning light and Leigh couldn't look away. If anything about a man could be ethereal, then Sean's eyes were just that.

"I like crows," Leigh said hollowly. "They're intelligent."

A sudden crashing coming from the direction of the cottage startled her.

Innes, his hair wild and his face streaked with soot, broke through to them. He saw John Valley and halted. His arms fell to his sides and his face became rigid.

"Tell us," Leigh said, as gently as she could. She liked Innes's ebullient personality. "What happened?"

Slowly Innes raised his head and looked from one to the other of them. "I chased him off. That's it. Some crazy little fae in purple satin rushed down to your place, Niles. I was leaving something for you and Leigh. He stood on my shoulder and hissed in my ear. He said you two were his protectors."

Innes's audience didn't have anything to say.

"He said—the fae, that is—he said some guy was on Leigh's roof doing something to her chimney and wanted me to deal with it. And the guy was there, just like the fae said. I scared him off—almost all the way up here—then went back to see what he'd done to the cottage, if anything."

Innes noticed the disapproving look on Niles's face. "Stop looking at me like that, dammit. I dragged him off the roof and gave him some shoves. I didn't"—his attention returned to Valley—"hell, look at that. I didn't do it. We left all that behind."

"Where's Percy?" Leigh said. "The fae?"

"How should I know? There's a pile of soot in your living room and some dead crows. Like those only dirtier." He pointed at the birds on the ground.

Niles grabbed her hand and went rapidly downhill toward the cottage with the other two men trailing behind.

"We need to call the police," Leigh said, the cold air snatching her breath away.

"Let's get the whole picture first," he said. "No one can help John Valley now."

"Look," Innes said, loping along easily despite the mess underfoot. "I didn't do—"

"We know you didn't," Niles said. "But who did?"

"Whoever it was wanted it to look like us," Sean said.

"What good would that do?" Niles said. "No one around knows...aw, shit. If a word gets dropped in the right place and the authorities make some inquiries, we could be unlucky enough for them to hit some big-mouth paper pusher willing to talk about special ops and a contract operation no one is supposed to know much about."

Leigh's heart beat faster and harder. At the cottage, Niles put her into Innes's hands and opened the unlocked door.

"I'm going in," she told Innes and Sean. She held up her hand, showing the seal, and they took a respectful step backward.

Niles would have to learn to accept what their union meant. He was not the boss where she was concerned.

She ran into him as he was coming back out of the cottage. "I'm going to take a look," she said, and evidently he heard the edge to her voice, because he didn't try to stop her.

Apart from a putrid smell of soot and two more dead crows spilling from the fireplace onto the floor, there was nothing to see.

Outside again, Niles took a leap, gripped the edge of the roof, and landed on it lightly. He disappeared for what felt like a long time before he slithered down again with two black plastic bags.

He held up one. "More sacrificed birds." The other he set down carefully. "We'd better give Percy a medal. That's what Mr. Valley intended to use to start his chimney fire. You were supposed to get home, Leigh, go inside, and get scared out of your mind by birds and flames shooting out of your fireplace. Call 911."

Leigh realized she was shaky. Everything that happened to her now carried some horrible risk. What would happen next?

She searched for her phone. "I don't know what I did with it. Someone better call me or I'll never find it."

Niles used his own phone to call her. "I might as well make the call to the cops, too."

A phone rang in the cottage. Leigh ran inside and found it on the floor. "I'll make the call. It's my house and I should do it."

The phone rang again before she could dial. "Leigh, this is Gib," came her brother-in-law's voice.

She slowly rejoined the others. "Hi Gib. Is Jan okay? It's pretty early."

"You know that's not why I'm calling. How are you? Not hurt? Please say you're not hurt. Jan and I are on our way over."

Leigh switched her phone to speaker. "I'm not hurt." She felt three men watching her closely but didn't look at them. "What made you think I was?"

"The fire, of course. It's a good thing the fire department could notify us as next of kin. Where are you now? What kind of sicko would do a thing like that?"

She looked at the others then, at their serious and disgusted faces.

"I'm at the cottage," Leigh said.

"How badly was it damaged?" Gib asked. "Wait until I've finished, Jan. She's worried about you, Leigh."

"She's a good sister."

"I expect the fire trucks are in the drive," Gib said. "I'll park at the top and walk down. Can you believe it? Setting birds on fire and stuffing them down your chimney? Just to try to frighten you into selling."

Leigh sat down on the snowy porch, not caring how wet or cold she was. "And the fire department called to tell you this?" She grappled with what this call meant.

After a short silence Gib said, "They were pretty muddled up when I talked to them, but that was the gist of it. I don't blame them for having difficulty believing what happened. The cops will have to track down whoever did this. We want you out of there, Leigh. Jan won't sleep again with you on your own there."

"You want me to sell and move in with you?"

"You know we do. You need us. Hell, we need you, too. You're all the family we've got."

She looked out over the water, toward Camano Island.

"I couldn't live on your kindness, Gib." The word "kindness" stuck in her throat.

"We'll work all that out. You let me take care of your finances. They'll need managing and you don't need the stress of that."

chapter THIRTY-FIVE

Dr. Saul VanDoren's clinic, located in a rambling three-story house at the end of Gulliver Lane, was not what Leigh expected. If she had gone in to find a gaslight atmosphere complete with buttoned leather examination couches she wouldn't have been surprised.

Instead, the VanDoren Clinic and Lab was a modern, streamlined series of rooms, most with closed doors. The one open examination room she passed sparkled with immaculate stainless steel equipment and a whole lot of white.

"Come through to my quarters," Saul said. He still wore the heavy, hooded coat he had had on when he caught up with them at the bookshop, where they had gone to check up on Phoebe.

After a couple of hours with Langley's Police Department, tough men who wore baseball caps with POLICE emblazoned across the front in white, Leigh and Niles had been allowed to leave and take Jan with them. Gib chose to take off without a word about his plans, and without his wife. There was no solid evidence against him, and unfortunately, knowing more than he should about a fire that hadn't happened wasn't a reason to hold him.

Leigh made repeated requests for Jan to stay with her, but Jan wouldn't agree. Leigh feared her twin somehow felt partly to blame for her husband's actions.

Sean had learned from his buddies at the volunteer fire department that no one recalled talking to Gib. In fact, there had been no call about a fire at Two Chimneys at all. Still, none of his weird behavior put Gib under police suspicion of murder since he had plenty of alibis to confirm he hadn't been anywhere near Whidbey until he arrived after calling Leigh.

Leigh agreed with Niles and Sean that Gib seemed to know a whole lot about the efforts to get her to sell her property, and that money had to be at the bottom of whatever had gone on between him and John Valley. They had ideas about a possible plot between the two men, but no evidence.

Right now, Sean was over at Read It Again to keep an eye on Phoebe. Jan was with them.

"I shouldn't leave Jan very long," Leigh said. "She's got to be even more upset than the rest of us."

"Sean will take care of her," Niles insisted. "She's a lot better off with Phoebe than with Gib."

"Don't worry," Leigh said. "I agree with you."

Sally and Phoebe had shown up at the police station offering to take Leigh and look after her. That offer had been gently refused, but battered Phoebe had zeroed in on Jan—with help from Sally, who gave the whole "help in the bookstore" spiel. And to Leigh's amazement, Jan agreed to stay and work with Phoebe for at least a few days.

The police let them go with warnings that they'd be hearing from the Sheriff's Department as John Valley's death was investigated. The theory that he had been crushed by a falling tree didn't seem to be off the table.

Leigh and Niles followed Saul down a flight of stairs to the lower level of the house and into a room furnished sparingly with outrageous Biedermeier pieces. Saul waved them to a lime green couch with roll pillows at either end and gilt-encrusted legs that rested on the gleaming ebony floor. The cartoonish, early-nineteenth-century splendor suited the elegant Saul.

"I saw your hand," Saul told Niles and glanced at Leigh. "Would I find the matching mark on you?"

She held up her palm and he nodded, smiling slightly. "Times can only get more interesting," he said.

"You've got a reason for wanting us here?" Niles said. "Other than to congratulate us on our match."

Saul inclined his head. "But I do congratulate you. You, Leigh, are Deseron?"

She nodded. "How do you know?"

"A friend told me, but you've no need to worry. Your secret is safe," Saul said. "Truly, I find your kind fascinating. The ones who got away. Slipped through the fingers of the paranormal community to become supposedly extinct. I don't think we shall see more than artificial periods of calm while the forces who are bound to hate you decide how much harm you can bring to them."

"Leigh is not alone. She never will be," Niles said brusquely. He held Leigh's hand.

"Of course not," Saul said. "And if I can be of any help, you only have to call. Use her."

For an instant Leigh didn't know what he meant. Then she became aware of Skillywidden on her shoulder, pressed against her neck while she looked at Saul.

"Use her?" Leigh said. "The cat?"

"Not just any cat, I assure you." He tilted his head to listen to drops of yellow crystal pinging together around an unlit hurricane lamp. When the sound stopped he continued, "Sally has given Skillywidden to you for a purpose. The little one is of the Communicator Class of fae and she is a shapeshifter. Don't be fooled by her charming, restrained demeanor. She has fire in her."

Leigh put a hand up to the cat, who licked her fingers.

Saul laughed at that, then quickly sobered. "I brought you here because I have disturbing news. My tests have taken longer than I hoped but now I have some answers. Unfortunately, they are very bad. They spell a difficult future until we find a way to neutralize your werewolf friends, Niles."

"They are no friends of mine," Niles said sharply.

Leigh placed her hand on Niles's knee, hoping to calm him and avoid an angry outburst. Whatever Saul had learned, they needed to hear. And Leigh also needed to hear Saul's answer to a question that had been plaguing her.

"Saul," she began, "you are not an average vampire, are you?"

For a long moment Saul stared into space. "I go my own way," he said at last.

Leigh looked at his smiling mouth where no glittering fangs showed. "But are you...like that terrible Colin?" she asked in a hushed voice. "Do you drink from..."

"No, not like him. I exist on whole blood intended for transfusion but past pull date. After all, a man must guard his honor. I am a maverick vampire, a loner with no slaves or interest in the world I never wanted to enter. I am not a danger to you, Leigh. I promise you that. Now. Let's discuss what I've found out about Rose."

Niles shifted to the edge of the couch. "I was pretty sure it was you who carried her away that night."

"Yes. She was already dead but there was no point in arousing panic among the humans. I dealt with her disposal—after collecting specimens." He shook his head slowly. "The wolves will retreat when they find out what we know. But only temporarily, until they feel safe continuing."

"Rose is in Alaska," Leigh said.

"I'm sorry, but no." Niles shook his head. "I couldn't tell you until I knew why they were covering up the death."

Leigh wished the bad news would stop coming.

"Explain your findings," Niles said to Saul.

"Rose's blood had me intrigued at first. I knew there was something that shouldn't be there but nothing was immediately clear."

Niles let out an impatient growl. "Just tell us."

"I *am* telling you. What was introduced into Rose was animal blood—werewolf, I believe—although there hasn't been an opportunity to get the specimens I need to be sure."

Looking from one man to the other, Leigh jumped up. "How did she die?"

"The animal blood killed her. It caused a general infection of the blood allowing for clots to develop. One clot to the brain could easily have killed her. There were many. And there may still be something even more sinister to be found."

"Is Violet like her?" Niles asked. "What if the others who were taken are walking around like time bombs? Waiting for a clot to hit the brain?"

"Then they are in serious danger," Saul answered. "But we can't know without investigation and we can't investigate without explaining why we want to. What would you say if someone asked to test your blood to see if—" Saul paused and raised his arched brows. "Your situation is different, but with a full human, a question like that would make them call the police. They would say you were mad."

"So what do we do?" Leigh said.

"Nothing until the ones who left most recently show up again, dead or alive."

Leigh felt sick to her stomach. "What if we're wrong? What if the others really have just left town? That's possible, isn't it?" Even as she said the words, Leigh held little hope there was any truth to them.

"This is how it is in our world, Leigh—your world, too, now," Saul said. "And I believe all of this is an experiment in progress. So far some of the human guinea pigs seem to have passed their tests with flying colors, walking among other humans with no sign of being different."

"Molly," Niles said. "Molly was missing for a while, too. And she's gone again now."

"I have other thoughts about Molly," Saul said. "And I hope to have a chance to prove myself right or wrong." He poured white wine into two glasses. "For my guests," he said. "I can't risk scaring them off with glasses of red wine."

Leigh took the glass he gave her and went to stand behind the cerise velvet slipper chair he had used. "Where do the fae creatures fit in?"

"Are they being used?" Niles said, all of his focus on Saul's knowing face. "Cover for the wolves who know the fae would never consider them capable of misleading them? Would that be possible?"

The pupils of Saul's eyes were opaque, with a reddish hue. "If the werewolves have pulled that off—even by accident—this world of ours is heading for a violent war of revenge. The underworld has its pecking order. No one makes fools of the fae—or whomever the fae answer to. There is always a higher force."

"Why would the wolves introduce their blood into humans in potentially lethal doses?" Niles said.

"Hard to know," Saul said. "This pack hates humans, and if they can use them to destroy themselves, so much the better. Perhaps the plan is to create a Trojan Horse to gradually undermine humanity—at least in this place— from the inside."

"Humans they can use as puppets later?" Circling the windowless room, Niles fell into deep thought.

"And it won't matter to them how long it takes to make enough puppets," Leigh said quietly. "They have plenty of time."

"Unless they don't have plenty of time anymore," Niles said. "Unless they used to but now they don't."

Saul nodded.

"Because of me?" Leigh said. "And the Deseron? I see both sides of the veil and pure humans can't. And I am not an experiment. I am compatible with the werehound. There must be others like me, you know." She thought fleetingly of Jan. "Deseron will help the hounds bond with humans, integrate with them. Your strength and numbers will grow while the wolves are still trying to get control."

"They have never wanted to be human," Niles said. "We have, or most of us. There is always a rogue. But these werewolves have always used, then destroyed, humans."

"You will win," Leigh said. "You and Sean and the others—and Saul. You will."

"I love your confidence," Niles said without a shred of humor. "We have a lot of enemies to contend with."

"But perhaps Leigh's confidence is all we need," Saul told him. He had grown almost transparently pale. "I must ask you to go now. Please, Niles, watch this woman carefully."

"I intend to," Niles said.

"And pray the wolves make a mistake," Saul added, stretching out on the green sofa and pulling a black satin coverlet over him. "I am on your side, hound. And I'm ready to fight." He pulled the coverlet over his head. From beneath it he said, "The ultimate answer may be to win the humans' trust. Together, forces for good overcome all the odds."

chapter THIRTY-SIX

READ IT AGAIN WAS IRRESISTIBLE. Floor-to-ceiling book stacks, cozy if threadbare chairs, a big potbellied stove hissing and popping in the center of the room, and hot cider and chocolate standing ready with home-baked cookies. Niles saw the moment of pleasure on Leigh's face and wished he could make sure she always smiled.

And he would, dammit. There might be dangerous times, but he would never doubt his power to control them, and neither would Leigh, if he could build her trust.

She pulled on his arm.

"Hey, shorty," he said, looking down his nose at her. "I need to be alone with you."

"We've been busy," she told him. "It isn't over yet but we'll be alone soon. We'll make sure we are."

"Your sister and Phoebe are comfortable with each other."

"Jan needs some good friends." Leigh's grip on him tightened.

"What about Jan?" Niles said. "Is she Deseron, do you think? She's your twin."

"When she's ready, we'll find out if the two of us are alike in every way." Leigh massaged his arm and kissed his hand absently.

"Jan's going to come and stay with me," Phoebe announced from the center of the room. "And be a book-seller now and again when I can trick her into it."

Murmurs of approval followed.

"She wouldn't come to me, but perhaps that's just as well." Leigh stared at Niles. "Where is Sally?"

"I don't know." He didn't see her anywhere in the big room.

"Something's coming," Leigh said. "I can hear it."

He shook his head, listening, hearing the wind rattle windows and the familiar sounds of his own hounds, whom he could always contact. But nothing unusual was coming toward the shop that he could tell.

A rush of cold swept in as the door opened, setting the brass bell jingling.

Violet almost fell into the shop, but she was laughing rather than showing any distress. "You won't believe what we've been through," she said. "I hope we haven't worried everyone. The van broke down in the middle of nowhere. It's a long story but we're all fine."

"Violet! Thank goodness!" Phoebe exclaimed. "Did the others—"

"They've gone home," Violet broke in on Phoebe. "They all have work to get back to."

She should be windblown, Niles thought. Or at least more visibly ruffled if there was some long, dramatic story to be told.

Tall, brown-haired, and pleasant to look at, Violet threw down her big purse and opened it wide. "Come and look at all this."

Bars of candy, packets of chips and gum, wrapped cookies, they all spilled out. "These are what we've been living on." She shoved her hands in her pockets and sighed. "We would have starved if he hadn't found us."

He? Niles looked toward the door again and stopped breathing.

The man who stood there was very familiar, but ought to be a ghost. Maybe he was a ghost. Niles turned to Sean, who stood, motionless.

"My God," Sean muttered.

"Is it him?" Niles said, his vision blurring. Shock immobilized him.

"Niles. Sean," the man said. "Damn, I've missed you guys."

Gary, the werehound they all thought had been kidnapped and killed in the Middle East many months earlier, exuded vitality. Blond with light blue eyes, a square jaw and athletic body, he looked the all-American guy. And that's what he had been before he'd been turned into a werehound. Niles didn't remember the exact circumstances of his transformation. Those details hadn't mattered during combat.

"It's me," Gary said. "I thought you'd be glad to see me."

"It's great," Sean said, but without a lot of enthusiasm. "It's a shock. We thought you were dead." Niles could see him trying to think his way through this development.

"Where have you been?" Niles said. He shouldn't want to take this man by the throat and shake him, but that was his immediate impulse.

"Escaping one group of captors after another and making my way back from the most Godforsaken pit of a place in Pakistan." He went to Niles with his arms spread wide.

It was Sean who dragged Niles into a bear hug with Gary, while silently warning Niles to keep his cool and wait for Gary's explanation.

"Who's the lady?" Gary said, indicating Leigh. "My mate, Leigh," Niles said. "We are sealed." He heard the challenge in his own voice.

More slapping of backs followed and Gary said, "Congratulations—both of you." He smiled at Leigh.

"We'd better call all the hounds together," Niles said. He forced himself to keep the tension from his voice. There were many more questions about where Gary had been, and why it had been impossible to get a message to his team.

Mind track should have been possible, at least while they were all still in the same area, yet none of the hounds had been able to reach Gary.

"Give me a little while to settle down before you get the others," Gary said. "I'm beat. This hasn't been easy, any of it. But I'm glad to be back."

"Try some hot cider," Phoebe said, all warmth as usual.

Gary accepted a mug and walked to the far side of the room where he sat heavily in a chair and leaned his head back. He closed his eyes.

"This is too much," Sean said. "How could Gary just happen to find the missing women? That's one hell of a coincidence."

"Exactly," Niles agreed. "I don't get it that he just

walks in like this. We haven't heard a word about him since the day he was kidnapped."

Niles shoved aside thoughts of the emotional hell he had been through.

Leigh could sense Niles's discomfort, and she took him in her arms. "You never told me the full story about Gary."

"It isn't a subject Niles likes raised," Sean said. "He blamed himself for what happened."

Violet chattered on about being marooned in the wilderness, and Phoebe led her to a back room where they could talk alone. Curious about the returned hero who didn't seem as wildly welcome as he should be, Leigh disengaged herself from Niles and went to sit on the arm of the man's chair.

Gary opened his eyes and smiled at her.

"Do you mind if I ask how were you captured?" Leigh knew such a bold question might normally be considered rude, but normal was a concept that no longer seemed to exist in her world.

Gary's blue eyes, much paler than Niles's, were troubled. "I thought my brother hounds would be asking that question by now. It was bizarre and it happened so fast." He bent forward to look around. "Sorry, but is there a restroom?"

"It's through the storeroom," Leigh said. "Come on, I'll show you."

chapter THIRTY-SEVEN

IN THE FRONT OF THE BOOKSTORE, Niles paced. Why couldn't he just celebrate Gary's returning from the dead and stop feeling resentful of his own pain?

Because something didn't sit right.

He crossed his arms and stared at the floor. He just couldn't get his mind around the idea that Gary had survived and lived to get back—without an apparent mark on him. Why wouldn't he have made contact as soon as he got away, or as soon as possible after that?

And how did he happen upon Violet? She also unsettled him with her vague story of mashed tires and no way to get in touch. Everyone had a cell phone.

She was another of the kidnapped group. Who knew for sure what she was now?

"Where's Gary going?" Niles asked Sean as he watched Leigh lead him from the room.

"Back with Phoebe and the others, I guess," Sean responded.

Tamping down the urge to run, Niles calmly headed for the back, catching Sean's eye on the way.

Sean followed. Part of a window showed between stacks of books. Niles looked out of the windows and grabbed Sean.

"Son of a bitch," he ground out.

For an instant Niles had seen nothing but a snow-covered field with stands of firs in the distance. Using the full capacity of his sight, he made out an oversized were-hound with Gary's distinctive black and ginger markings, running among the trees.

Leigh hung from his jaws like a rag doll.

They came together at the fringe of the forest.

Niles, Sean, Innes, Ethan, and Campion stood with Piers and Renny, who had made it in from their lone stations on neighboring islands, and Simon was on his way from a more distant point.

Gliding over the snowy field came Saul, with two other men in dark clothes. They joined the hounds. "Can you see anything?" Saul asked Niles.

"A gathering of the wolves on a hill surrounded by sparse trees. They must want to be seen or they would stay in the forest. I'm going to get Leigh back now."

"We will help you," Saul said. The only introduction he gave his two companions was, "These are friends of convenience. Reliable in return for favors we all understand. We need every one of us here."

He and the two other vampires spread out, keeping slightly behind the hounds and distributing themselves as evenly as they could.

"Let's go." Niles started to run.

"We have to change," Campion called out.

Niles wanted to; more than almost anything he wanted to change, but he was stronger as a man than as a were-hound and he needed that strength. It no longer mattered if his enemies knew it. "I will go as I am," he told the others, who made no comments. Not all of them had greater power as men, but they had all chosen to use their hound forms to cover their identities when they were forced to attack.

Around Niles, the running men—with the exception of the vampires—became great, muscular dogs with bared fangs, and the animals gathered speed.

In trees close to the hill the wolves gathered, nine of them by Niles's count, and Gary.

"They have the advantage," Niles said. "They intend to kill us as we go up that hill."

Clenching and unclenching his fists, he watched while Gary, with Leigh on her feet now, pushed her face down in the snow. She looked helpless among the wolves.

"I'm going to push them to react." Niles walked out of the trees, cupped his hands around his mouth, and yelled, "D'you feel safer hiding behind a woman, Brande?"

"Don't forget I know you," came Gary's familiar voice in Niles's head. *"I know how your mind works. You're soft. You've killed but you hated it."*

"I was talking to Brande," Niles said.

"Talk to me. Brande has made me military leader here. I have a proposition for you. An exchange. You for the woman. Walk up to us slowly while the rest of the team backs away."

Niles started to walk immediately, trying to formulate a plan as he went.

"Don't do it," Sean snarled into Niles's mind, leaping

beside him. He ran in front of Niles. *"He doesn't intend to let Leigh go. They want to kill both of you."*

"I know that." Niles turned to the rest and said, *"Stay where you are."* He exchanged glances with Sean and then with Saul. Their struggle was obvious but they nodded and Saul whispered, "Have it your way."

Once more Niles turned and leaned into the slippery incline. He went steadily uphill until he was within feet of Gary and Leigh.

"I'm here," Niles said. "Leigh can go down now."

Gary continued to stand with the claws of one paw holding Leigh where she was.

"Go back!" she cried. "What difference does it make which one of us dies?"

"Let her go," Niles told Gary. "Don't add dishonor to everything else you're guilty of."

With a swipe, Gary hit Leigh in the back, sending her rolling and tumbling across the snow to a wolf who grabbed her up in his jaws and shook her.

"Come on, come on," Gary called to Niles. *"Just you and me, buddy, like it used to be, only this time the best of us is going to win. You thought you could always be the leader and I'd follow. Not anymore."*

He lunged at Niles and knocked him backward with the first blow.

"Get Leigh," he shouted to the others, but he was immediately overrun by the team's pounding feet that soared over him before Saul hauled him up.

"She'll be taken care of," Saul cried.

Gary charged and Niles blessed his own agility, side-stepping the bull-like approach and lunging to grab him by the neck.

"You really believe that myth that we are stronger as men?" Gary sneered into Niles's mind. *"You're a fool but why should I argue?"*

"Some of us are!" Niles cried.

Gary twisted free of Niles's grip and took his arm between snarling jaws, dug in murderous fangs.

Niles tasted his own blood, spurting from deep puncture wounds.

With the fingers of his free hand, Niles drove into Gary's nostrils, clamped onto his muzzle, and yanked upward, breaking bones and dislocating the jaw.

Gary's howl climbed to an endless scream. He lashed out, beating at Niles.

Withdrawing his hand, Niles struck again, and only once, with two fingers into Gary's eye sockets. He drove deeper and the hound keeled over backward, legs flailing, until the moment when Niles connected with the brain.

With the tearing away of his hand, Niles turned his face away from splattering blood.

Gary was dead.

Without pausing, Niles continued his uphill rush, searching for Leigh. His arm hung useless at his side and he clasped the wounds, kneaded them, stopped the bleeding. He turned in circles, still looking for her, bending his weakened elbow, feeling the trickle of returning strength.

Another wolf came at Niles. Their bodies locked together and Niles whipped the enemy onto his back, laying bare the vulnerable belly.

Niles knew this one was no match for him. His own strength only swelled and his arm approached complete healing. He caught the wolf by the throat, swung him around above his own head, and heard the creature's neck snap.

As Niles had known they would, the wolves sprang then, howling their war cries.

Everywhere he looked, there was blood. But it became mostly wolf blood. The three vampires fought, each of them with two hounds as partners, and the hounds struggled on, making the best of their lesser height to land wounding gashes to bellies, the backs of legs, and feet.

Gradually the wolves lost ground.

Adrenaline rushed through Niles. With Saul between them, he and Sean rushed Brande. The hounds' jaws were wide and slathering. The lightning movements of the vampires turned back Brande's every attempt to thwart the attack. Another wolf joined him.

Too late.

Saul lifted Brande over his head and smashed him down.

They were winning. Spurred by triumph, the team and the vampires drove the larger pack back.

This would be the last time werewolves would prey on unsuspecting victims on this island.

There was Leigh, on the ground again beneath the foot of Brande's wolf, Seven. His fangs could have been bared in laughter, only he started to lower his head toward Leigh and Niles knew what was about to happen.

"No!" He leaped, clawing the air to reach Seven. The wolf's teeth were already hooked in Leigh's clothing. Niles snatched at that slathering mouth, tore it away and Seven with it.

A broken snag of a tree, driven into the ground during the fight, was something Niles only saw from the corner of his vision, but his instincts didn't fail him. With his help, Seven landed on the snag and Niles dragged him over the frozen bladelike wood. It ripped the wolf open from neck to groin, laying his belly wide and spilling its contents on the churned snow.

Niles yelled at Leigh to run, but Saul already had her and was pushing her down the hill.

Yet another wolf reared up to strike and Niles leaped to meet him, then paused, his leg in midair. He heard the attacking cries of his brother hounds, the sounds of the vampires' whip-strong limbs swishing through the air, but that was all.

Before him, lifted from the ground, the werewolf pack hung, frozen in their fighting positions, their wounds congealed, no blood flowing anymore, no spume flying from their fangs.

The team grew still.

Exquisitely slowly, the wolves blurred and receded, their bodies frozen in their last positions, being sucked away toward the forest on the other side of the hill. And the bodies of their dead floated after them.

Niles flung around. "Something's doing that," he said, not caring that the battle had left him naked. "We had them but something's saving them."

"Not saving them," a voice sang out across the hill. "Not from you, but *for* me."

A short distance away stood the woman Niles recognized from Gabriel's on the night Phoebe was hurt. Tarhazian, Sally had called her. Gone were the odd Victorian clothes, replaced by a black velvet coat that touched the ground and a crown of glittering black gems. Her angelic face made a mockery of her stance, with arms upraised and fingers poking toward the disappearing wolves.

"How fortunate that we meet again," she said. "So sorry to stop you from finishing the wolves, but you will be grateful. They have already done a great deal of damage. But you know that. Without them how would we find out exactly what they've done and deal with it?"

The stare she gave Niles was not pleasant. "Of course, we cannot be sure the fae and the hounds will agree on how the story should end for the wolves—or if it should end."

"Come, Sally," Tarhazian said, and Sally materialized wearing a tightly pleated muumuu in her favorite red. "You've done well to lead me here," Tarhazian murmured.

Any thought of attacking the Fae Queen would have to wait, Niles realized. He owed Sally too much to risk her life in whatever might happen.

Sally didn't look toward Niles and the spectacular group of naked men who stood with him. She said to Tarhazian, "I'll be glad to visit my old friends again. It's been a long time."

"And it will be much longer yet," Tarhazian said with a sly smirk. "Until I don't have any more use for you here."

Sally bowed subserviently, but Niles saw her unhappiness.

Brande and his pack had completely disappeared, taking their wounded and dead with them. Tarhazian and Sally also faded into the night.

Leigh arrived at Niles's side and pushed an arm around his waist. His team seemed unconcerned at having her stand among their nude bodies.

"Can you still see them?" Saul asked Leigh quietly.

"Yes," she said. "I see them all. They don't look like wolves anymore. They're men and they're talking as they go and arguing." She turned her face up toward Niles. "Who were you speaking with?"

"A powerful Fae Queen," Niles said.

"One who fortunately isn't our enemy. Yet."

chapter THIRTY-EIGHT

LEIGH! IT'S DARK and cold down here."

Leigh clung even tighter to Niles, clutching a big blanket around them. "I warned you to travel as a hound," she told him. "All that fur keeps you warm, not that you ever feel the cold anyway. And I'm not complaining about your dress code." She held him so close they stumbled.

"It's your icy skin I'm thinking about," he told her.

They had climbed down the stairs from the bluff to his home—her home, too, Leigh realized, but she had insisted they were going onto the beach. The tide was low and a half-moon showed in shades of lemon and gray through a membrane of royal blue cloud.

Only a short distance from the moon, that royal blue cloaked to black.

"I want to take you inside," Niles said, holding her close. "Aren't the pebbles hurting your feet?"

"I've got shoes on. You're the one who's barefoot." She giggled. "And bare-assed."

"Leigh!" He sounded genuinely shocked.

"Not ladylike," she said, running a hand over the part of him in question. "I don't mind if you want to go without clothes all the time. At home, that is. I don't want any other woman seeing you."

"Thanks—I think."

He rubbed her back and she sucked in a sharp breath. Saul had worked on her with his healing hands before they left the others. Energy had flooded back into her body, but the bruises and some of the cuts would take a little longer to go away.

Leigh gazed over fine ripples on the inky water, ripples edged here and there with fluorescence. "This is why I'm here," she told Niles. "Chimney Rock Cove, the waters and what's beneath them. And what comes from that rock out there."

Niles was more interested in trying to keep Leigh covered up than in anything she said.

Time to show him what she was coming to believe. The fountainhead of the Deseron, supposedly extinct but far from it, lay out there.

They reached the water's edge and she kicked off her shoes.

"Please, Leigh. I think you're delirious. Aren't you hurting? Aren't you exhausted?"

She reached under the blanket to caress him. "Not at all. But I feel as if I'll explode with joy, and I feel very, very sexy."

He groaned. "Then we definitely need to go to the cabin."

"Why?"

"Just because we do. I'll take you to bed and love you till you are exhausted and pass out from weakness."

Leigh put first her toes, then her feet into the water.

As she stared out, a pattern of glittering silver formed. It came to rest at her feet but spread straight out to where the rock was and opened in a circle as if to surround it.

And the water was soft and warm, caressing her skin, beckoning her deeper.

She wrapped the blanket around Niles, touching her nose to his when she saw how dark and troubled his eyes were. "It's all right. Sometimes even the strong have to be led."

In a swift move she tugged her sweater over her head and ran her fingers through her hair, shaking it and reveling in the sensation of faint breeze slipping around her neck.

Her jeans followed the sweater and she stood there in the faint moonlight in nothing but her flimsy bra and panties. And she struck a pose just for him until he made a grab for her.

Leigh hurriedly waded out of reach. In water almost to her knees, she unhooked her bra and tossed it away.

"Leigh," he moaned. Then he was quiet for a moment before he said, "You sparkle. What is that? Little points of light flashing from all sorts of places. Are you a witch? Have you been keeping a secret from me?"

Her panties were removed with less grace and she fell up to her neck in that sparkling water. "This is all mine," she called. "Until I can find the mystical missing Deseron master to take over and teach me the ropes, I'll just have to go on instinct. Instinct pulls me into this water, into this light. If I sparkle"—the hand and arm she held up gave off bright flashes—"that backs up what I'm telling you. I feel strong here. I'm getting stronger with every moment. I don't hurt—except for needing you. Come in, Niles."

He threw the blanket aside and ventured into the water, heading straight for her.

Leigh turned away and waded as fast as she could, then broke into a strong sidestroke, trying to draw him as far from the shore as possible. "Do you see the path on the water?"

"Yes, but I don't know how. I've never seen anything like that before."

"It could be that now we are mates, you will have some of my powers." She trod water. "Do you think that means I'll start being able to turn into a hound?"

He broke his stroke but only for a short while before driving forward again and reaching her. He tried to stand, but the water was too deep and they clung together, legs tangled together, holding each other's faces.

"You will never become a hound," he said, and she drew back at the anger in his voice. "It was forced upon me, and helping to make hounds acceptable, desirable even, became my job. And with your help, I'll succeed. But what happened to me will not happen to you. I want you as you are—always."

Running her hand along his jaw, Leigh smiled. "Hah, look at you." She pointed to his shoulders and arms. "You've got the magic shine, too. Mm, I think I could slide all over you."

Taking her by the waist, Niles held her still and gradually raised her until her breasts settled on top of the water. "Ah," he said softly. "Now there's a sight to make me think about all kinds of slippery, sliding things."

He grabbed her against him and kissed her open-mouthed, moved his tongue to touch as much of the inside of her lips and cheeks as he could reach.

Leigh's core burned and pulsed.

She slid one knee between his legs, all the way up until she felt the rigid length of him.

Niles kissed his way from her lips over her jaw and bent her gently backward to smooth her breasts with his palms between.

The words he whispered were indecipherable.

His kisses traveled in a line between her ribs, down her belly, to her center. He held her almost out of the water to tease her with his tongue until she flipped around and grasped his shoulders. "Make love to me," she said.

"You've managed to make mush of my brain," he told her, holding her bottom with both hands and urging her against him. "But not so much I can't think at all. You should be freezing."

"But I'm not. Feel me."

"I have felt you. I am feeling you. You're not and it's crazy."

She flipped upside down in the water and drew his penis into her mouth, as much of it as she could. He struggled not to let his desire get the better of him and managed to haul her up to the surface again.

"You'll drown, little minx," he said. "In we go, now."

Leigh slid up and down his length, catching his most vulnerable parts between her thighs with each pass.

"What's wrong with here?" she said, guiding the tip of him just inside her. She loved the way the strong lines of his upturned face shone by moonlight. Slowly she inched him deeper inside her, not stopping until he gripped her waist and buried his face in her neck.

"There's no protection," he muttered. "I don't want to risk a child until I know more. We risked it before, but I won't lose you in childbirth. Nothing is worth that."

He kissed her neck and she took advantage of the opportunity to thrust herself all the way over him. Whipping her legs around his hips, she locked her ankles together and held him there.

"How am I supposed to resist you?" He was breathless.

"If there's a child, there's a child. Not that it's likely so soon."

"Perhaps not, but...Leigh, there are no more werehound females left. Part of my original quest to find a human mate was to find someone strong enough to be the mother to my children. But that has no meaning to me anymore. I just want you. The risk is too great. If I have you, I have everything."

Leigh had learned much about risk in the past few days. She could see in Niles's eyes that his concern was genuine, but her need for him—to build a future with him—was stronger. Wrapping her legs even more tightly around him, she urged him toward her center.

He gave a single thrust into her and she cried out.

"Niles, without you I don't have anything. Please, this is what's meant to be—us together. I am not a hound. Eventually, if we are meant to have a child, it will be different. Don't worry about it now."

The silken waters ebbed and flowed around them, folded over their bodies. Pressure mounted in Leigh's body, pounded through her, throbbed, ached, burned all over again.

Niles didn't talk anymore until much later, after they lay on top of the damp blanket, on top of the beach pebbles, enfolded in the warm, tingling light from the sea.

This was the beginning...

She's a feline shapeshifter. He's a werehound.
Together, they are perfect—and lethal.

Please turn this page
for a preview of

Darkness Bred

Available in December 2012

Prologue

IT WAS ALREADY too late.

Before the bouncer let him in, before the doors to the club closed behind him, before he walked through a crowded hallway toward silver lights pulsing in time to mind-pounding music and a wildly spinning stream of shining reflections around magenta walls—it was too late.

A man hustling a woman up the stairs from the side-walk outside had looked back at Sean Black and stood still for the beat of one long, triumphant stare. Then they had gone inside.

And Sean had followed like a jumper to the edge of a cliff.

He could never forget that face, the sharp, predatory features, the sneer creased across his almost lipless mouth. In the back room of a saloon in Creed, Colorado, Sean had saved the man's life, and in thanks, the man as good as took his.

"Why, Jacob O'Cleary, as I live and breathe," a smoke-stained voice ground into Sean's ear. "What a surprise to see you. Small world, as they say." The man had waited for him to follow, known he would. Holding the elbow of a young brunette whose eyes were too big for her face and scoured a puffy purple underneath, he walked ahead into the surging crowd.

Hearing his birth name for the first time in far more than a century jolted Sean. Jacob O'Cleary—the only name this ancient werehound knew him by.

Walk the other way, Sean.

Only he couldn't, because it was already too late.

Trolling San Francisco's Chinatown late on a Saturday night didn't happen by accident, not to Sean Black. Whispers through his own hidden world that a dangerous hound known only as Aldo had been sighted in the area, and was asking about him, had brought Sean to the city. He expected to spend days, maybe even weeks tracking Aldo—not to all but fall over the guy.

But of course, Aldo had planned it that way. He needed to taste the power of dominating a superior intellect again, and that could only mean that Aldo had begun to deteriorate. Sean could restore him.

Once through the entry hall, the place was bigger than it looked from the outside, with rocking, rubbing bodies smashed together on a central dance floor and tables all around the edge. There were booths for those who wanted privacy, and plenty of stools along a long bar for parties less concerned about their conspicuousness.

Sean looked around and quickly identified a number of vampires and a shapeshifter in drag. What the shapeshifter might be without the curly red wig and four-inch heels would take Sean longer to figure out. The vamp groupies, male and female, were impossible to miss. Their fawning advances on those they desired were sickening, but the often degrading looks, touches, and even painfully administered physical rebuffs didn't stop them from pleading again to be used.

With the exhausted and scared-looking woman balanced on a stool, Aldo stood at the right end of the bar. A tall, thickset man with oiled black hair that made a heavy blunt-ended helmet curving to his earlobes, he would be hard to miss.

Other patrons, most of them high almost to insanity, gaped but still had enough sense left to give Aldo plenty of space.

Aldo leaned back, bracing his elbows on the bar, staring straight at Sean. They hadn't seen each other in over a century, but the look in Aldo's hooded, red-brown eyes said he didn't doubt his power over the hound he thought of as little more than his escaped slave. Aldo expanded his chest and flexed muscle inside a skin-hugging green T-shirt.

Only he was not as massive as Sean, and neither did Aldo share—nor was he aware of—the rare twist that helped bind Sean and the rest of his team together.

Like his alpha, Niles, and some of the others they regarded as brothers, Sean had even more deadly strength as a human than as a hound.

Sean braced his feet apart and crossed his arms. With his eyes he dared the other one to try proving his superiority.

Aldo pulled the woman off her stool and she winced.

Sean had no doubt that her tight-fitting sleeves hid bruising—or that when she was naked, her voluptuous little body would be covered with marks of domination.

Tears shone in her eyes, eyes that Sean realized didn't focus. He took a step toward the couple. Aldo virtually held his companion up. From the way she started to slump, Sean figured she would fall without support.

"How've you been?" Aldo said, his nostrils flaring despite the wider grin on his mouth—only on his mouth. He came closer, shuffling the girl along with him. "Let's see. Where was it we last met?" With one pointed forefinger, he tapped his chin.

"Do you need help, ma'am?" Sean asked the woman quietly. "Just say the word and I'll get you out of here."

"He always was an interfering fool," Aldo said, leaning down to put his head close to hers. "Don't worry, Lily. I'll make sure he doesn't take you from me," he tutted. "Still trying to pick off other men's women, Jacob? I would have expected you to be more mature by now."

Sean saw it then, what he had feared, the oblivious stare some drugs brought. Lily blinked slowly at Aldo and leaned, her face turned up to his.

"What's your game this time?" Sean said. "She needs to go home."

"She belongs to me," Aldo said through his teeth, his lips barely moving. "What I want, I own. You know that."

"Why are you here now?" Sean asked.

"I came for you."

Sean laughed. "Generous of you, but no thanks. I've got all the friends I need."

"Friends? I need no friends. You and I have unfinished business. I want you and you belong to me."

Sean forced down the urge to take this vermin by the throat. He ought to get out while he could, yet he could not leave Aldo with his helpless victim, and neither could he go without attempting to turn this vicious animal into a toothless joke.

With his fingers sticking into Lily's thin arm, Aldo moved to pass Sean.

"Leaving so soon?" Sean said. "Why did you come at all?"

Aldo's awful grin split his face again. "Did I say I was leaving?" he whispered hoarsely. "The fun has only just begun. Look around you. Everyone shares here and I must share Lily." He swept one arm wide. "My entertainment first, then theirs."

"Let her go," Sean said. He made sure that although his body might seem relaxed, every muscle and nerve was ready to spring.

Lily's belt came undone easily and Aldo dropped it on the floor. With one tug he unsnapped her jeans and yanked them halfway down her hips. She flapped her hands at him ineffectually.

Whatever Aldo had given or done to her was making Lily increasingly disoriented and helpless.

Pushing a hand inside her skimpy white shirt, Aldo squeezed a pale, bruised breast until the woman moaned with pain.

"Enough," Sean said, keeping his voice low but penetrating enough to get to Aldo. "If you want to push someone around, try me." He beckoned with both hands.

"Who could ask for anything more?" Aldo said, and

his red-brown eyes turned hot. "But sometimes a man wants to be chased. You come and get me this time."

The breath Sean drew in took long enough for Aldo to slash his claw down the front of Lily's body. Sean reacted instantly.

He sliced the side of his right hand into the narrow space beneath Aldo's nose, and drove hard.

Aldo shook his head, blood flying from his nose, and bared his teeth. "Defending a whore's honor," he said. "How touching. She's here because she wants to be. Do you think I looked for something like her? She wants me and what only I can give her."

He threw Lily into the arms of a gawking, spotty kid who looked underage. This one held her up and gazed, fascinated. When he parted his lips, a double row of sharply pointed teeth showed and his ears began to elongate. He was some sort of fae.

Sean made a move to grab the woman away, but he felt as much as saw Aldo swing something through the air and whirled around in time to block a bottle heading for his own face.

The powerful hand that held the bottle connected with Sean's shoulder and glass shattered, hung in the air in a net of glittering shards, then sprayed over the nearest patrons.

Only in the farthest reaches of the club did people continue to dance and laugh, and ply themselves with whatever made them feel invincible.

Scuffles broke out, and shrieks. People bled from glass-inflicted wounds, most of them small, unlike the one on Sean's shoulder that soaked his shirt.

Sean's arm would heal soon enough. No time for giving in to pain. He hauled the woman away. Aldo was using her because he knew Sean would intervene to help her. Regardless of why she was here, or what choices she might have made, now she was suffering because of him and she was his responsibility.

The music stopped, but the screaming and panic raging around him rose like a shifting wall of sound. Weight on his back, pressing him down on Lily, infuriated him, but he dared not show the full extent of his strength. To do so would mean that too many questions would circulate and an advantage could be lost to his team forever.

"Two choices," a familiar, gravelly voice hissed into his ear. Aldo lifted Sean's head by the hair and slammed it down on Lily's. Then, under the cover of a confusing scuffle, landed a kick to the vulnerable spot at her temple.

Sean managed to make enough room to stare at her face, at her glazed eyes. They were the eyes of death now. "You've killed her," he shouted, breathing in blood from his own nose. "You've goddamn killed her!"

"How can an upstanding man like you make up such lies?" Aldo ground out. "You attacked her and I'm trying to pull you off. And that's what the police will believe if you don't do what I want."

"Get out of my way." Sean heaved upward but Aldo clung to him, his face stretched into its foul, lipless grin.

"Too bad about that," he said, jerking his head toward Lily's corpse. "A little collateral damage. All I'm after is you. We only have seconds. Join me and you'll never be attached to any of this. Refuse and they'll get you for murder—if the crowd doesn't tear you apart first. There are enough of our kind here to do it."

"I'm not your kind," Sean spat out. "The answer's no. I'll take my chances."

"Change your mind—now," Aldo said, his smile gone. "I made you, and you belong to me."

"Never."

"I'll hunt you, Sean. No matter what kind of noble little life you think you've created, I'll always be there to take it away. You'll never be free of me."

Sean stared into Aldo's cold eyes. Sirens wailed faintly in the distance. "I'll die before I give in."

THE DISH

Where authors give you the inside scoop!

♥ ♥ ♥ ♥ ♥ ♥ ♥ ♥ ♥ ♥ ♥ ♥ ♥ ♥ ♥ ♥ ♥

From the desk of Stella Cameron

Frog Crossing

Out West

Dear Reading Friends,

Yes, I'm a gardener and I live at Frog Crossing. In England, my original home, we tend to name our houses, and the habit lives on for me. Some say I should have gone for Toad Hall, but enough said about them.

Things magical, mystical, otherworldly, enchanting—or terrifying—have occupied my storytelling mind since I was a child. Does this have anything to do with gardening? Yes. Nighttime in a garden, alone, is the closest I can come to feeling connected to the very alive world that exists in my mind. Is it the underworld? I don't think so. It is the otherworld, and that's where anything is possible.

At night, in that darkness, I feel not only what I remember from the day, but all sorts of creatures moving around me and going through their personal dramas. I hear them, too. True, I'm the one pulling the strings for the action, but that's where the stories take root, grow, and spread. This is my plotting ground.

In DARKNESS BOUND, things that fly through tall trees feature prominently. Werehound Niles Latimer and widowed, mostly human, Leigh Kelly are under attack from every quarter by fearsome elements bent on tearing them apart. If their bond becomes permanent and they produce a child, they can destroy a master plan to take control of the paranormal world.

The tale is set on atmospheric Whidbey Island in the Pacific Northwest, close to the small and vibrant town of Langley, where human eyes see nothing of the battle waged around them. But the unknowing humans play an important part in my sometimes dark, sometimes light-hearted, sometimes serious, a little quirky, but always intensely passionate story.

Welcome to DARKNESS BOUND,

Stella Cameron

♥ ♥ ♥ ♥ ♥ ♥ ♥ ♥ ♥ ♥ ♥ ♥ ♥ ♥

From the desk of R.C. Ryan

Dear Reader,

Ahh. With QUINN I get to begin another family saga of love, laughter, and danger, all set on a sprawling ranch in Wyoming, in the shadow of the Grand Tetons. What could be more fun than this? As I'm fond of saying, I just love a rugged cowboy.

There is just something about ranching that, despite all its hard work, calls to me. Maybe it's the feeling that farmers, ranchers, and cattlemen helped settle this great nation. Maybe it's my belief that there is something noble about working the land, and having a special connection to the animals that need tending.

Quinn is all my heroes wrapped into one tough, rugged cowboy. As the oldest of three boys, he's expected to follow the rules and always keep his brothers safe, especially with their mother gone missing when they were children. In tune with the land he loves, he's drawn to the plight of wolves and has devoted his life to researching them and to working the ranch that has become his family's legacy. He has no need for romantic attachments...well, until one woman bursts into his life.

Fiercely independent, Cheyenne O'Brien has been running a ranch on her own, since the death of her father and brother. Cheyenne isn't one to ask for help, but when an unknown enemy attacks her and her home, she will fight back with everything she has, and Quinn will be right by her side.

To me, Cheyenne is the embodiment of the Western woman: strong, adventurous, willing to do whatever it takes to survive—and yet still very much a beautiful, soft-hearted, vulnerable woman where her heart is concerned.

I loved watching *the sparks* fly between Quinn and Cheyenne.

As a writer, the thrill is to create another fascinating family and then watch as they work, play, and love, all the while facing up to the threat of very real danger from those who wish them harm.

I hope you'll come along to share the adventure and enjoy the ride with my new Wyoming Sky trilogy!

R. C. Ryan

www.ryanlangan.com

♥ ♥ ♥ ♥ ♥ ♥ ♥ ♥ ♥ ♥ ♥ ♥ ♥ ♥ ♥ ♥

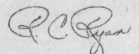

From the desk of Bella Riley

Dear Reader,

When my husband I were first married, one of our favorite things to do was to go away for a romantic weekend together at a historic inn. We loved to stay at old inns full of history (the Sagamore on Lake George in the Adirondacks), or windswept inns on the Pacific Ocean (the Coronado in San Diego), or majestic inns made of stone in the middle of a seemingly endless meadow (the Ahwahnee in Yosemite Valley). Now that we've got two very active kids, we have slightly different requirements for our getaways, which are more active and slightly less romantic...although I have to say our kids put up with "Mommy and Daddy are kissing again" pretty darn well! Fortunately, my husband and kids know that my favorite thing is afternoon tea, and my husband and son don't at all seem to mind being the only males in frilly rooms full of girls and women in pretty dresses.

As I sat down to write the story of Rebecca and Sean in WITH THIS KISS, I immediately knew I wanted it to take place in the inn on Emerald Lake. With those pictures in my head of all the inns I've stayed at over the years, I knew not only what this inn looked like, but also the many love stories that had been born—and renewed—there over the years. What's more, I knew the inn needed to be a large part of the story, and that the history in those walls around my hero and heroine would be an integral part of the magic of their romance. Because when deeply hidden secrets threaten to keep Rebecca and Sean apart despite the fireworks that neither of them can deny, the truth of what happened in the inn so many years ago is finally revealed.

I so enjoyed creating my fantasy inn on Emerald Lake, and I hope that as you're reading WITH THIS KISS, even if you aren't able to get away for a romantic weekend right this second, for a few hours you'll feel as if you've spent some time relaxing...and falling in love.

Happy reading,

Bella Riley

www.bellariley.com

♥ ♥ ♥ ♥ ♥ ♥ ♥ ♥ ♥ ♥ ♥ ♥ ♥ ♥ ♥

From the desk of Jami Alden

Dear Reader,

Who hasn't wished for a fresh start at some point in their lives? I know I have. The urge became particularly keen when I was starting high school in Connecticut. Not that it was a terrible place to grow up, but an awkward phase combined with a pack of mean girls eager to point out every quirk and flaw had left their scars. Left me wishing I could go somewhere new, where I could meet all new people. People who wouldn't remember the braces (complete with headgear!), the unibrow, the glasses (lavender plastic frames!), and the time my mom tried to perm my bangs with disastrous results.

In RUN FROM FEAR, Talia Vega is looking for a similar fresh start. Granted, the monsters from her past are a bit more formidable than a pack of snotty twelve-year-olds, and the scars she bears are physical as well as emotional. But like so many of us, all she really wants is a fresh start, a new life, away from the shadows of her past.

But just as I was forced to sit in class with peers who remembered when I had a mouth full of metal and no idea how to wield a pair of tweezers, Talia Vega can't outrun the people unwilling to let her forget everything she's tried to leave behind. Lucky for her, Jack Brooks, the one man who has seen her at her absolute lowest point, will do anything to protect her from monsters past and present.

And even though I got my own fresh start of sorts

when I moved across the country for college, I sure wish someone had been around to protect me from my mother and her Ogilvie home perm kit. I don't care what the commercial says—you CAN get it wrong!

Jami Alden

www.jamialden.com